# THE PLUME HUNTER

## Renée Thompson

Torrey House Press, LLC
Utah

First Torrey House Press Edition, December 2011

Published by Torrey House Press, LLC
P.O. Box 750196
Torrey, Utah 84775 U.S.A.
http://torreyhouse.com

International Standard Book Number: 978-1-937226-01-5
Library of Congress Control Number: 2011936385

Cover photos: *Great Egret* by Greg Downing, naturescapes.net; *Campsite Dawn* by Guy Tal, Guy Tal Photography, www.guytal.com.
Back cover photo by Jill Carmel
Cover design by Jeff Fuller, Crescent Moon Communications

For Jena and Maya, in thanksgiving of their
devotion to the natural world and their
stewardship of the land.

*The mercantile business did not suit me.*

— John James Audubon

# THE PLUME HUNTER

# CHAPTER ONE

The scent of simmering beans and ham hocks brought two marsh dwellers into their camp, the old one short, the young one tall, shotguns resting on their shoulders. Fin McFaddin felt the men before he saw them, some sixth sense kicking in before he heard their feet rustling in the grass; he sat up warily, anticipating their arrival.

His best friend Aiden had just shoveled a spoonful of hot beans into his mouth, so Fin stood and greeted the men. "You're the ones we heard toward sundown," he said, "shooting beyond the cattails."

The older fellow nodded. "Yep, that whar us."

Fin eyed the man, noted the hickory-stained crevices lining his mouth, and the tobacco tucked behind his bottom lip. He hadn't but ten strands of hair, which stretched across his scalp like fingers clutching his head, and his hands were thick as beefsteaks. Arthritis seized his thumbs so that they curled inward, straining toward his palms. He had a hump, too, sprouting from his backbone. Fin guessed he was fifty or so, although he couldn't have been that old and navigate the marshes. Likely he was forty, one foot inside the grave.

The younger fellow had a stretchy face and hair that hung to his shoulders; he looked nineteen, or so — Fin and Aiden's age — and walked with a limp. He wore rough denims and a flannel shirt, and a straight-cut woolen jacket. Both men's coats were stained with old blood, and stunk of skunk and onion.

"We seen your fire," said the older man, who introduced himself as LeGrande Sharp. He declined to offer his hand.

"Smelt your supper too," said the younger one, who called himself Axel. He gave no last name, just set his eyes toward the pot on the fire and licked his wind-burned lips.

Fin told the men who he was, then indicated his friend with a nod. "This is my partner, Aiden Elliott." Aiden set his plate down, rose, and held out one hand. The older man's eyes twitched, and he hesitated, but he shook it. The younger man just stood there.

Aiden wasn't sure what surprised him more: that Fin had referred to him as a partner — for they'd formed no business agreement at all — or the grip of the old man's hand. Fingers as gnarled as his shouldn't hold any tension at all, yet LeGrande's contained a fair amount of power.

Neither Fin nor Aiden offered the men supper, but seeing as how the strangers demonstrated no inclination to leave, it seemed in their own best interests to feed the vagrants and get them on their way. Fin asked if they'd eaten. The old man said they hadn't, and readily accepted Fin's offer of a plateful of beans. Fin dished them each a spoonful, threw some ham on top.

"If you got coffee in that pot," said LeGrande, nodding toward the fire, "me and my nephew would take some."

Fin splashed them each half a cupful. The one called

2

Axel said he'd take some sugar, but Fin said they hadn't any. It irritated him that these strangers had no supper of their own to go to; as it was, he'd already parted with four nice chunks of ham.

Once the men had eaten, they rested on their elbows, relaxing beside the fire. Axel slipped one boot off and held his foot a few inches from the flame. His big toe, rimmed with blood, stuck through a hole in his sock; he had rubbed his toenail raw against the leather of his boot, a situation most men suffered from at one time or another. Boots got wet and then they shrank, sometimes two sizes smaller.

Aiden slipped his hands into his pockets. "What brings you men to Malheur?"

"We're taxidermists, up from Klamath country," said LeGrande. Anyone with an understanding of the great outdoors knew the term was marsh talk for plume hunters: men who shot birds for the millinery trade in New York and San Francisco. "Hunt herons mostly, but grebes is good too — grebes, terns, and cormorants. We trekked to Malheur to shoot little whites — kilt sixteen this morning." He looked around the camp, eyed the handful of pelican skins stretched between two poles near Fin and Aiden's tent. "What you men into?"

Fin was quiet a moment. He didn't trust the man, thought he resembled the stocky green heron that ate the babies of blackbirds. "We never put a name to it," he said, infusing his voice with nonchalance. "Mostly we're collectors." This was only partly true; Aiden was the devout collector, while Fin preferred hunting birds — sometimes his chest thumped so hard when he stalked them that he could barely contain himself. Once, as a boy, he'd gone stiff inside his trousers before he'd ever pulled the trigger, and though he was no more than twelve at the time, the event so astonished him that he hid behind a tree until his head cleared and his blood ran cool and his hands held still again. He understood his body's reaction to hunting birds was a heat he couldn't control, yet he never confessed his feelings to anyone, lest they think him ungodly or demented.

"I'm an öologist myself," said Aiden.

"Öologist?" said the gangly one, the one with no last name.

"Egg collector," Aiden told him, adding, "Fin takes mostly bird skins. We're considering starting a society once we venture back to Portland—a club of sorts, where we'd exchange eggs and discuss ornithology, if we'd a mind to."

Fin pursed his lips and glanced at the ground; he and Aiden had never discussed any such thing. While it was true they had come to the marshes of southeast Oregon for profit *and* for study, Aiden's goal was scientific and based primarily on learning. Fin, however, needed to shoot birds and sell their feathers so he could help support his mother. In all likelihood Aiden was following Fin's lead, trying to assuage LeGrande's concerns, persuade him they weren't rivals; the man didn't look like he'd take kindly to competition.

Aiden's comment seemed to satisfy LeGrande, and he settled deeper on one elbow. Scooting back from the fire, he yanked the bandana from around his neck, mopped his face, and stuffed the large red square into his pocket. He pulled a flask from his vest, popped the cork and sucked hard at its contents, shrinking the whiskey by one quarter. Declining to offer so much as a swallow to anyone else, he let loose a low grunt. "I ain't no öologist," he said, drawing the word out in a way that told of his disdain, "but I know birds. Shot terns and herons and pink curlew all the way down to Florida. Worked for a feller name of Cuthbert, though I ought to have hired my own crew—"

"Made bigger money if you had," Axel interrupted.

Fin glanced up at the mention of money, although his head never moved and his features feigned indifference. Aiden caught the shift in Fin's demeanor, and knew without a word there was no pretending about it: Fin wanted to know more about the financials, the *money* end of pluming. Being Fin's best friend, Aiden wanted to help him get it figured out, if only to assist Willa McFaddin, Fin's widowed mother.

Aiden leaned forward, set a naïve and somewhat ignorant quality to his tone, and asked how pluming worked, exactly.

LeGrande swigged his whiskey. "You know how it works. Got you a mess of scalps o'er thar." He nodded toward the pelican skins, then frowned distastefully. "You ought to waited a day before you skinned 'em, though. Blood leaked all over the feathers, and you've likely ruint them."

"Well, we're no experts," Aiden said, letting the comment dangle. He hoped LeGrande would bite.

"No, you ain't no experts," LeGrande agreed. He took another swig, held the brew in his mouth before it slid down, and then grimaced as the liquid stung the pipe inside his chest.

"Not 'til you been at it as many years as my uncle do you get to be an expert," Axel volunteered. He picked at his toe and squeezed it until blood spurted out; an oozy yellow substance followed, which even a fellow as hearty as Fin found difficult to watch.

Aiden nodded at LeGrande and smiled. He kept his mouth shut and waited for the liquor to do its work. LeGrande helped the process along by draining the bottle. "White herons, you take only the longest plumes right along the back. Snowys, you take the back, throat, breast—"

"Don't forget the head," Axel put in, glancing up from his toe and looking at Aiden. "Uncle L's got him a whole shack of head feathers."

LeGrande sniffed, and dragged his hand beneath his nose. "Thirty ounces gives you a packet, and once you got a packet, you got a business too."

"How many herons do you have to kill to make a packet?" Aiden wanted to know. It was a risky question, and Fin, at least, worried LeGrande might not answer. But the man sat up, and it seemed he might well go there, for he was the professional and Aiden the amateur, and a scientist, at that.

"Four herons make you an ounce, so what's that? Hundred-twenty birds or so?"

Aiden whistled.

"How much you get for an ounce?" Fin asked, emerging from his silence.

The marsh dweller clammed up, which meant he wasn't as far gone as they'd hoped. He was a shrewd one, and even with a dozen swigs of souse in his belly, he'd never surrender information as sensitive as that. But Axel missed the cloud passing over his uncle's face and blurted, "Thirty-two dollars, and in case you can't cipher it, that's more than twice the price for a single ounce of gold."

LeGrande's mouth went tight. He stood, walked over to Axel and kicked him, hitting the young plumer squarely on the toe. Axel yelped, and his eyes began to water. "What'd you do that for?" he cried.

"Get up," LeGrande told him, and then turned to leave.

Without a word Axel stood, then hobbled off to join his uncle, his boot held loosely in one hand. The men disappeared into the brush, neither offering so much as a thank you or the simplest farewell.

"You could put your boot on, at least," Aiden called into the darkness.

But Axel didn't stop. Aiden looked at Fin and said in a

low voice, "That old man's going to thump his nephew when they get back to camp. I'd stake my life on it."

Fin nodded, and with sympathy in his voice, said, "A man can't help it if he's stupid." He stood with Aiden a moment, peering into the distance before walking over to a log. He sat, poured the dregs of his coffee onto the fire, then leaned back as the coals hissed and sizzled. He and Aiden were quiet a long time, each recounting in his own mind the incident just past. The fire began to die down, and before the light was lost, Fin leaned forward, picked up a stick, and scratched numbers in the dirt. He whistled low. "If that figure Axel spouted is accurate, we're talking $960 for a package of plumes. Have I got that right?"

Aiden took the stick from Fin, tallied this and carried that, drew a line across the dirt. "You've got it right, exactly."

Astonished, Fin sat fully upright. "It would take three years to earn that much at Gilchrist's."

"It's a fortune, alright."

"You had that kind of money, what would you do?"

"Get myself to Berkeley and pay my tuition—college is expensive, you know."

"You aim to do that anyway, and your pa will surely help you."

That Aiden would receive assistance from his father for his first year of school while Fin toiled at Gilchrist's in downtown Portland didn't embarrass him one bit. "I guess I'll have to think on it," he said. "Why? What would you do?"

"Leave the mercantile for good, fix it so my mother can quit the laundry business, or at least get her into something that's not so hard on her back." He looked up at Aiden. "I'd buy a boat, too, and maybe a bigger gun—kill ten thousand birds and make myself a rich man."

"Won't be a heron left at Malheur, if you do."

"If I don't kill them, LeGrande will. Why should he make all the money?"

"You'll hang onto your hat a whole lot longer if you stay out of that man's way—hang onto your head too."

"I wear a cap," Fin said, chuckling. "As for my head, I've got no plans to lose it."

He made light of the situation, more for Aiden's sake than his own. He knew in his gut LeGrande Sharp was bad news, but he knew too he could take care of himself—that he *had* to take care of himself, since he had so few options: either he returned to a job he despised at the mercantile, or risked riling the old-time plumer. The latter held greater appeal.

He slept very little that night. Thinking of Aiden and their boyhood days, he realized that even at twelve he had known he would never get enough of the sights and sounds of the natural world, of berries dripping on the vine. At thirteen, fourteen, fifteen—and all the years thereafter—he had lain awake, listening for the murmuring of the great Mount Hood, and the call of America's Great Basin. After his father died, he told his mother he was leaving. "I'm heading for the opposite side of Oregon, to make us a better future."

Small violet moons glistened beneath Willa McFaddin's eyes. She had known this day was coming, but still she asked, "What have the marshes got that the forests don't? I wish you'd just stay home."

"We talked about this, remember?" he said, not unkindly. And because he couldn't help himself, he spoke of his deepest yearning. "I've heard rumors of a stork-like bird that stalks the grasses of Malheur, and geese so thick they rush to roost with a roar that bursts the ears. I've heard of white herons, and little whites, and pelicans, too. And a diver called a grebe."

"Grebe?" said Willa. "I can't quite picture it."

"It's got a red eye, and a neck as long as a snake."

"Well, I don't like that," she countered at once, and they shared the smallest laugh.

Now, as the sun crested on the cattails of the high-desert marsh, Fin got up. The clatter of ducks and geese was deafening, and he wondered how Aiden could sleep through the din. While he made a breakfast of flapjacks, coffee, and freshly caught trout, he again thought of his mother. Told himself his goal was justified, for not only would he make a better life for both of them, but he'd pursue his love in the process. It was a common-sense decision.

The fragrant scent of frying fish roused Aiden from his bedroll. He got up, wandered groggily to the log by the campfire, and sat in the morning sun.

Fin handed Aiden his food, then cleaned his own plate in short order. He might have licked it, too, had he been sitting alone, but Aiden had manners and would chastise him soundly, and the morning was too nice to endure a saw as loud as that.

After Aiden finished his coffee, Fin said he wouldn't return to Portland with him at the end of summer, as planned. "I want to travel to Lower Klamath, join up with LeGrande and his nephew, Axel."

"You can't be serious," Aiden told him.

"I want to learn the ropes, is all. Get the feel of serious pluming."

"Then teach yourself, like you've always done. You don't need LeGrande Sharp to show you how to hunt birds. You learned that years ago."

"Not on Klamath, I didn't." Fin stood, walked over to the fire, and poured himself more coffee. "LeGrande's from there," he said. "He knows the birds and their haunts. If I ask him real nice, he might hook me up with some market hunters. I'll learn that business in the fall, shooting birds for the restaurant trade, then switch to pluming come March or April."

"Don't do it, Fin. No good can come of it."

"I've got to, Aiden, I need the money."

"Well you're a fool, if you do."

"In case you forgot, I've got no father back in Portland to sustain me."

"All right," Aiden said, "I'll give you that. Just know that by the time you've had your fill of LeGrande Sharp and dragged yourself back home, there won't be a bird left in the sky. You'll have shot them all, you and your cronies there."

"What difference does it make if I shoot birds for money or for science? Either way, they'll die."

It was a dig, and Aiden knew it. "The difference is I'm collecting eggs and skins in the *name* of science," he argued, "for understanding and for knowledge. You're making no contribution at all, just killing for the sake of a dollar." As soon as he said it, he regretted it, as the remark came out more bitterly than he intended. He took a breath, started again. "Sooner or later, this carnage, this killing for profit, will be illegal, Fin. Where will you be then?"

"Well, it ain't illegal yet, Aiden, and I plan to take advantage."

"There are other ways to make a living—photography, for one. It's the future, Fin, photographing birds instead of shooting them. I plan to take it up myself one day, arrange my photos in a booklet and write an essay or two—"

"I've got no talent for writing, or picture-taking, either. And I sure don't see no money in it."

"There may not be much in the beginning, but the better

we get, the more people that hear of us, well—can't you see? Our names in some scientific journal, atop an article or two?"

"I'm no photographer," Fin repeated, "nor writer, nor conservationist. I've got no qualms about hunting, nor thoughts against it, either. It's what I love, Aiden, and no amount of reasoning will make me change my mind."

"Have it your way, then. But what you're doing is wrong, and I sorely wish you'd see it."

In that moment, something radical shifted between them. Fin had always believed their friendship was capable of withstanding even the deepest wound, but he understood now that this fracture in their relationship was likely beyond repair. He had no wish to make things worse than they were, however, and so he bit his tongue and walked toward the tent.

"That's right," Aiden said, his tone brittle now. "Turn your back on me. While you're at it, turn your back on everyone who loves you, and awaits your return, for I imagine they're all dead to you now."

Fin slowly turned. "What's that supposed to mean?"

"I promised your mother I'd see you safely home. And in case you're interested, she isn't the only one longing to see you. Maggie is too. She's loved you her entire life, as you well know. You give her a chance, she'll make you a fine wife one day."

All this time Fin thought Aiden was on his side when it came to Maggie Elliott. But it turned out blood was thicker than water, just like they said it was. "I don't love your sister like that, Aiden. I've never once held otherwise."

Fin might have said more, but he wasn't one to turn a knife once he'd plunged it. He clamped his mouth, packed his gear, and set out to find his plumers. Before he left, he asked Aiden to tell his mother that he would send money as soon as he was able. And though he might have made some other choice had he a mentor to guide him, he had no advisor, save his beloved friend, to tell him to be careful.

# CHAPTER TWO

The millinery on Front Street in Portland's Harker Building featured an elegant showroom where Aiden's mother, Blythe Elliott, shopped. The store's interior was spacious and inviting, with polished wood floors, an oriental carpet, and a full-length mirror for viewing. On each side of the wide red carpet a counter stood—the first eight feet long, the second just under twelve—and in two corners armoires reigned, with no fewer than eleven shelves apiece.

Mrs. R.C. Ryan, the shop's proprietress, offered ready-made and custom hats in the most becoming styles. Twice yearly, she traveled to Paris and New York City, returning with new ideas and the most fetching productions, featuring fur, feathers, and flowers. As the shop's sole designer, Mrs. Ryan served as the arbiter of feminine opinion, assessing each patron based on width of face and length of neck, encouraging the use of *aigrettes*—the long, beautiful plumes of big and little herons—to lend height to upper features and provide dignity and elegance.

Mrs. Ryan employed four assistants: the first, a young woman with shapely fingers who handled fancywork—the application of feathers, ribbons and flowers—and a second, who operated the machines and constructed specialty wire frames for custom orders. The third worked as the shop's straw and crown sewer, and the fourth performed the duties of cutting, crimping and lining. Mrs. Ryan insisted on neatness, accuracy, and delicacy of touch, and no worker remained long in her employ if she proved remotely careless.

Mrs. Ryan herself examined each completed hat, turning it in her hand and eyeing every detail, occasionally sending it back for further adjustment when it failed to please her. She demanded perfection, and perfection she got, and it was this quality that ensured not only her reputation, but her ability to command up to fifty dollars per hat. For those with less money to spend, or whose husbands weren't professionals—as Owen Elliott was—there was always Gilchrist's; the mercantile sold ready-made hats for five dollars each.

Blythe adored the milliner. "Mrs. Ryan," she intoned, extending both hands and clasping the woman's upon striding into the store. "My daughter Margaret and I have a function to attend, and need to look our best. What have you got that's marvelous and exciting? Something new from Paris, perhaps?"

Mrs. Ryan looped her arm through Blythe's. She led her toward the store's largest armoire, and while Blythe considered a sealskin toque—a large cap with a full crown and rolled brim, suitable for a vibrant matron—Maggie wandered toward the shorter counter, where shocks of emerald green and royal purple captured her attention. There were hats constructed of felt and tulle and gathered velvet, all trimmed in lace and feathers. There were round hats with Mercury wings, and flat ones featuring gardens: dried apples and apricots and slender string beans, and blood-red pomegranates. On the opposite side, on the longer counter, sat hats with ostrich feathers; some were clipped, some curled, and some were broadly fanning.

Maggie found each hat captivating, and then saw the one she would die for. Crafted of brown felt and shaped like a hunter's cap, it featured the bodies of six plump hummingbirds, their heads and throats a deep rose red, their bodies gray and green. Each bird was perched on a small stick at something of an angle, its wings neatly folded. She glanced at the price tag, and seeing it was marked twenty-five dollars, picked up the hat, walked over to the full-length mirror, and placed it on her head. She stood, transfixed, staring at her reflection.

Mrs. Ryan took note instantly. Stepping forward, she said, "My goodness. I'd not realized how much you've grown, Margaret. You look stunning in that hat."

"I'm eighteen now," Maggie told her, smiling. "You haven't seen me in a while."

Mrs. Ryan turned toward Blythe. "Just look at her, will you? She's become a woman, it seems, and a lovely one at that."

Blythe too stood in front of a mirror, an oval encased in a wooden frame that showcased her upper body. She adjusted the sealskin toque on her head, glanced over one shoulder and casually regarded Maggie. "Mmm," she said, tilting her head, and then said nothing more.

If Mrs. Ryan found Blythe's reaction peculiar, she merely bit her lip. Maggie took no notice, however, and stood one minute more, gazing into the mirror. She'd not asked for a thing in her life, aside from the love of Fin McFaddin, but she badly wanted this hat. It was for a special meeting of Aiden's, and she wanted to look good for his friends. Sadly, Fin would not be among them.

Maggie hadn't seen Fin since she was fourteen, a dreamy-eyed schoolgirl who had clung to the belief he would come home one day, perhaps when the leaves turned brown. That was four years ago, and in all the time he hadn't sent her as much as a single letter. In the early days, he'd written to his mother. Willa had shared those notes, knowing how much Maggie longed to hear from him, but when he never asked after her, never told Willa to give her his regards, Maggie understood he might never see her as she wished him to, although she refused to give up on him.

When Aiden had first returned from his travels, he had told her of the time he and Fin had spent in Malheur's marshes, how smoothly things had initially gone, and how roughly they had ended. Aiden's face colored when he described the argument they'd had. "Fin's working as a plume hunter, if you can believe it," he'd railed. "He flat-out refuses to make the distinction between collecting birds for scientific purposes, versus killing them for profit. Mark my words, Maggie, someday Fin and men just like him will empty the sky of birds."

Maggie had laughed at that. When she realized her brother was serious, she'd said, "Aiden, that's impossible."

"Haven't we already lost the great auk?" he'd said. "And what about the passenger pigeon? That bird has been blown almost entirely from the sky."

"What about blackbirds?" she'd wanted to know. "There must be millions left of those."

"There are, Maggie, but that's not the point."

She stood quietly after that. Even at fourteen, she'd understood Aiden had missed the point just as much as she had. He stood ready to blame everyone but himself for the disappearance of birds, unable to see—or admit, either one—that scientists and oölogists were as guilty as plumers for wiping out whole species. A body couldn't run around, snatching up eggs to stick in museums, then cry, "The skies are all but empty!" As far as Maggie could tell, there were still plenty of birds left in this world, and as long as there were six to pin to her bonnet, she was happy to put them there.

"What do you think, Margaret?" asked Mrs. Ryan. "Shall I box it up for you?"

Biting her lip, Maggie glanced at her mother. Blythe nodded. "Yes, please, if you would," Maggie told Mrs. Ryan.

Blythe asked Mrs. Ryan to box hers, as well, and then sat for a custom fitting since she needed a hat for a formal occasion.

Mrs. Ryan produced a measuring tape from her pocket, and placed it around Blythe's head, just above the ear, holding it firmly but not too tightly, exactly where the hat would sit. She jotted a few numbers on a slip of paper, and when that was done, asked Blythe if Margaret should be measured too. Blythe said yes, while Maggie said no, adding she had everything she needed.

"Don't be silly, Margaret," said Blythe. "A woman can never have enough hats."

So Maggie, too, sat for a custom fitting.

On arriving home, the women found Owen Elliott sitting in his stocking feet at the kitchen table. A mortician by trade, and the owner of the local mortuary, Maggie's father had no wish to bring ill will upon his family by tempting Luck and Fortune. Not once had he opened an umbrella inside the house, walked under an open ladder, or crossed the path of a black cat. His mother too was superstitious, and because she refused to wear shoes in the house, he also declined to do so. She had died when he was seven, so he'd never had the opportunity to ask the reason for her shoelessness; he had always assumed she thought it unlucky, so he thought it unlucky too. He'd not yet been able to persuade his wife to go shoeless outside of the bedroom, although Maggie delighted in walking barefoot, if no one was around.

He held a saltshaker in one hand, and having spilled a few grains, brushed them into his palm and tossed them over his shoulder. "Ah," he said, eyeing the hatboxes when Blythe and Maggie walked in. "So you've bought more hats, have you? What did you pay for them?"

"Nothing," Blythe said, strolling breezily by.

"How did you manage that?"

"I told the milliner to send the bill to you."

Owen laughed heartily, as he more than anyone appreciated his wife's cleverness. "Brilliant, Mrs. Elliott," he told her, popping a boiled egg into his mouth.

Maggie planned to show off her new hat at the meeting of the Oregon Öology Society, the OOS, Aiden called it. The society was Aiden's idea entirely, something he'd thought up while camping in the marshes of Malheur. The society was meant to showcase his scientific findings and to sell and trade blown eggs to organizations with similar affiliations: institutions and museums and such. He'd formed the OOS just two weeks after returning from Malheur, and had placed ads in magazines such as *The Oregon Naturalist*, which explained who and what he was:

> AIDEN ELLIOTT. FIELD ORNITHOLOGIST
> AND OÖLOGIST. EGGS COLLECTED, SOLD,
> AND EXCHANGED.

Maggie had wondered how the eggs were blown. Aiden told her there was a trick to it, that Morris Kiff, the local curio-shop owner, had some years earlier shown Fin how to do it, and in turn, Fin had shown Aiden. Morris had also demonstrated the art of preserving skins, which were saved flat or round. Maggie wondered about that, too, and asked Aiden what the difference was. He told her a flat skin constituted the back of a bird—sometimes called a scalp—while a round skin looked like a bird intact, minus its innards and eyes.

"A bird without eyes?" Maggie had ventured, for the notion seemed downright eerie.

"A cotton ball sits where the eye once did," Aiden explained, "although it doesn't do much to improve a bird's appearance." He went on to say that Fin had once stuck cloves in a bird's eye slots, making the creature look star struck. Neither he nor Maggie spoke for a while, as they contemplated Fin. And then Aiden smiled. He told Maggie that he had once blown out the contents of a blackbird's egg, with Fin instructing him to prick a small hole in the center—never on the end, as Fin himself had mistakenly once done—and then make the hole larger still, using a small drill.

"Now stick the pipe into the hole," Fin had told him, "but barely now, you hear? Let's see what happens."

Aiden had leaned over, his hollow pipe ready to go.

"That's right, now stick it in and blow. You'll get the hang of it."

Aiden gave it a try, and to his surprise, the juicy parts spilled right out.

Fin showed him how to rinse the egg, demonstrating how to hold it between two fingers and with a syringe force a little water in, then again blow out the contents. "Bugs and mice not so apt to injure an egg, if it's clean," Fin had said, expertly setting the orb on a swatch of batting to dry.

Every now and then, they gathered eggs that were close to hatching. Such occasions required that they drill a larger hole before puncturing the embryo with a hook. The first time Aiden tried it, he ran the hook through the shell on the opposite side and ruined it.

"Fin told me to concentrate," Aiden said to Maggie, "to pretend I had a gun in my hand, and it was fixed upon a warbler. I was no natural, I'll admit, but when I tried a second time, when I really focused, it was easier. I washed out the soft parts, which the embryo hadn't yet absorbed, filled the egg with water, and set it in a box to percolate. Once decomposition set in, the chunky parts popped out."

"I would like to have tried that," said Maggie.

"Requires more practice than you'd think," Aiden told her. "I was never as good as Fin was, but my delight was in the recording of data, as Fin disliked it so. I took great care to log into my journal all that Fin transcribed—nest location and condition of the eggs, whether fresh or partly incubated. Each egg needed cataloguing too, and on the side with the hole, I wrote the catalogue number in fine black ink, and on the opposite side, the set number, and number of eggs contained within that set. I'll tell you, I thrived on the activity. 'I could do this all day long,' I bragged to Fin, and he said, 'I could surely let you.'"

Maggie could hear Fin say just such a thing, and it was the memory of his voice, so self-assured, that had kept her going. That and his smile—when he chose to give it—and the way he appeared when he tilted his head and his hair hung over one eye. It seemed he was always in need of a haircut, yet disheveled as he was, it was his casual air that she admired. Most women wanted men to throw flowers at their feet; Maggie wanted someone different, a man who wasn't so desperately feeling, who kept his notions to himself. In that respect, Fin was her opposite, just as he was Aiden's, and it was that which drew him to her.

Maggie knew her brother missed Fin, and that he wished he were around to accompany him on his birding expeditions. Aiden had become something of an expert himself these days, when it came to blowing eggs. He now sold and traded everything he found in Portland during the summer months, and each fall, after returning to school in Berkeley, he combed the hills of California and did his collecting there.

Morris Kiff took over Aiden's duties as president of the OOS when Aiden left for school, relinquishing them each spring when Aiden came home again. The society met once a month in Morris's house. By the summer of 1897, the organization's membership had swelled into the forties. Women were not as a rule invited to OOS functions, so the upcoming meeting served as an exception.

The gathering was to be held in Bradley Hall, since the event was expected to be crowded. The day's speaker, a curator from New York City, had sent a note to Aiden beforehand, specifically requesting that men bring their wives and sweethearts along for the afternoon's presentation. The reason behind the man's request remained a mystery, which made it all the more appealing, so turn out they did, in droves. Someone had leaked word that there would be a drawing, a door prize of a dollar, although why Aiden Elliott would provide such a luxurious award no one specifically knew.

Morris was upset when he heard about it, as the society hadn't extra funds to spare. Aiden took the news in stride. "We never said we'd cough up a dollar," he told Morris, coolly. "It was a rumor from the get-go, and I'll be the first to tell them so."

"Likely you'll do it with a tomato stuck on your nose, for soon as they figure out you've no prize to give them, they'll fling that much and more."

Aiden considered this. "We'll get a bigger crowd if they think there's cash to be had," he said, seeing by the look on Morris's face that the man not only disagreed, but also suspected Aiden had started the rumor. "Okay, look," he went on. "We may get a few new members out of the deal, and once everyone has settled in, we'll simply apologize, tell them it was some scallywag who spread the falsehood. And then we'll make it right by offering one of Tula's pies."

"I doubt that will appease them, Aiden, but you're the president. Do whatever you want."

To that end, Aiden paid Tula, the Elliott family's housekeeper, two bits to roust a few refreshments. She accepted the offer as soon as Aiden presented it, for she enjoyed pie making, and was good at it.

The entire community thought Aiden's parents, Blythe and Owen Elliott, a regal pair. His father looked more a king than the owner of a mortuary, with his gray beard and frock coat flowing, his nose as long as a scepter. Blythe's own nose was almost as lengthy as her husband's. A great gob of hair, as curly and wild as her children's, had a habit of bunching up on one side of her head, resulting in a rather lopsided appearance so that she never looked royal so much as acted it. She was naturally aloof, and as unlike Aiden and Maggie as a queen from two elves propped on a toadstool.

It wasn't four weeks after Fin's father, Edward McFaddin, had died that Aiden had come home after bird hunting with Fin to find his mother at the top of the stairs, flinging socks over the banister.

"Darks go in that pile," she'd said to Maggie, who stood at the bottom step. "Whites go…whites go…" She glanced down, and noticing Aiden only then, said, "Where do the whites go, dear?"

The question took him by surprise; not only were those the first words she'd uttered to him since dinner the night before, but he had no idea about whites, darks, or anything in between.

"How about there?" he ventured, pointing to an empty spot on the floor.

"Ah," she said, and over went the bed sheets.

It turned out Willa McFaddin had been to the house that very day, offering her services as a laundress and earning two dollars and twenty-five cents a month for a pile collected on Monday, washed on Tuesday, ironed on Wednesday and delivered in tidy bundles on Thursday afternoon. Three families a week, supplemented with Fin's bird money, meant she could support herself while Fin was in Malheur country. She only needed to secure a commitment from someone like Blythe Elliott to attract the interest of others, as she'd put it, adding, "if you'll take me on, I know Mrs. Souter will too, and maybe Mrs. Beckwith, and her oldest daughter as well, for your husband's name means something in this town...yours too, of course."

"I've got a woman now," Blythe had told her, "though I admit she complains sorely of her workload." Each day, Tula swept the floors and dusted furniture, and when she wasn't doing that, she was beating rugs, and polishing brass and copper fixtures. Mending came after the supper dishes, and Fridays were for baking.

"I'll gladly ease her burden," Willa volunteered, "starting Monday morning."

"All right," Blythe agreed, "let's give it a try." She asked what she needed to do, beyond informing Tula that Willa was taking over the laundry.

"Separate your clothes, is all. What I call whites some call coloreds — it would help me greatly if you'd make the decision on your own."

And so Blythe had done just that, which is what she told Aiden when he asked why she was flinging laundry over the banister. "I've hired Willa McFaddin," she said, "and she's asked me to sort our clothes, which is precisely what I'm doing."

"Why don't you have Tula do it?"

"She informed me laundry is no longer her concern, and if I hope to retain her employ, I best figure it out on my own."

Neither Aiden nor Maggie seemed surprised by Tula's pronouncement, or that their mother had allowed it. Blythe wasn't one to fire a maid any more than she'd chastise Maggie, for that was Owen's job. So often as a child Maggie had burst through the door at half-past six, dragging in all manner of debris — dead leaves and lichen and bits of dried moss — her face flushed and sweating. If Owen hadn't already seated himself at the dinner table and draped his napkin over one knee, he'd greet her at the door with a thump to her head, remarking, and rather dryly too, "How nice of you to join us, Huckleberry Finn."

When Blythe had chucked a wad of fabric toward Aiden that day, saying, "Kick that over to the darks, will you, dear," Maggie had glanced down at her brother. He saw in her eyes the consternation he himself felt, as it never occurred to either of them that the Elliott household would pay the McFaddins to wash Tula's laundry. But if it bothered Blythe, a body never knew it. She tossed one last armful of her husband's trousers over the railing, and then asked Aiden to stack the piles on the porch where Willa McFaddin could find them. And then just like that, she disappeared, for the Brontës were calling and she had a book to read.

Despite Willa's help, Tula still had plenty to do, but

assisting Aiden was a pleasure. She willingly made pies for his meeting—a meeting which continued to perplex Aiden. Why Frank M. Chapman had requested the gathering in the first place was still a mystery, although secretly Aiden hoped Chapman planned to recognize the society for its work. Chapman himself was a collector and if anyone appreciated the value of quality skins and eggs—not to mention their contribution to the scientific method—it was the curator from New York City.

At five minutes of four Aiden stood at the back of the room, greeting the attendees. The hall was large and airy, the ceilings tall and broad. The floor was lined with tidy rows of wooden chairs, and there was a podium up front. At the far side of the room there were three long tables with punch bowls and trays of gingersnaps. Tula's pie sat as a centerpiece, the crowning glory of pastries. Aiden had asked her to make her best effort, and turn out a winner she did, piling a mountain of golden-tipped meringue atop a pond of lemon-custard. A woman told her husband it looked just like the Matterhorn, to which he replied, "Feller could ski it, if he'd a mind to, then eat it afterward."

A sign propped on the end of one table encouraged society members to jot their names on a calling card, then drop it into a fishbowl, since there would be a door prize; the man who made the Matterhorn joke dropped his name in first, and a dozen others followed.

It was four o'clock exactly when Maggie walked into the room. She wore a white silk blouse edged with opalescent beads, a brown skirt, and her little hat, of course. She hadn't realized Aiden's meetings had grown so popular, and was surprised to see so many people there. Despite his time away from Portland during the winter months, it seemed he'd made headway in the field of ornithology, as his supporters were all too glad to rally around and cheer him. Many of their wives and sweethearts had come for the meeting too.

The blonde-haired woman from Guthrie Park was there, wearing a dress hemmed with the heads of two hundred purple finches. Aiden had told Maggie about her, when he'd first come back from Malheur. It seemed he and Fin had shared stories on that trip, anecdotes of their younger days, and Fin had confessed he'd once kissed the blonde-haired girl, but the kiss had left him listless. It had hurt Maggie to hear that story, and she wasn't certain why her brother had told it. Likely he was trying to steer her away from Fin, and persuade her to love another.

Maggie gazed at the woman, thought her beautiful. She wondered if Fin would be disappointed to learn she had gotten married, tied the knot with a lumberjack, who wasn't even handsome. Maggie's eyes drifted toward him then, and settled on his form. He was as big as the legend, although he owned no ox and walked with a limp. As far as Maggie was concerned, the blonde woman didn't know what she'd given up; Maggie wouldn't have let Fin go if Paul Bunyan himself had proposed.

She squeezed into the knot of people, angling between men in bowlers and women in outsized hats, nearly all of them decorated with wings of birds fastened at their brims. Some hats bore the bodies of entire pigeons, and there was one with the head of a great-horned owl, which sported dark, vacant eyes. Maggie recognized Fin's neighbor, Mrs. Gary, who wore a hat bedecked with moss, leaves, and a nest lined with lamb's wool; inside, a goldfinch sat in earnest incubation. Most impressive was a bonnet containing no less than thirty *aigrettes* leaning breezily outward, as if succumbing to some wind. No man could walk alongside it without receiving a tickling to his chin.

Maggie took in the sights and sounds, the perfumed soap, the wayward drift of tobacco. She felt every inch a grownup, and it did a body good to know more than one eye traced her path as she sauntered toward her brother. If she couldn't have Fin, maybe she'd have some other young man, although no one else appealed.

"Ah, here's my sister, Margaret," Aiden said, when she finally came upon him. He held out his arm and drew Maggie in, introducing the stranger beside him. "Maggie, I'd like you to meet Mr. Frank M. Chapman, an ornithological expert, if ever there was one."

"It's a pleasure to meet you," said Maggie, offering her hand. Chapman accepted it warmly, hesitating only a moment as his eyes wandered upward, to the birds adorning her hat.

"The pleasure is mine," he said, brushing her hand with his lips.

The gesture struck Maggie as wildly continental. "I've never known a man to kiss a woman's hand before," she blurted giddily. "Makes me a feel a tourist in some far off place, like London or Paris, or Rome."

Aiden coughed into his fist, and turned three shades of crimson.

"I've not yet been to Paris," Chapman told her, "although I'm sure it's as lovely as they say." Glancing at Aiden and then back at Maggie, he smiled, charmed.

The man's lively gaze told Maggie she'd captivated him, and so she planted her eyes demurely on the little fig that was Frank M. Chapman. If she ever hoped to move past Fin, she had to flirt a little. This man would make good practice.

Aiden approached the podium and called the room to

order, requesting that everyone kindly take a seat. Maggie chose a spot near the front. There was a rustle of petticoats and a bit of throat-clearing, as the crowd began to settle. When someone in the back hollered, "When you gonna draw names for that dollar prize?" Aiden wasted no time addressing the unfortunate rumor. A murmur went up, and he quickly pointed out that they had seen Tula's pie, hadn't they, and could anyone argue it was a fine substitution?

The man doing the hollering sat back with his face pinched and his arms crossed, while a rotund fellow named Dickman called, "Then let's get on with it and draw the names right now. I got a feeling I'm the winner, and I'd like to have a bite before the meeting commences."

Dickman's wife said, loud enough for all to hear, "See he doesn't win, will you, Aiden? Robert's trousers barely button as it is." How the crowd laughed at that.

"Tell you what," Aiden put in, drawing confidence from the happy gathering. "I'll allow our distinguished guest to draw our winner upon the meeting's conclusion." And when all heads nodded and the room went quiet, Aiden happily sighed.

"Good afternoon, ladies and gentlemen," he started, speaking in earnest now. "Welcome to the monthly meeting of the Oregon Öology Society. It's a privilege to have with us today the bird curator of the American Museum of Natural History in New York City, Mr. Frank M. Chapman. Mr. Chapman is the pioneer of museum exhibition techniques, and is here to speak to us of his impressive work, as well as his expertise in ornithology."

Aiden licked his lips. "In his original correspondence, Mr. Chapman asked that we invite the ladies of the community to attend this afternoon's meeting, which we've done — although I confess we've yet to learn the specifics of the invitation —"

here, the women tittered and the men smiled and nodded, for they were eager to learn the reason for the turnout. "Without further ado, may I present to you, Mr. Frank M. Chapman."

The audience applauded as the man strode toward the podium. He wore a tweed town suit, a knotted tie, and a vest beneath his jacket. Maggie watched him trot up the steps, thinking as much as she might have wished it so, he was nothing compared to Fin; he was thirty if he was a day, with thinning hair and a forehead so high a body could skate across it. Now that she'd taken a moment to truly examine his features, the way he carried himself, she could see he was the kind of man who'd want a proper lady. One with a pedigree.

No, he was too genteel for Maggie's taste, and wasn't the least bit like her. Aiden, though, was Chapman's twin, in mannerisms and desire; it was clear her brother had fallen in love, for there he sat, clapping wildly and beaming like a madman.

Chapman clutched the podium with both hands. "Thank you for having me, and for your introduction, Mr. Elliott." He smiled at the crowd. "As my colleague has indicated, I'm here today to speak to you about my experiences, primarily my foremost affection, which is ornithology."

All eyes were focused on Chapman, although a few blinked admiringly at Aiden, since he was the one who had arranged the speaker's appearance.

"I'll begin by first telling you about my work, for I am not infrequently asked, 'What do you do at the museum? Do you stuff birds?' If a curator of ornithology is true to his name, his first duties are the care of the collections under his charge. Each specimen must be identified, labeled, catalogued, and given its proper serial number before being stored in such a way that it will always be immediately available for examination.

"The mounted birds are then placed in the cases of the exhibition halls. The usually far larger number of unmounted skins—those resembling dead birds—are placed in containers which protect them from insects and dust, as well as from the bleaching effects of light, which detracts from their scientific value.

"Doubtless the uninterested will call this work dull, but to me it is an endless source of pleasure and information, as it brings intimate and constant association with specimens."

Chapman paused, holding his chin just so. "Now, I bring this up because I'd like to tell of a survey I conducted in New York City during two February afternoons in 1886. At that time I was a banker and amateur ornithologist, and was inspired by the formation of an organization, a group known as the Audubon Society—which I'm sad to say disbanded a few years ago, but may soon be regrouping—to secure information concerning the number and kinds of birds that were worn on women's hats.

"As I strolled Fourteenth Street, notebook in hand, I recorded, when I could identify them, the names of birds seen on the hats of passing women. In the light of existing conditions, the result seems incredible. It is probable that few if any of the women whose headgear formed part of my record, knew that they were wearing the plumage of the birds of our gardens, orchards and forests."

He gazed out at the sea of women and smiled, albeit benignly. In return, the women smiled back, eager to learn of Chapman's intentions, and confident they'd be included in some significant and meaningful way.

"Permit me to share with you the results of that survey."

He sucked in his cheeks while thumbing through his notes. Finding what he was looking for, he peered into the crowd. "I counted no fewer than 174 birds perched in various states of repose — 40 species in all, among them four robins, twenty-three cedar waxwings, fifteen snow buntings, twenty-one terns, and sixteen bobwhites. That this alarmed me I'll tell you frankly, for 542 of the 700 hats I tallied were garnished with feathers, the most elegant of which were the beautifully curved plumes we call *aigrettes*." Here, he gazed pointedly at the woman in the audience with the hat sporting dozens of long white feathers. "More specifically," Chapman went on, "three of four hats were decorated with feathers of dead birds."

The woman smiled weakly. She, along with everyone else in the room, began to sense where Chapman was going. She shifted in her seat.

Chapman let his statement linger. "The prevailing ignorance of bird life is demonstrated by an existing indifference to bird destruction, and by the almost universal habit of wearing the stuffed bodies of our familiar songbirds as hat decorations. I understand that your bonnets bring both you and your admirers joy, ladies, but you must understand that behind your feathered hats lie a trail of bloody slaughter."

The audience erupted, and the woman's husband stood. "You've got no right to spout such opinions, Chapman. I don't care if you're a curator or a camp cook — it's an unseemly thing to say."

"Unseemly or not, sir, it's a fact. Each winter scores of market hunters scour the shores of your lakes in southeast Oregon, murdering waterfowl for the restaurant trade. Come spring, plume hunters finish the job, and soon enough they'll wipe herons from your state altogether, just as they've done in Florida." Here, he looked at Aiden. "A groundswell of discontent has sprung up in the East, young man, and is aimed not only at plume hunters, but oölogists as well. Your society would do well to concentrate solely on scientific endeavors and separate itself entirely from the commercial aspects of collecting."

"Now hold on," Morris Kiff interrupted. He had to shout to be heard from a seat in the back. "The whole reason I belong to this organization is to promote my business—that's what I do, you know, buy eggs and skins and other memorabilia, and sell it across the country. How am I to make a living, if you cut off half my trade?"

"Birds must be made real," Chapman said, "before we can expect to appeal effectively on their behalf. They don't exist merely for the sake of commerce."

"What would you have us do?" shouted someone else. "A good many of us here collect at least some skins and eggs, and it's Kiff who buys our wares."

"I for one have taken up photography," Chapman said, "and find it quite relaxing. Why don't you and your compatriots shoot photographs instead of bullets? In that way you can instruct and inform, without the destruction that collection requires."

Aiden blinked, for that was precisely the suggestion he'd made to Fin four long years ago. Yet he had never considered himself an abuser—not the way that Fin was—so he'd not applied his own advice, or even bought a camera.

"What kind of plan is that?" shot a rattled voice up front. "There isn't one of us here who knows a thing about so-called picture-taking."

"All I'm saying is we must develop a concern for our wildlife heritage," Chapman said, "and to birds in particular. Reaffirm the ethics of sportsmanship, otherwise our flying creatures will go the way of the great auk and Carolina paraquet, and who among us wants that?"

"And where do you fit in, Chapman?" hollered the fellow in the back. "You're only too happy to spout conservation, but I reckon you collect more than your fair share of artifacts for your museum in New York City. I'll wager you've shot more birds than the lot of us here have shot in our entire lifetimes."

"The difference," intoned Chapman, raising his voice to speak above the din, "is that I'm not gathering eggs nor shooting birds merely for the *sake* of collecting. I am furthering the understanding of ornithology. My endeavor is purely scientific—and with science comes truth and understanding, one bird skin at a time."

Maggie sat up, for it was precisely the point she had once raised with Aiden. Chapman's response was Aiden's own, and when she glanced at her brother now, she saw his cheeks ignite.

The woman with the long white feathers jumped from her seat and stood alongside her husband. "If you'll recollect, Mr. Chapman, we women were *invited* here today—and by you, I might add. None of us came with the notion we'd be attacked, and I for one think it ungentlemanly to imply we're nothing but heartless killers."

"Hear, hear!" barked her supporters.

It seemed all eyes were on Aiden now, and that the stares were disapproving. He adjusted his necktie and swallowed. Despite his discomfort, he stood to address the crowd. "I don't believe it's Mr. Chapman's intention to attack anyone," he said. "He too is our guest, and we owe it to him to hear him out."

Chapman glanced at his notes and then looked up again, unfazed. He turned to the woman in the hat, and spoke calmly to the crowd. "Ladies and gentlemen, if you'll kindly allow me. I have one more point—*please*."

The woman stood straighter, as it was to her that Chapman directed his plea.

"It is not my intention to attack, but to inform," he told the woman, "for it is women such as you who control entirely this story's outcome."

"How do you mean, Sir?"

"It is *you* who wear the hats, *you* who can closet them tomorrow."

For ten minutes now Maggie had listened to Chapman insult every woman in the room. Every man too. She shot her hand into the air and waved. "Mr. Chapman," she called. When he didn't immediately respond, she stood. He saw her then, and motioned to her with a nod.

"With all due respect, Mr. Chapman, even Yankee Doodle wore a feather in his cap."

Chapman smiled. "So he did, Miss Elliott, so he did."

Maggie thought she'd gotten the best of him, but he requested permission to tell a second story. "If I may?" he said, and so she slowly sat. Someone in the audience groaned, begging for brevity.

"I've an acquaintance in Boston," he began, "a woman named Harriet Hemenway. We've had a number of discussions of late, and it is this good woman's contention that women who wear birds on their hats look silly, and as long as women look silly, they'll be perceived as silly, and for that reason never acquire the right to vote." Chapman didn't specifically state that Maggie looked silly with her hat full of hummingbirds, but when he glanced her way, the implication was clear.

Having heard enough, Morris Kiff stood too. "If you're talking about Maggie Elliott, I don't think she looks silly at all. I think she looks just dandy—in fact, I love those little birds atop her hat, and the next young man that brings me one will get double the normal pay."

Though a handful of women clapped in appreciation,

Morris's outburst disturbed Aiden deeply. As the society's part-time president, Aiden thought Morris ought to have held his tongue, not to mention a more congenial point of view. He turned toward his sister, then called above the crowd, "You want the right to vote one day, don't you, Maggie?"

"I've never really thought about it, Aiden, but yes, I suppose I do."

To everyone's surprise, the woman with the feathered hat pulled the bonnet from her head. "I want my voice to be heard, just as the voices of men are heard," she said, handing the hat to her husband. "Stash that in the attic with your wartime souvenirs, for I won't have anyone telling me I look foolish the day I cast my vote."

Her husband's mouth fell open. "You won't *live* long enough to vote," he said, and though he'd not meant it in a cruel way, that's the way it sounded.

The woman opened her mouth to protest, and seeing that things might well spiral out of control, Aiden quickly stood and directed his comments to his sister. "Maybe you could do likewise, Maggie? Shelve your feathered bonnet?"

Morris wouldn't hear it. He strode toward the front of the room, and standing in the middle of the aisle, said, "Maggie's your sister, Aiden, and if anyone was to stand up for her, I would think it would be you." His eyes darted toward Maggie. "Aiden ought not criticize you in front of this crowd or any other—nor should his friend, Chapman here." He looked over at the man, his eyes ablaze and his mouth set hard. "I know you think it's a sad thing to kill a living creature, but killing is God's way. He created animals to sustain us, whether it be our livelihood or as food on our tables. It's not a sin, but a means to support our families."

"It is a sin, when it's wasteful," Chapman countered, "or

when you enjoy it a little too much."

"You mean to tell me you've been hunting and collecting all these years, and you never once enjoyed it?"

Chapman took a moment to shape his words. "I admit that as a boy I rejoiced each summer in the ringing call of a bob-white," he said earnestly, "and with equal joy killed it in the fall. But I'm a boy no longer, Mr. Kiff. To my way of thinking, I've given you two excellent illustrations of the existence of savagery and sentiment in man's imperfect nature."

Morris scowled. "I ain't no savage, any more than Dickman there, or the lady with the hat." All eyes went to the woman now. She'd recovered from her husband's insult, and confessed to the crowd she'd never given a single thought to *how* feathers got on hats: they'd always simply been there. And then she spoke to Morris.

"Mr. Chapman raises a point. Perhaps it is a cruel practice, and we women, at least, ought to consider abandoning it."

Morris clenched his jaw, as he was too much the gentleman to argue with a lady. He bowed. "Ma'am," he said, then slapped his hat on his head and strode out the door.

A line had been drawn. It was up to each individual to decide which side he stood on. About half the crowd got up and followed Morris out. The rest remained, willing to at least discuss the pros and cons of Chapman's theory. Dickman spoke on behalf of a handful of those who just like him had stayed, wanting a chance to win Tula's pie. "I hope this don't mean there won't be no drawing," he said.

Aiden hesitated, assessing the mood of those remaining. It seemed opinions were generally with him—or at worst, undecided—and so he seized the chance to win over those he could.

"Well, why not?" he announced. He marched forward,

smiling determinedly. Snatching the bowl from the table, he hoisted it into the air. "I told you at the beginning of this meeting we'd have a drawing, so let's go on and have it." And then just like that, Aiden's future constituents—meaning the men in the room, for women wouldn't vote for many years to come yet—clamored around the fishbowl, hollering, "C'mon, Chapman, pluck my name from young Aiden's bowl there, if you'd be so kind!"

When Chapman picked a name and announced Snub Cunningham the winner, the blonde woman's lumberjack limped up to accept the pie.

"He ain't even a member of the OOS," Dickman groused.

Snub must have felt embarrassment at that, for he had come to the meeting with the notion he'd win one dollar. Now he'd have to fork over two bits or so, just to make amends. He held up the pie with one hand. "I ain't no egg collector," he said sheepishly, "but how's a donation sound?"

Aiden clapped the fellow on the back, said he'd gladly take his money, and all seemed satisfied.

Maggie marveled at Aiden's ability to win over a crowd. Chapman, for one, clearly thought him special, or at least a man with talent. And Aiden had already made clear his feelings about Chapman, for he'd gone on endlessly about the man before he ever arrived. It was "Chapman this" and "Chapman that" until Maggie thought she'd wring Aiden's neck for all his nonstop clucking.

She knew Aiden had previously met Chapman through a mutual acquaintance in Berkeley, that they'd hit it off at once. When Maggie asked what would compel Chapman to travel from New York City to Portland just to attend a meeting, Aiden had said he supposed it was to ask him to get involved in the Audubon Society. And then Aiden showered her with those details too, drenching her with information about the organization, how a fellow called Grinnell—who'd named the society in honor of John James Audubon—had formed it. The group folded for a variety of reasons shortly after it was founded, and it was Chapman's goal, as well as that of others like him, to get it going again.

After the meeting, while sipping a cup of punch and nibbling a cookie, Maggie watched as the man chatted with Aiden. Every so often Chapman glanced her way. As soon as he and Aiden concluded their conversation, he strolled over, hands in his pockets, to have a word with her.

"I must apologize for criticizing you in front of your peers," he said, bending slightly forward in his bid for humility. "It was never my intention, as Morris Kiff implied."

"I guess you read my thoughts then," Maggie said, biting into her cookie.

He opened his mouth to speak, then apparently thought better of it. He smiled, rather kindly, Maggie thought. She expected to see some superiority there, but saw sincerity instead. It surprised her, and so she offered him a cookie, which he accepted. He took a bite, and when he spoke again, it was to compliment her brother.

"Aiden's a good man," he said, "a man with a great deal of potential. I've seen his writing, and for a man of only twenty-three, he expresses himself quite well."

Maggie thought about telling Chapman that Aiden talked a whole lot more than he wrote, but then she supposed he'd figure it out on his own.

"I've encouraged him to pick up a camera, just as I have done," Chapman went on. "It would be quite a boon to the Movement if he'd add a few photos to his essays to introduce Easterners to birds found throughout the West."

"Movement?" Maggie asked.

"The reorganization of Audubon," Chapman clarified. "Not that he needs to make a career of photography, mind you, just pursue it as a hobby. Your brother's calling is politics. That's where he'll make his mark."

All this time Maggie thought it was but a reverie of Aiden's, to be a senator. She recollected how she had once caught him practicing speeches in the forest, soliloquies without aim or focus, featuring himself as the protagonist, a man called *Argonaut*. She had stepped noisily from behind a tree—pretending she'd only just arrived when she'd been watching all along—asking what an Argonaut was exactly. Aiden told her it was an adventurer engaged in a quest.

"Well, what quest are you on?"

"I haven't figured it out exactly," Aiden said sheepishly, for the truth was he hadn't fully grown into his ambition and had only known it as a dream, some distant goal to be someone, an American hero, perhaps. And now Chapman had confirmed it. Bit by bit, it seemed Maggie's brother was becoming the man he'd always dreamed of: powerful and recognized, admired by the people.

She thought too about Fin and the Audubon Movement, and how it might affect him. It wasn't a good thing to be a plume hunter now, and it seemed that Fin's situation, whatever it might be, would turn from bad to worse. And while it did not bode well for him, it was good for her; when he got wind of the Audubon Movement, no doubt he'd come home again.

# CHAPTER THREE

Fin had no specific idea where to find LeGrande Sharp or the nephew he called Axel, but he knew they'd go where the money was, and so he headed south to Klamath, arriving in early fall.

Southeastern Oregon was a peculiar land. Gone were the fir canopies of Portland's forests, the clouds of pewter and purple. This was a place of sagebrush and greasewood, of rim rocks and sharp stony edges. Here, the sky gleamed white as Heaven, and the lakes resembled oceans. Lower Klamath, a body of water that straddled Oregon and California, looked a great deal like Malheur, with its bulrushes and knotted channels. The country was similar too: the edge of beyond, the middle of nowhere, although Klamath was prettier. Junipers dotted the countryside and hills traversed the horizon. A man had the ability to breathe in this basin, to fill his lungs with something more meaningful than simple satisfaction. Fin hadn't the talent that Aiden had to put it properly into words. All he knew was that he was in the midst of it all, thrilling to the fall migration.

He had tried to describe the event to his mother before he'd left Portland, saying, "There's a place called Klamath, where more birds than you can imagine rest and nest and eat all they please. Come springtime, they hop aboard a flyway—a current of air like a magic carpet that runs from Canada to Mexico—and head all the way to Alaska. In fall, when it grows cold in the northern country, they fly home again. Some say birds have navigated that route for a thousand years or more."

Nearly everything he knew about birds had come from hearsay, or from *Lattin's* catalogue of eggs. Having no real bird book to flip through, he had pored over the names of birds in the slim pamphlet and by this method identified the creatures slicing the sky: a ring-necked pheasant, for example, fit its name exactly, as did a red-tailed hawk. But a cedar waxwing wore a mask and a brown topknot and was too complicated to decipher.

Willa had wanted to know what he would do at Malheur, and at Klamath, too, if he ever made it that far.

"Shoot birds and sell their skins, earn us both a living. I'll need time to test it out—maybe five months or so. If I'm successful, I'll come home and hand you my money, but after that I'll be off again, to ply my trade for good."

"But what if you're not? Successful, that is."

"I'll come back anyhow, and hang my hat at Gilchrist's."

Now that he'd landed at Klamath, he was confident he'd never work at the mercantile again. He'd find his success here, make all the money he and his mother would ever need. As for going home to deliver it like he said he would—well, he couldn't do that now. He had to take up with LeGrande while the taking was good, and he hoped his mother would understand. He hoped, too, Aiden would soften the blow when he spoke to her, but that was probably wishful thinking.

Every day of Fin's first week at Klamath, the heavens exploded with glinting wings and duck calls. Even the swans were talking, chattering among themselves the way that humans do. Fin planned to shoot as many as he could. He started with a mallard and then a pintail, inspecting each one after he'd shot it, as he'd seen Aiden do. He'd never taken a moment to marvel at their beauty, for he wasn't curious in the way that Aiden was. But he had some time and so he took it, running his fingers along the short, smooth feathers of each duck's belly, and stretching out its wings. The mallard was truly something, its shiny green head glowing black and purple. He understood the appeal the feathers might have to a woman, why she'd wear them on her hat. But it was the curly-cue at the base of the rump that made him smile, for it was the sort of curl a mother would fashion atop her baby's head.

He plucked the three feathers that comprised that swirl, and wove them through the side of his cap. And then he plucked one more and held it, twirling it between his fingers. Every few seconds it vibrated slightly, and so he tilted it this way, and then that, to see what would happen. It quivered again, and he thought that's how it was for ducks, when they took off in the wind.

He stuck that feather next to the others, and then cooked both ducks over a medium flame, until their skins crackled and burned. His mouth began to water. He ate one bird that night and saved the other for the next day's meal, then shot a canvasback and cooked that too, finding it as flavorful as anything he'd tasted.

Since his first night at Klamath he'd slept in his bedroll on the ground, snoozing low beneath the covers like a nighthawk in its nest. He wanted to see the stars in all their glory, lustrous as opals against a black velvet sky. So many nights in Portland the clouds swept in and covered the stars completely. Now, when Fin looked to the sky, he marveled at the heavens, relished the wind whistling in his ears and the cold against his skin. But there was an ache, too, a sort of melancholy over the way he and Aiden had parted. He missed his friend, although it was clear the two of them had grown apart. When he closed his eyes, he pictured Aiden in their boyhood days, the two of them stuck together, despite their differences. But that was then and this was now, and the time had come to move forward.

The morning of the third day, the marsh was blowing steam, and there was a dusting of snow on Mt. Shasta, which glowed majestically from the south. It was now too cold to sleep unprotected, so Fin broke out his tent and set it up, calling it a day as soon as the sun went down. In two weeks' time, he saw and heard no human. Yet the waterfowl were spectacular, green-winged teal and cinnamon teal banking over the marsh. There were pintails too, and canvasbacks, and more mallards than he could count. If ducks were dollars, Fin supposed he'd soon be as rich as Rockefeller.

On day nineteen, he began to worry. Here he'd left Aiden at Malheur and come all the way to Klamath with the notion he would work with plumers and market hunters. He'd heard that when the birds were flying, a man could bag over one hundred ducks a day. But even if he shot only a dozen or two, there was no one at present to whom he could sell them, and so he sat, awaiting the arrival of the others—whoever they might be.

And then one day, as he lay snoring in his tent, he awoke to gunfire. Bolting upright, he thought it nighttime at first and then realized he had it upside down, that the sun was just now rising. Throwing back his blanket, he pulled on his boots, grabbed his gun, and took off at a wobble across the frosted field, forgetting his jacket and escaping in his shirtsleeves. The morning air bit his ears, and his backside too, and he dashed back to grab his coat, his hot breath warming the hairs inside his nose.

He followed the reports of at least half a dozen guns, and spotted a knot of men. Three were in a boat, and two stood on the shore. Fin approached from behind, not wishing to stray in front of a bullet. As soon as the opportunity presented itself, he called out to the men, told them he was looking to join in and were they willing to let him? It wasn't their permission he needed so much as their contacts; a pile of ducks laid on the beach, and no doubt they knew someone with the cold hard cash to buy them.

The taller man yanked himself around and eyed Fin, and then elbowed his companion. The shorter man twisted for a look-see. As soon as Fin caught his silhouette, he recognized the hump growing stout as a tree stump between the man's shoulders and knew it was LeGrande Sharp. The younger fellow was Axel, LeGrande's nephew.

The older man slogged through the water toward Fin, his rifle in one hand. "What you doing here?"

"Thought I'd take up with you."

"Ain't got no group of your own to get to?"

"Not as yet, I don't." Fin kept his eye on the man's gun. "Thought I'd start with you." He sounded as brave as any backwoods boy, but the truth was he felt nervous around LeGrande. He wasn't about to let the old buzzard know it, however, and so he walked up to greet him, held his hand out like LeGrande was a friend, and he was pleased as punch to see him.

LeGrande hesitated, and when he shook Fin's hand no smile crossed his lips. He looked around. Seeing no one, he said, "Whar's your friend? The feller what called you partner?"

"We split up," Fin told him. "I left him at Malheur, although I suppose he's in Portland by now."

LeGrande again peered into the distance. "Whar's your boat?"

"Ain't got one."

"Wagon?"

"Ain't got that, either."

"If you ain't got a boat and you ain't got a wagon, how was you planning to fetch your ducks and haul 'em?"

Fin confessed he hadn't thought that far ahead, that he was of a mind to join up with a team of market hunters at Klamath, and learn the trade before investing in equipment. Come spring, he said, he'd turn to pluming, when the feathers of grebes, terns, and herons were at their finest. Then, he'd shoot ten thousand birds, for he was a dedicated hunter.

LeGrande scratched the spiny whiskers on his neck. They could always use another shooter, he said, but because Fin wasn't bringing anything to the table except a gun and a shoulder on which to tote it, it would cost him. "We fetch three dollars for every dozen teal we bring in, five for mallards, seven for pintails and nine for cans." LeGrande was talking canvasbacks, of which Fin had already eaten half a dozen; he quickly calculated the profits he'd consumed and wished he'd downed a few teal instead, although they were harder to chew. "We'll tally what you bring in," LeGrande went on, "and you'll turn over half your earnings—"

"Half!"

"That's the way it works, boy. You don't like it, you can find some other bunch to shoot for, though they ain't likely to take kindly to no interloper." LeGrande leaned forward and spat, letting the remark sink in.

"All right," Fin said, "but come springtime, I aim to set out on my own, hunt herons and collect plumes. I'll have a boat by then, and I'll do my shooting on the north end of Tule Lake. There won't be no reason to share a cut with you, nor anyone else, and any money I earn will be my own." It was a risky venture, giving LeGrande what-for so early in the game. But Fin understood the value of a dollar, and knew he'd never strike it rich if he split his earnings with every market hunter and plumer this side of Salt Lake City.

LeGrande grunted. He told Axel to get a move on, take the newcomer with him. Fin propped his gun against his shoulder and followed the younger man toward the water. "Be sure to keep your knickers dry," LeGrande taunted. "Wet drawers is hell to sleep in."

For a while, at least, Fin did manage to keep them dry, thanks in part to the warmth of the afternoons. Klamath in November was a beautiful season, and though the temperature in the morning hovered around thirty degrees, the days could bring a sunburn. The willows lining the creek banks shimmered golden-yellow, and the bulrushes at the marsh's edges had gone all rusty brown. The only green that Fin could see came from the junipers in the distance, but the marsh itself shone strikingly blue, and reflected the rolling hills.

The red-tails were in, and the marsh hawks too, and hundreds of thousands of pintails. There were gadwalls and scaups, and ducks called buffleheads—Fin hadn't known what they were or what to call them, until Axel pointed them out. There were canvasbacks too, and all fall and winter Fin worked alongside LeGrande and Axel, shooting as many as he could. He counted twenty camps of hunters lining the borders of Lower Klamath and Tule Lake, the latter an expanse of water ninety miles around. Every man capable of squeezing a trigger bagged dozens of birds a day.

It was exhausting work. The men toiled from sunrise to sunset, but even so, Fin greeted the marshes and fields of frost with a bold and eager heart. Never had he worked so willingly, or so hard, hunting down and killing every water bird he could find, for nothing satisfied him so much as stalking birds and shooting them, relishing the thrill he received when they spun circles to the ground.

He'd bought a chokebore gun from a fellow with black pinfeather whiskers sprouting from his chin. The man came with his wagon to the hunters' camps three days a week. He collected the ducks that Fin and Axel and the others had stored in the canvas bags he'd sold them, and which he then hauled to California.

Fin wanted to know where in California those birds got to once the driver had picked them up. The man said they were freighted to Montague, then expressed to San Francisco, where just as Fin had heard, some pretty lady in a restaurant picked at a drumstick without once sucking the marrow. "Waste of a good duck, if you ask me," said the driver, a speck of tobacco lodged beneath teeth stained garlic yellow.

That season alone, men along the lakes killed one hundred and twenty tons of waterfowl. Fin did all right too. Despite splitting his earnings with LeGrande, he was able to send a good amount of money to his mother, although do so required an additional two percent to ensure "safe delivery" of his funds, week after week, to the post office in Merrill.

He sent his money with the driver of the duck wagon — he seemed a trustworthy fellow — including with his cash a note to his mother. In this letter Fin told her he was sorry he'd not come home as he said he would, but he had decided to stay where the money was, in an effort to secure their futures.

While on the topic of money, he reminded her to get hers to the bank, knowing she'd be tempted to hang onto it, arrange it in a little tin box before stuffing it beneath her mattress. It wasn't that she had anything against banks. She'd just never had enough to park there, and what she did have, she preferred to keep at home. More than once Fin's father had scolded her, told her a lumpy mattress was the first place a robber would look, if he came in search of money.

"If a body needs twenty-two dollars so badly he'd steal it, I'd give it to him," Willa had told him, not once looking up from her mending.

Along with his cash, Fin sent his mother a bit of news as well, a brief description of the routine he'd fallen into; how all fall he'd worked as a market hunter, and would continue doing so through early winter; how in spring he'd switch to pluming. He wrote too of the men he'd met, leaving out the unsavory characters like Axel and LeGrande, whom he considered swamp desperadoes, and concentrating instead on those like the wagon driver, though men as good as him seemed few and far between. The handful he'd met were more like LeGrande, possessive of their squares on Klamath Lake and not too keen on sharing. He also told of the tundra swans and snow geese and white pelicans too: birds spilling from the sky as thick as confetti, their bills as orange as marmalade, their wingtips dipped in charcoal.

When putting words to paper, Fin sometimes thought of Aiden, how his friend was likely to view the creatures as lords of some gay, feathered kingdom, characters for the journals he kept and wrote about on his journey. Fin saw them differently. Watching birds had yet to stir his blood as much as shooting them.

All through that frosty season, as he trudged the shores

of Klamath and Tule lakes, he came to regard the region as the greatest rendezvous for ducks he'd ever see; most times he couldn't begin to count them, so densely did they cloud the skies with their dark, fluttering wings. And as he tracked them with Axel, learned the trade, and got to know the man, he understood that the thrill of the hunt was likely the only thing he and his cohort had in common.

Axel hadn't but three years of schooling and couldn't add two apples if he held them in his hands, yet he knew more about stalking birds than Fin would have imagined. Axel told Fin how, as a boy, he'd scoured the mangroves of Florida, gone up to the Carolinas and back down again. From there he'd hit the Sunk Lands of Arkansas, and now here he was, rowing the lakes of Oregon and California. Along with his uncle and their stringy companions, Axel speculated that they had killed enough geese, ducks, and prairie chickens to stock every café in the world. Come springtime and early summer, he'd slaughter grebes and herons, pluck their feathers and then sell them to the millinery trade, as quick as he could kill them. The only bird Axel refused to shoot was the one called sandhill crane.

"Cain't tell you why," he confessed one evening as he, Fin, and LeGrande sat around the campfire. "I could shoot ever goose between Arkansas and Alaska, though I ain't actually been that far north. Just never been able to shoot no crane is all."

"You're sentimental is why," LeGrande said. "You never grew no backbone."

"Did too," Axel argued, his thin face puckering.

LeGrande leaned back and grimaced. The man complained every day of the cold, saying it robbed his fingers of their freedom, and bothered his hump too. He shifted his feet, dipping his toes toward the fire and rubbing them 'til they warmed.

Axel wasn't one to argue with his uncle. He'd seen the effects of other men's arguments, how they generally led to some disfigurement or other. A man named Mazzoni had got his nose bit off when he lost a hand of cards to LeGrande and made the mistake of calling him cheater; another was said to have lost a testicle to LeGrande's Bowie knife. Axel took that tale for a rumor, however, wondering how a man could walk straight if he hadn't but one ball flapping against his thigh.

Axel looked up at Fin, something akin to sadness in his eyes. "Don't suppose there's a bird you can't likely shoot?" It wasn't a question so much as a comment, and Fin saw at once how Axel wished it so.

Fin contemplated how best to put it. Confessing he did would earn him a sigh of disgust from LeGrande, but there was one bird for which he held a soft spot. And then maybe because the fire had warmed his tongue, or because he was lonely, he came out and said it.

"There's one I shot when I was a boy, a kingfisher, if you know it." Axel nodded while LeGrande showed no interest at all, just gazed at some dark hole in the tules. "Spotted him on the naked branch of a willow," Fin went on, "a pert little fellow, looking high and peckery—"

"Peckery?"

"Sort of top-heavy and standing about yey high," Fin said, "like a woodpecker might do. Had wings as blue as midnight, and a reddish bellyband. A funny topknot too." Here, Fin gathered his hair with his fingers, making a sort of haystack with it.

Axel hooted, and Fin got the idea LeGrande might have laughed too, if he hadn't been so all-fired determined to stand apart from them.

"He was just sitting there," Fin went on, "clacking at a

tadpole, his whole body thrusting forward with the effort of every squawk. I liked him straight away—admired his spunk and vitality..." His voice trailed off as he lost himself in the reverie of that day. He recollected how he'd been walking along the river where a stand of cottonwoods grew, admiring leaves as they shimmered gold and brown. A few fluttered to the ground, spinning softly as they fell, making no sound at all. The air smelled of dust, and the land was cool and dry. He recollected too how his family had been a threesome then, his father still alive, how Aiden was his best friend, his one and only companion.

"Don't quit now," Axel put in, his face aglow in the firelight. "Tell what happened next."

"I shot him is what happened. Fished him from the water and laid him on the bank. Seeing him like that, his feathers wet and mangled, jangled my insides and got me feeling blue. I can't tell you why I regretted shooting that bird. I just did." He settled his gaze on the coals.

Axel's eyes glossed with moisture. Fin's story gripped him somehow, and he coughed and looked the other way, then jumped up and beat a trail toward his tent.

LeGrande snickered. "Now look what you done," he said. "You set the boy to blubberin." The marsh dweller sat, lumpish and greasy, against a burned-out log. He was probing a tooth with a pick he'd whittled from a twig of juniper.

There was something about LeGrande that rubbed Fin's fur backward, made him want to glance over his shoulder whenever the plumer was around. Fin would have to give Aiden his due. His friend had called LeGrande exactly what he was: a body who would allow his resentments to build, and then take them out on others.

Now, when Fin looked at LeGrande, he saw a man who

was not only willing to abuse his power, but to withhold his sympathy, and anything else a nephew might look for in the way of kindness from an uncle. Fin regretted he'd let his guard down, that he'd allowed LeGrande to see his tender side, for LeGrande had no tender side; the man wasn't one to let on he had fear or a soft spot, either one, and it troubled Fin that the man now sported an advantage. In the future, he'd be more careful about the secrets he let spill.

A few days later, the sky bloomed indigo and purple. A short while later it turned gray, and a squall rolled in and riled the birds. Thousands of geese took to the air, tilting sideways as they flew. And when the sun surged forth and ignited their wings, the country stood a dream world.

Fin marveled at Klamath's beauty, and might have marveled the whole spring through, had a cloud not marred his view. The cloud had a name, which Fin called LeGrande; he suspected that the man had stolen money from him, since he'd tallied in his head the ducks he'd shot, and kept the memory there. When LeGrande slapped cash into Fin's hand, it hadn't the heft it ought to. It had happened before, and back then Fin had clenched his jaw and let the matter go — he needed LeGrande, and his connections, to earn a decent living. This time, though, he had a response, and plainly spoke his mind.

"That don't feel like fifty percent," he said. "You're sure you counted right?"

LeGrande's eyes went slim as a cat's. "I can count well as I can shoot. You like to call me on it?"

"I won't call you on it. But I told you when I joined up with you, it wouldn't be forever. I'm changing our arrangement."

"How you plan to do that when you got no wiggle room?"

"I got enough, I guess."

Fin's tone was as bold as LeGrande's, although he didn't

feel that brave. A body could push LeGrande just so far before the man pulled his gun and showed it; but saying nothing would get Fin nothing, except maybe a tour of the poor house. He told LeGrande he'd give him twenty percent of his future earnings—keeping the extra thirty for himself—if the man would part with Axel for perhaps one month or so.

"I need him to introduce me to the northern shores of Tule Lake," Fin said, adding, "that place is as twisted as this one here, and I need to get my bearings."

"That ain't what you signed up for."

"Well, I didn't sign no contract."

The men stood, glaring at one another. Fin made the first move. "Look," he said, "ain't no law says you got to take my offer. Lloyd Blackman might go there." Lloyd was a plume hunter with a camp nearby, and old as Mississippi. He wasn't the best marksman, but he could sit sturdy in a boat and point out grebes at least as well as Axel.

"Ain't no law says I will," said LeGrande. He strode toward a low-lying tangle of sagebrush and then put his foot on a rock. Turning, he spoke to Fin. "I'll take your deal," he said, "but not because I got to."

*Right*, Fin thought, but did not say. *You've got five million options.*

Fin stuffed his cash into his pocket, and turned to look for Axel. He spotted him squatting next to the campfire near their tent, stirring a pot with a wooden spoon. Axel was studying its contents, as if uncertain what it contained: it might have been laundry, might have supper, but when he leaned in and touched his tongue to the spoon, he smacked his lips and smiled. Looking up and seeing Fin, he said, "Mmm…rabbit. You want a taste of it?"

"I ain't hungry yet. I guess I'll wait a while."

As he watched Axel, he doubted he'd ever call him *friend,* although the man was tolerable enough. He wasn't cruel, as LeGrande was, and was generally cooperative, although he wasn't close to brilliant. More than once he'd spoken up at precisely the wrong moment, like that day back at Malheur, when he'd let go his uncle's secrets and LeGrande had kicked him for it. And it wasn't more than a week ago that he'd crawled from his tent, sporting a lumpy eye with a glossy black ring around it. The thing was swollen as big as a sweet plum, with only a crack to see through. Fin was curious, but made no inquiry about it. As it turned out, he didn't have to. Axel caught him staring.

"I run into a tree stump," he said, "in case you're wonderin."

"I ain't wondering," Fin said, although it was clear Axel had not considered the improbability of the remark, how stumps didn't grow as tall as he was, and if they did, they weren't stumps at all, but snags. Axel refused to look again at Fin, just gazed across the lake with that swollen eye, and pulled his mouth up tight.

Why Axel held loyalty to a man who used him as a whipping boy Fin could not comprehend. "All right," he confessed after a while, "I am wondering a little. Wondering if it was LeGrande maybe popped you one. Seems to me you could knock his teeth out, you wanted to. Your arms are tight with sinew."

"I ain't one to sock my uncle."

"After what he's done to you?"

Axel poured a cup of coffee and then sat on a rock with a slanted surface, finding it a comfortable lean-to. The sun was just beginning to rise, and the sky was streaked with gray. The world smelled damp and loamy.

"LeGrande's the only family I got," Axel told him. He

looked at Fin with hazel eyes, eyes that had likely seen a lifetime of hurt before he was ten. Although he was Fin's age, he looked thirteen, with his bare feet and smudged face, his hair in need of combing. "I wasn't but two or three when my mama died, and I don't remember much. She fell into a well, trying to grab a bucket. Pa was the one that found her. Pulled her out and seen by her mangled hands she'd fought to save herself. Not long after, he put a bullet in his head. LeGrande said Pa didn't want to live without her."

Fin looked up, wondering if his own father would have killed himself over his mother, had she been the one who'd died. He thought not, as he'd never seen the man so much as hold her hand, or kiss her, although once he'd seen him carry her to a picnic he'd arranged on a blanket behind the house. The gesture had warmed Fin's heart. His mother had asked for little in her life, and this kindness from his father had made her blush and laugh.

Axel carefully slurped his coffee, so as not to burn his tongue. "Mama was LeGrande's sister, and he came and fetched me and raised me as his own. I seen a long time ago it wasn't his calling. He wasn't soft and cuddly, like my real pa was. He's always been a hard man, and don't take to sniveling babies." Axel's brow folded, as though he wished things had been different. "Riles him I ain't as tough as he is, and I reckon he aims to change me. He might succeed, one day."

Fin didn't think that would happen. Though it was true a man could change, Axel hadn't the hide that LeGrande did, nor did he seem apt to grow one. Fin had no doubt that Axel felt he owed his uncle, but nowhere was it written he had to endure LeGrande's cruelty just to even things out. Tolerating a beating was no payment for anything at all. Nor did Fin believe it was courage Axel lacked, but confidence. LeGrande had likely hammered the notion into Axel's head that he hadn't a brain at all. Likely Axel believed him.

There was a time early on when LeGrande had tried a similar strategy on Fin, telling him no rooster from Portland would amount to anything, no matter how loud he crowed. It wasn't the remark about Portland that irked Fin, but the comparison to a yard bird. He came back with the tart reply he wasn't a rooster, but a fighting cock, and would go ten rounds to prove it.

LeGrande sniggered, but his eyes grew small. "Someday I just might let you."

Fin suspected that day *would* come, though he didn't know when or where. And so he watched his step, and held one eye secure beyond his shoulder.

By the middle of May, last year's cattails began to green up and grow tall. Birds arrived by the tens of hundreds of thousands: Ross's geese and Canada geese and grand white pelicans. The sky all but rained snow geese.

Four days after the geese touched down, in sleet that spit for hours, the wagon driver from Merrill arrived with a load of canvas bags. Most plumers stored their grebe skins in bales, although a few preferred to stash them in bags the driver had brought, just as they did ducks for restaurants. The driver was a hunter too, but mostly he shot creatures he nicked at the side of the road with the rifle beneath his seat. He'd stacked a collection of coyote, bobcat, and raccoon pelts in one corner of his wagon, stating his willingness to bargain at every stop he made.

"Like to sell you a coonskin to make yourself a hat," he said to Fin one day.

"I won't wear a hat that's got a tail on it."

"Dan'l Boone won't either," the man observed. "That he will is just a rumor."

A dog stood on the other side of the driver's wagon, lagging toward the back. A curious-looking creature, it possessed curly hair, a broad head, and a hide the color of tree bark. Its tongue hung out, although the day was chilly and had a bite to it. "See you got yourself a boyfriend," Fin said, chuckling.

The man was bundled in a tobacco-colored jacket, a swatch torn from the elbow where the stuffing poked out. He wore a gray forage cap, a boxy affair like a young soldier's hat. He shifted in his seat to better see the hound. "Critter been following me since daybreak. Lost its mama, I reckon."

"You name him yet?"

"Ain't a he, it's she," he said. "Ain't got no tallywhacker."

Fin was leaning against a tree, his back to the wind, hands buried inside his pockets. His ears ached, and he wished the driver was selling nice wools caps, instead of varmint hats. He turned his collar up, hunched his shoulders to ward off the cold, and watched the dog as she looked here and there, clapping her jaws like she was hungry.

He had a bit of mallard jerky nestled in his pocket, a snack he'd saved for later. He dug it out, squatted low on his haunches, and whistled. The dog lifted her head and sniffed the air, but wouldn't come closer. "C'mon," Fin urged. "I'll share a bite with you."

"You can keep her if you like," called the driver. "I got these sacks to sell." He too turned up his collar, then snatched a bobcat skin from the back of the wagon and threw it across his lap. He waved a farewell with one finger, snapped his reins, and turned the wagon around.

Fin was about to holler he wouldn't keep a creature that refused to eat from his hand, but then the dog ambled over.

After a bit more coaxing, she accepted Fin's morsel, and he complimented her on her soft mouth, and rubbed the top of her head. "You a bird dog?" he asked. He thought she looked like one.

She raised the little nub of fur that was her eyebrow, and wagged her tail. Fin patted her again, and gave her the rest of the jerky. He called her Josie, for no reason other than it popped into his head at precisely that moment, and he liked the sound of it.

He hadn't realized what good company a dog was, or how watchful she would be. She was smart too, as he soon discovered. After he first got her, Axel bumped into camp to tell him they'd been on a scouting trip, and would be off the next day to hunt grebes. Josie barked when she saw him. Holding her tail high, she bared her teeth, trotted backward, and kicked up a spray of dirt. Fin hollered at her to calm down, and reluctantly she complied. But when LeGrande showed his face a short time later, she raised her hackles and growled. Fin understood she carried the same sixth sense that he himself possessed, and he liked that in her. LeGrande warned Fin he'd shoot her, if she ever caused him trouble.

"She won't give you no trouble, if you let her know you're coming. Same with you, Axel."

Axel laughed—the notion of warning a dog of anything at all went against the grain. "What do you want me to do? Carry a horn, toot it from the bushes?"

"No, but you can tramp the ground a little, and make some noise."

And so Axel agreed to slap the weeds, while LeGrande refused to compromise. "Just keep her out of my way, McFaddin, or I'll knock her in the head."

Not trusting LeGrande to behave like a human, Fin took

Josie everywhere. The first day he and Axel went grebe hunting on Tule Lake, she was the first to jump into the boat. She gave them no trouble at all, demonstrating she was eager to please and remaining still when Fin told her to, while they rowed along a channel. There was a slight ripple to the water, aided by a breeze. When they'd first started out, near the end of the lake where the water was shallow, the air had stunk of sulfur. But the farther they rowed the better it got, and if a man used his imagination, he could say it smelled sweet as a morning meadow.

Tule Lake resembled Lower Klamath, just as Klamath resembled Malheur. But it had nooks and crannies that Fin didn't know, and so he relied on Axel to fill in the details. It wasn't more than an hour before Fin had most of it down, including the sway on the horizon like a woman's hip, were she lying on her side. Then there was the giant willow with two bald eagles, watching with yellow eyes. Once or twice they lifted their wings, poised for flight, but when the men passed without molesting them, the sentries held their posts.

As Fin and Axel closed in on a colony of Forster's terns, and another of frothy herons, Fin maintained they ought to stop and shoot the herons at least. Axel fixed his gaze on a spot in the distance, for it was grebes his blood was hot for, and grebes he aimed to kill. "What about the terns?" Fin asked, hating to miss the opportunity to make some easy money—wings and tails of Forster's terns were worth forty cents apiece.

"We'll catch 'em later," Axel told him.

There was an unusual authority to his voice, and so Fin sat back, accepting Axel's tutelage. He looked back toward the woman's hip, marking the hill in his mind, and in that instant knew he didn't need Axel as much as he thought he did. He realized he could leave the men tomorrow, if he had the notion. But doing so would infuriate LeGrande, and stir a pot of trouble. Yet Fin knew too that he was good at pluming, that he was capable of making real money on his own. Despite the funds LeGrande had stolen from him, Fin had bought the boat he and Axel sat in now, as well as the skiff they dragged behind it. He used the smaller boat as a trolley of sorts to haul birds and skinning supplies. Even so, he kept these thoughts to himself. Whatever he told Axel, Axel would tell LeGrande, and the last thing Fin needed was some steely-eyed marsh dweller seething over lost profits.

Fin was still thinking on this when they came upon a bulrush mat about an acre wide. By Axel's count, the floating mass supported eight hundred nests or so. Unaware of their presence, two feathered divers sprouted up and with kinked necks sprinted across the water in an impressive courtship dance. They were late getting to it, Fin thought, for most birds already had a handful of eggs nestled beneath their bellies, and some had hatched their babies.

Hundreds of birds flew every which-way, and the terns and gulls clamored so, their calling hurt his ears. He didn't know whether to look up, or down, and so he simply sat, trying to take it in.

Axel laughed, amused by Fin's consternation. He rowed alongside the floating island, paused, and then set the oars down. Waving one arm in an arc across the landscape, he said, "You can walk across this part here, but you best watch yourself or you'll step into a mushy part and sink in over your head."

"Walk across it?"

"It's made up of old tule stalks, mostly. There ain't no sod beneath it. I spent the night on one not two years ago. Might have stayed a second night, if I hadn't burnt it down. A breeze come up in the middle of breakfast, and caught the place on fire. I slapped it 'til my hands was raw, and then jumped into the lake." He paused, as if recalling the blisters he'd earned that day, and then his mind seemed to skip to a different place and he turned and pointed north. "Row toward the mouth of that slough over yonder," he said. "I got a trick to show you."

Fin took up the oars then. When they reached the slough, Axel gathered some canvas and a rope and rigged up a blind. The men sat behind it, and it wasn't long before a knot of birds the size of three small boats swam toward them. Fin's heart thudded, and he smiled. Axel nodded, they opened fire, and mass confusion ensued. Grebes flew off while others flew in, not knowing what to do. The birds hadn't yet learned to fear shotguns, and in short order Fin and Axel had killed forty-seven grebes.

Smoke from their guns burned their eyes, but they kept going despite the stinging, reloading and shooting, and quickly reloading again.

Axel tied two dozen of the dead birds together so they formed a chain of sorts, and flung it across the channel. Serving as a barricade, it prevented the remaining birds from escaping into the open. Fin couldn't cipher why the others simply didn't dive underwater to escape the blockade, but something about the device confused them. When they swam in circles, panicked and uncertain, Axel and Fin shot a hundred more.

Josie knew her job exactly. She stood erect, quivering, awaiting Fin's command to go. Fin recollected how as a boy his own legs had shaken when he spied a target, how sometimes even now he could lose himself to some far-off place with the thrill the hunt provided. He released Josie, watched her leap into the water, scoop up the birds, and fetch them to him, thinking it uncanny he'd found a dog that loved hunting as much as he did.

"Likely some market hunter owned her before you," Axel said as he, too, watched Fin's dog with wonder. "Bet he misses her now."

After they'd gathered the grebes, Axel said he knew of an old cabin in an abandoned stackyard where they could skin their birds. "Let's get to it then," Fin said as he loaded the trolley and headed off to find it.

The place was situated on a bona fide island, an anchor of dirt beneath it. Fin wasn't the superstitious sort, but he didn't like the looks of it; the shack was missing a chunk of its roof and had no windows at all. Wind had blown the door off its bottom hinge so that it sat topsy-turvy, and the breeze drifted through like a ghost.

The boat's prow rammed the bank. Fin untied the rope to the trolley, hopped out, and pulled the smaller boat to shore. Josie's tail slapped the air. He told her to come along, and she too jumped out, her nose at once on the ground.

Empty shotgun shells and feathers were scattered around a burned-out campfire, and an oar with the tip of its handle gone lay propped against the cabin. The place was still and quiet. Everything about the shack tickled the hairs at the back of Fin's neck. If he had been alone he might have climbed into his boat and left that very minute. He glanced over at Axel, but if the man thought the place peculiar, he didn't show it. Leaning over the trolley, he filled his arms with the grebes they'd killed, and dropped them onto the shore.

Axel's nonchalance infused Fin with courage, and he walked over to the shack. Hefting the better part of the oar and gripping it in one hand, he walked through the door, pausing while his eyes adjusted to the dark. The stench of rotting flesh hit him instantly, and he snagged a bandana from his pocket and held it to his nose. The place was alive with the clamor of buzzing flies.

Fin glanced over to a chopping block and spied a pile of wings about two feet high. Just beyond that, scattered on the ground, lay a hundred or so grebe carcasses, feathers ripped from their breasts. Their naked bodies undulated, as if by magic. Fin stepped forward cautiously, gripped the oar, and nudged one of the birds. He half expected the creature to fly toward him, but it sat tight, its body stiff and its eyes bugged out, and he knew for certain it was dead. He flipped it over, found a thousand maggots roiling about, feeding on the corpses. He lunged back, saliva pooling in his mouth, the soft spots beneath his ears stinging wildly. Heaving, he bolted for the door.

Axel looked up from the trolley. "What's got into you?"

Fin scrambled toward the back of the shack, bent low behind the building and vomited until nothing but bile flowed. His breath came in short, jagged spurts, and he waited to see what else would come out, the taste in his mouth so bitter he began retching again. He thought he might pass out.

Axel appeared from around the corner, Josie behind him. He leaned against the building and watched Fin. "Never took you for no heaver," he said, flummoxed.

Fin wiped his mouth and tried to concentrate. Axel took Fin's silence for some painful memory, something he could relate to. "You thinking on your kingfisher?" he asked. "The one with the mangled feathers?"

Fin brought himself up to his full height, and lumbered past the plumer. He didn't go back into the shack, but piled his grebes outside, near the burned-out fire. As he skinned them, he thought about what he'd seen in the shack, and his reaction to it. He'd run with market hunters for months now, but until that moment the killing hadn't fazed him. He wondered how he could react the way he had, with all that burned inside him.

Josie lay at his feet. She nuzzled a small pile of loose feathers, sneezed, and then laid her chin on crossed paws.

Axel soon joined him. When they finished skinning the birds, he suggested they leave the skins to dry. "You all right to head out for the rest of them grebes?" he asked. Fin didn't respond. "Fin?"

He looked up then. It was a moment before Axel's question registered, and then he nodded. He stood, climbed into the boat, and whistled for Josie, but as it happened, they left too late in the afternoon and had no luck at all. Likely they'd scared off the birds with their earlier shooting, and so they set up house in the middle of the marsh, claiming as their home the roof of a former muskrat house. The structure stood a foot above water and nearly five feet across, and was made of marsh debris—stems of reeds and water plants, sturdily compacted with mud.

Axel crawled from the boat onto the creature's palace, flattening the top with his feet. Fin spread a blanket he'd pulled from the boat, and the men sat atop it. Axel chuckled and looked at Fin with a broad smile, wagering it wouldn't be long before they sank, fully clothed, into the water.

The rat-house lasted until sunset at least, when they heard the report of gunfire. Axel's smile was gone now. He glanced at Fin. "How far away you make it?"

It was the first Fin had spoken since the grebe shack. "Mile?" he ventured, gazing toward the horizon. "About that, I'd say."

"You see now why I was hot to fetch them grebes? Herons was temptin'—and we'll get them yet—but we ain't alone on this lake. First light of day, we best get back to our skins, before the others find them and load them on their boats."

They ate no supper, just called it a night, each man drifting off to sleep. Thunder awoke them at midnight. Fin roused with a crick in his neck, sitting up on one elbow, uncertain what had stirred him. Axel asked if a storm was coming, and Fin said it was. Lightning flashed in the distance, a bold and crooked bolt that shivered against the sky, and then the rain came. The first drop landed on the back of Fin's neck, the second on his nose. Stumbling from his blanket, he meandered more or less sideways off the platform, landing in muck to his elbows. He figured as long as he was there, he would cover the boat with canvas, and when that was done, he crawled back onto the platform. Axel was up by then, crafting a tent from blankets. Fin slipped under the makeshift protection, and the men spent the rest of the night sitting back-to-back, peering into the darkness. Josie lay squinting in the downpour with her head down.

Shortly before sunrise the men stood with stiff knees, their trousers damp and scratching their inner thighs. They didn't speak, cold as they were and tired too, just gathered their gear and stashed it in the boat. By the time the sun crested, they'd begun to thaw a little. They looked around, and it seemed the marsh was reborn, the sky alive with birds. As they headed back to the skinners' shack, Axel turned congenial.

"That was some night," he observed. "I don't like to get that wet, unless I got my clothes off."

Fin made no comment. He dipped an oar into the water and held it, his back toward the sun. The warmth loosened his neck and massaged his spine, and made him feel more human. Despite this small comfort, he wasn't inclined to engage Axel in conversation; the man talked too much as it was, and Fin didn't feel like chatting. Yet if he himself refused to talk, he'd start to think, and that was no good either.

Twice during the night, Fin's mind began to creep toward the run-down shack and the bodies rotting there. That the grebes had riled his stomach continued to confound him, for never before had he recoiled from the sight of a naked bird. Try as he might, he could not put his finger on the specifics of his upset, and so he told himself it was a solitary thing, the bothering deep inside him. But when he and Axel returned to the shack to pick up their skins, Fin refused to look at the dwelling, fixing his gaze on the marsh instead, and the birds he planned to kill there.

By summer's end, he fetched a bundle of cash for the grebes and terns he'd shot. He gave LeGrande his cut, twenty percent for Axel's instructions, and kept a bit for himself. He sent the balance to his mother. For the first time he included no note with the cash. His head was empty and his heart cold, and he had nothing clever to say.

In time, he left LeGrande just as he said he would, and set up camp at Tule.

# CHAPTER FOUR

It wasn't long before Aiden realized that his mentor, Frank M. Chapman, was right: the OOS had become a liability, and so he disbanded it, holding the opinion, as Chapman did, that collecting eggs for collecting's sake must be abandoned altogether. "Public opinion has turned against us," he told OOS members before he dissolved the group. "We must endeavor to find new ways to pursue scientific study, and put a dollar in our pockets."

Yet not once did he acknowledge a link between the work of men like Chapman, who continued to collect eggs and shoot birds solely in the name of science, and the desperate straits of so many birds. Nor would Chapman acknowledge it either, perhaps because he was too in love with his work to draw that logical conclusion.

But Morris Kiff saw it, and necessarily adapted.

Like most men, he disliked change, but he was a savvy businessman and if Frank Chapman, Aiden Elliott, and other men like them aimed to turn the tide on the private end of the bird business, he aimed to keep one step ahead of them. He sold his stock of skins and eggs at the curio shop and began to carry painted penny postcards and picture books instead, both of which his customers snatched up as soon as he unboxed them. Mountains were a popular postcard feature, and Kiff offered miniature pastels of Mt. Hood, Mt. Shasta, and Castle Rock, which wasn't technically a mountain but a haystack of jagged granite that climbed nearly to the stars.

Aiden too developed new interests and bought a camera, as Chapman suggested he do. When he wasn't studying, he was up in the hills, shooting photographs. He published his first ornithological paper on the birds of California while still a student in Berkeley, circulating as companion pieces two crisp and well-exposed photographs of great blue herons. He wasn't making much money yet, and his father Owen continued to support him. From time to time Aiden felt a twinge of guilt about this, knowing Fin was still in southeastern Oregon, killing birds to make a living. Fin's endeavors were by far the tougher go, and when Aiden lamented to his father that he wasn't yet prepared to pull his own weight, Owen clapped his son's shoulder. "You're an investment, Son," he said, adding, "I have every confidence you'll pay off one day."

Not wanting to disappoint the man, Aiden worked hard to make it true. He corresponded with Frank Chapman, who helped him however he could, talking up his talents among the ornithological elite, including T. Gilbert Pearson, William Brewster, Robert Ridgway, William Dutcher, and Elliott Coues. Chapman encouraged Aiden to correspond with Harriet Hemenway, as well, the Boston woman whom he'd mentioned that day at the OOS meeting, now almost one year ago. She'd taken up the mission to revitalize the Audubon Society in earnest, and it was toward this endeavor — launching societies in Oregon and California and states in which a great deal more help was needed—that Chapman wished Aiden to work. He also encouraged Aiden to take part in the proceedings of scientific societies, serve on committees and directorial boards, and delve deeper into politics. "You do that, and your contribution to the Movement will be handsomely rewarded."

Aiden embraced it all. He believed it was possible to further enlighten the public by exposing them to photographs of birds they'd not seen before, at least from the perspective of a telephoto lens. He'd had quite a lot of practice, hauling his camera up Douglas firs, photographing tanagers and flickers and various birds' nests. One sunny weekend in March 1898, he packed his camera and lenses in a hard leather case, which he'd stuffed into a satchel containing a dozen glass plates. Slinging the pack across his back, he strapped his tripod to his bicycle and boarded a train for San Francisco. High above the city, on Mission Ridge, he planned to photograph a pair of golden eagles nesting in a sycamore.

Hopping from the train, he jumped onto his bicycle and steered toward the hills, pedaling until the shops and houses gave way to rustic wooden fences. Cows blinked as he rode past. He tipped his hat, eliciting stares from their liquid brown eyes while they stood and worked their cuds.

After another mile or so, he veered onto a rutted path that cut through a pasture. Bumping along, teeth rattling, he worried for a time about the glass plates in his pack. When he reached the end of the road, he propped his bicycle against a barn, checked the contents of his knapsack and found the plates intact. Adjusting his satchel, he set out the rest of the way on foot, since it was now too steep to cycle.

Photography was a hobby he'd come to adore, as it

allowed him to traipse the countryside, just as he'd done as a boy. A stand of eucalyptus trees swayed in the distance, filling the air with menthol. Insects buzzed, and a mud hen called from a distant puddle.

Aiden stood a moment, taking it all in. He fancied himself a scholar, in his gray vest and bowtie, and thought himself quite lucky to be hiking the country when he wasn't studying, to photograph birds. He was thinking on this still as he searched for his golden eagle's nest, striding through grass so tall it brushed his knees and thighs. When he found what he was looking for, he marveled at its size—the nest was four feet wide and two feet tall, big enough to hold a man.

He watched it through his binoculars and saw after twenty minutes or so that it was home to two adult eagles. Heart pounding, he quickly set up his equipment, rigging two ropes to the sycamore and then scaling it with trepidation. Hoisting his camera, he dared not look down, for the venture was beyond dangerous: the nest was cradled in a Y at the end of a branch, thirty feet from the ground. Plus, he had to contend with the birds. He fully expected them to stand and fight, but instead they retreated. The action confounded him, for he'd expected the eagles to defend their nest, as so many mammals would do.

He held his breath, adjusted his lens, and brought the nest fully into view. He snapped a dozen photos of two downy chicks, and when he was done, climbed carefully down from the tree. He was as happy as he'd ever been, and returned twice more over a ten-week span to capture the youngsters as they sprouted. The photos were magnificent.

And then one day, as he stood in front of the Berkeley campus, discussing with a friend the formation of a club where interested amateurs could meet to advance the study of ornithology, a woman sat nearby. As engrossed as he was in recounting to his friend his excursion to photograph the eagles, he didn't immediately see her. But then his cohort stepped aside, and Aiden spotted the girl. She sat on a bench, a book in her lap. Every so often she glanced his way, her eyes widening almost imperceptibly as he explained to his friend how he'd gotten his camera up the tree. Twice he caught her staring. Each time, she quickly dropped her gaze and studied her book, as though something of great interest lay between its pages. His breath left him as he took in the color of her hair, which shone vibrant yellow, and the delicate shape of her mouth. When she looked up a third time and gave him a tentative smile, he asked his friend if he knew her.

The man squinted, considering the woman. "She's in my music theory class—she plays the violin."

"Would you provide an introduction?"

The twosome walked over, and the man said, "I beg your pardon, but I believe you're in my music class—"

"Yes," she said, nodding. "I recognize you, too."

"My name is William Brickley, and this is my friend, Aiden Elliott."

"Hello, Aiden," she said, "I'm Phoebe Pembroke." She wore a shirtwaist blouse with leg-o'-mutton sleeves—huge affairs, a full yard of fabric at the shoulders alone, and with tight lower arms—and a brown tweed skirt. On her head sat a felt hat trimmed with ostrich tips, dyed three different shades of blue. She extended a slender hand.

Aiden's gaze lingered briefly on Phoebe's hat. He clasped her fingertips and brushed his lips against them, as Frank M. Chapman might do. If she found the gesture uncommon or unsettling, she gave no sign at all.

William Brickley smiled at Aiden and then turned to

Phoebe, bowed, and excused himself, saying he needed to get to class. Phoebe watched him go. She looked at Aiden and said, "I didn't mean to eavesdrop, truly, but I couldn't help overhearing. You really climbed a sycamore to photograph an eagle?"

"A pair of eagles actually, but it was their young ones I was after."

She considered this. "Weren't you frightened? Worried they'd strike you, or that you'd topple from the tree?"

"Yes on both counts," Aiden confessed. "But as it turned out, the adult birds were surprisingly docile, and never bothered me at all—perhaps because they live so close to civilization, and have grown somewhat used to humans."

Phoebe regarded him with earnest eyes. It was as if he'd tumbled from a cliff, the breath knocked completely from his body, and he knew at that moment he would one day propose to her. Before he'd given so much as a thought to how he'd accommodate the offer, he asked if she'd like to see his photographs. When she said yes, he almost sagged with relief. "I don't suppose it's appropriate to show you the photographs at my house?"

She seemed to consider this, and for a moment he thought she'd go along with the suggestion, but in the end, she said, "Why don't you run home, fetch them, and bring them back? I'll wait for you right here."

"I have a better idea—why don't you permit me to take you to supper, and I'll show you the photos over a meal." She accepted, and he told her he'd pick her up at her boarding house shortly after seven.

He called for her just as the sun dipped dusky in the sky, his curly hair slicked and fragrant with witch hazel. He wore a town suit with a crisp white shirt, and shoes of black patent leather. Phoebe had changed into a navy blue mohair dress with a high cream collar, and donned a velvet hat sporting a mourning dove sitting jauntily in the middle.

As they strolled toward Aiden's favorite café, a little place called Luann's, a breeze lifted a tendril of Phoebe's hair. Without any realization of the effect it had on Aiden, she drew it from her face with her fingertip, and went on with her conversation. His eyes held fast to the shape of her mouth, before drifting, languidly, to the curve of her nose, and then the shape of her ears, from which two small amethysts dangled.

She told him of her life, how she was the only child of a banker and a housewife, how she played two instruments, the piano and the violin, but longed to play a third—a mandolin, perhaps, or one they called a zither. How all her life she'd found the out-of-doors intriguing, but had been discouraged from exploring, for her parents were the protective sort, and rather stiff at that.

"I used to sit at my bedroom window," she told him, "watching robins build their nests. I always wanted a bird, a little canary or a finch, that would sit on my finger. But it seemed a travesty to lock a bird in a cage, so I never asked for one—although if I had, my father would have provided it, and in an instant, at that." She smiled, dropping her gaze to her shoes. After a moment she looked up. "I asked for a cat instead."

Aiden laughed, as he was altogether smitten with Phoebe Pembroke. He'd met her only six short hours ago, but loved everything about her: her honesty, her compassion, her interest in the natural world. "Are your parents fond of birds?" he asked.

"I don't know," she said, looking a little surprised. "We've never discussed it."

"And yet they named you after one of my favorites."

"Really? One of your favorites?"

He grinned. "Well, if it wasn't before, it is now."

"That's very sweet," she said, and he could see she meant it. "My grandmother's name was Phoebe. It's quite popular in England, apparently. Less so here."

He looked at her again, thinking she hadn't the physical characteristics of a phoebe—her hair was light-colored, whereas the little flycatchers were a dusky shade—and so her name was somewhat inappropriate. Her nature too struck him as shy and perhaps a little docile, despite her initial staring. Not at all flighty like the phoebe was, sallying from this perch to that, and generally flitting about.

"What do you study at Berkeley?" he asked, not wanting a moment to pass without learning more about her.

"I haven't actually declared, although I'd like to be a teacher. I long to make a difference in this world, and it seems the best way to do so is through children. The young mind rather than the mature one can more easily be taught," she said. "Don't you agree?"

Aiden hadn't a clue, but he did agree. "Absolutely."

"I wish I knew more about nature," she went on, her voice wistful now. "I'd love to teach children the things you know—about eagles and owls and such."

Not only had Aiden found the girl of his dreams, but a woman to whom an understanding of the natural world was paramount. That he could help instruct her occurred to him at once. Over a supper of steak and mashed potatoes, while he thumbed through his photographs, he offered to escort her to the eagles' nest, so she could glimpse one for herself. "We'll ride bicycles," he told her, "and if you don't know how to ride, I'll teach you tomorrow."

Phoebe laughed, and warmly touched his hand. "Though

I've not seen as much of the world as you have, Aiden, nor traveled far from home, I'm not altogether unexposed—I have ridden a bicycle at least a time or two."

They spent the next few weeks traversing the local landscape, and photographing birds. They were inseparable, and Aiden was attentive not only to Phoebe's needs, but to her yearnings too; in turn, she put him on a pedestal, wishing to crawl inside him, wear his skin as she wore her own, and know everything about him.

By early summer, when they'd been seeing each other for full two months, Aiden asked Phoebe to travel with him to Lake Tahoe. It was a test of her faith in him, since he had no chaperone to offer; he was certain she would insist on bringing a friend along, or at the very least, a cousin. She asked for neither. "I'm a grown woman, Aiden—I don't want or need a nursemaid."

On introspection, her response didn't shock him, since she had also hesitated on the day he met her, when she had seemed to take a moment to consider whether or not she'd go to his house unaccompanied. She did, however, tell him she wasn't entirely immune to public opinion, and asked him now to adhere to a level of propriety that he was happy to accommodate. He pitched a tent in the high Sierra, affording Phoebe every privacy while he slept under the stars. It was a solid plan, worthy of the gentleman he'd become, although it was more difficult than he'd imagined. He couldn't sleep with wanting her, and when she rose in the morning, the sun in her hair, he thought her the loveliest woman on Earth.

Each morning before breakfast, they hiked in the woods, and then again in the afternoon. In between, they sat at camp, leisurely sipping coffee and laughing as Steller's jays stealthily stole small bits of their food. On the morning of the third day, an unseasonable squall blew in, and piled snow around their ankles. Aiden tried to build a fire, but each time he got it going, the wind blew it out again. They sat together on a fallen log, blankets around their shoulders, Phoebe shivering 'til her teeth shook. Aiden shivered too. "This is ridiculous, Phoebe," he said, "let's crawl inside the tent." She leaned forward, looked this way and that, and seeing no one, got up and went inside the tent.

They lay in their camp clothes in the fashion of two spoons. Aiden looped one arm around her, hugged her to him and tenderly kissed her hair. She turned and kissed him, too, then laughed, saying his nose was cold. She lay next to him for a long while, bundled like a knot. As she began to warm, her body relaxed, and Aiden pulled her closer. She stiffened slightly, then gently turned toward him. "Aiden," she said tenderly, her hands on his face. "I love you more than life itself, but I need you to stay strong."

"There isn't a creature in all of the forest who cares what we do in our tent. Not a single human, either."

"I care," she said. "If you don't stay strong, I won't either. I need you to set the example."

This need she had for him, this dependence on him, filled him with affection and personal pride. He shucked the blankets, struggled to one knee, and took her hands in his. "I haven't nearly the strength you credit me for, but I'll wait, because you've asked me to. I love you, Phoebe, and if you'll have me, I'll marry you tomorrow."

Her eyes welled, and he kissed her hands. She accepted instantly.

In a letter to Maggie, Aiden confessed his love. "I've never met a woman like her," he wrote. "I can't tell you how many times she's wandered the hills with me, toting a box of glass plates and helping me set up shots. Never would I have guessed a woman as delicate as Phoebe Pembroke would take to the countryside, yet she begs me to bring her along. But this is the best part, Maggie—I asked for her hand and she said yes! I'm bringing her home for a few days after graduation, so you and our parents can meet her."

As quickly as Maggie could put pen to paper, she dashed off a note to her brother. "By all means, Aiden, bring my sister home!"

Aiden and Phoebe's train arrived late in the evening, after Blythe and Owen had gone to bed. Tula showed Phoebe to her room, and it wasn't long before Maggie fetched Phoebe, held her hand, and brought her down the hallway, into her own room. The two young women, dressed in nightgowns, gazed admiringly at one another. Phoebe sat on a stool at the dressing table while Maggie brushed her hair. "My goodness," Maggie marveled, sucking her breath in a bit, "it combs soft as satin."

"All my life I've longed for hair as wonderful as yours," Phoebe told her, complimenting Maggie's curls, which fell just beyond her shoulders. Maggie said she'd give it all to Phoebe if there was any way she could, since Fin McFaddin had often teased her about her hair, claiming it looked as though she'd slept under a log, then made her way home when townsfolk were dead, drunk, or sleeping. He'd once called her a woods elf on account of her unruly halo.

The memory of what Fin had said took Maggie back to her childhood, when she nine, Fin fourteen, and they had trekked to the woods with Aiden. The boys had tried to persuade her to stay home, but she had refused, and had marched like a soldier behind them. While she walked, she imagined how it was in the old days, when the smoke of wigwams clouded the air from Oregon to Oklahoma. She would have gladly offered herself up as Fin's squaw, had she and the boys been Indians. And if Fin had asked her to toil the whole day through, she would have done so, roasting acorns for his supper and baking plump, sweet dumplings for dessert, although where she would have found a fruit tree in those dark woods she couldn't rightly remember.

So many times she had begged to be Fin's slave while the three of them played among the pine boughs. When Fin asked for bread slathered in butter, she had fetched it from her knapsack as fast as her legs would carry her. And then one day, Fin startled her by saying he no longer wanted a slave, or an Indian squaw either. Maggie had stood as stiff as Chief Joseph then, her watery eyes fixed on him. "Tell me what to do different," she'd said, "and I'll do it, I swear I will."

"Ain't nothin *to* do, Maggie. I'm growing up, is all."

She wanted to grow up too, persuade Fin she was meant to one day be his bride. More than once he'd told her in his coarse voice he wasn't marrying a tomboy, since everyone knew tomboys weren't worth a lick in the kitchen.

Aiden was no better. He gave Maggie no more notice than Fin did. While Fin was collecting eggs, Aiden was sitting on a hollowed-out snag, his Winchester propped beside him. It seemed he was always scribbling in some notebook, and when Maggie sat next to him, he greeted her with a scoot in the opposite direction. She glanced over at the scratchings he'd made in his book, and he let go a hefty sigh. "Why don't you go home, find some girls to bother?"

She was fixing a sassy reply when a bird alighted in a blackberry thicket not too far from them. Its blue feathers and black crest gleamed, and her breath caught at the sight of it. It scolded her with a series of noisy chats.

She gazed desperately at her brother. "Let me shoot him, Aiden. I can hit him, I know I can."

"Just because you can hit a cow pie doesn't mean you can knick that bird."

"How do you know, if you never let me try?"

"If I let you, will you leave Fin and me to hunt on our own?"

Maggie nodded, breathlessly.

"All right," he said, handing over his Winchester. "Give it a try."

She gripped the stock of his rifle, hefted it against her shoulder, and held it there. Closing one eye and steadying the other, she sighted the bird just as she'd sighted dirt clods and tin cans, then slowly squeezed the trigger. The gun popped, and the jay flipped in the air. Landing on its back, it furiously pedaled one leg, and then the cycling slowed and stopped altogether, and the bird lay dead in the dirt.

Maggie shrieked, and ran to fetch her treasure. From down the hill Fin called, "What'd you kill, Aiden?" to which Maggie hollered, "I shot it, Fin! My very own blue bird."

Aiden went over for a look, frowning at the mess she'd made of the creature. "You shot its tail off."

Maggie didn't care. She scooped up the little bird and hugged it to her breast.

Fin dropped from the tree he'd been climbing and trekked up the knoll. He toted his canvas bag, its strap slung diagonally across his chest, and in his back pocket he carried a copy of *Lattin's* catalogue of eggs. Maggie remembered how in those days Fin collected eggs, just as Aiden did; it wasn't until they'd grown up that Fin's yearning turned to shooting birds, while Aiden's focus remained on the interests of his childhood.

"That's no bluebird," Fin said when he looked at Maggie's

bounty. He scratched his cheek, pulled the catalogue from his pocket and flipped through the pages. "I saw a bluebird in a dictionary once, and as I recollect, it's smaller."

"A lot smaller," Aiden agreed.

Maggie stood on her tiptoes, peering into Fin's book. Never once had he snatched it from view like Aiden sometimes had, although every now and then he twisted his body so she couldn't fully see it. "What is it then?" she asked.

"Blue jay, maybe. One they call Steller's." He handed the book to Aiden, opened his canvas pack and withdrew a nest he'd hidden there. Four buff eggs lay inside. "Pulled this nest from that tree down yonder," he said, nodding toward the pines. "Likely they belong to the mate of your bird there, Maggie."

Maggie and Aiden took a moment to admire the orbs with the slightly bluish tint. To Maggie's delight, Fin let her hold one. It was smooth and warm, and fit perfectly in the palm of her hand.

"We'll blow them at my house, then take them to Morris Kiff's," Fin told Aiden. "He'll be able to tell us what we've got."

"Maybe Kiff will buy them," Aiden suggested. Back then, Kiff still purchased blown eggs, feathers, stamps, geological specimens, and all manner of natural-history novelties, which he sold to his curio-shop customers, some from as far away as New York City.

"Maybe he will," Fin said, taking the catalogue from Aiden and flipping through it again. When he got to the page about jays, he pursed his lips and looked at his friend. "Eggs of the Steller's jay go for a dollar apiece—can you imagine that?"

Aiden whistled. "That's four dollars for the lot of them. You think he'll give you that?"

"Be something if he would," Fin said. He glanced at Maggie's bird and then over at his friend; it was as though his and Aiden's minds were one, and that single brain calculated what a dead jay might fetch them. They glanced at Maggie at the same time, and she hugged her bird protectively.

"You can sell your eggs if you want to, but I'm keeping my jaybird." She cradled the creature in the crook of her arm and kissed its scraggly feathers.

"At least let us skin it before it gets to stinkin'," Fin told her. "We'll treat it with arsenic."

But Maggie wouldn't hear it. She scooted home with that bird swinging in her apron, passing Fin's neighbor, Mrs. Gary, along the way. "What you got there, Maggie?" called the woman, and Maggie hollered, "My very own jaybird, Mrs. Gary!"

Maggie lay on the bed in her room, planning to enjoy her jay a little longer. Patting its head, she set it on her pillow, then grew drowsy and fell asleep dreaming of birdsong. In the midst of that cozy snooze she drew the creature to her, awaking two hours later with a scurrilous rash. She shot from bed, slapping furiously at her forearms. She jerked open the window, grabbed the jay, and chucked it into the weeds.

The next morning Blythe trotted her down to Gilchrist's to buy salve for her arms. The mercantile sat at the corner of Riley and Ridgeway, where the street was paved with wooden blocks; the blocks weren't straight but laid this way and that, and when it was hot, a tarry substance oozed between them. Maggie's mother could have afforded to shop closer to home, where the streets were paved in cobblestones, but she insisted on trading at Gilchrist's, where Fin's father worked. Edward McFaddin was an honest man, if not the most cheerful, and Blythe liked him since he wasn't one to pepper her with bothersome questions.

Maggie loved the rush of cool air that hit her cheeks

when she walked inside the store. She loved the way it smelled too, with its scent of cotton fabric and flowers. Vases of lilacs or freshly cut lavender—which Fin's mother Willa had cut and arranged, then sent to the store with Edward—adorned the long wooden counter.

Edward said hello when Maggie and Blythe walked in. "Come for a peppermint stick, have you?" he asked Maggie, striving to make conversation. It never seemed to come naturally, however, as he always forgot to smile. He turned to Blythe, and his eyes widened as they traversed the breadth of her hat; it was a stately affair with a wide sweeping brim that featured the wings of an Arctic tern.

"We're here to cure Margaret's bug bites," Blythe told him. "She slept with a dead bird."

Edward's forehead folded. "She slept with a bird?"

"A *dead* bird," Blythe repeated dryly.

Edward thought for a moment. He glanced toward the rear of the store, then back at Maggie. "My Fin have anything to do with this?" he asked, to which Maggie spouted, "Yes, sir, him and Aiden too." Yet the moment she cast blame Aiden's way, she regretted it, since Fin was more or less the culprit.

Edward hollered toward a room in one corner with a yellow curtain strung loosely across it. "Fin! Get out here and explain yourself to me and Maggie Elliott." He nodded at Blythe. "We'll get to the bottom of this yet, ma'am."

Fin parted the curtain and walked through the door. Even then there was an aura about him, some mystical air that surrounded him, and traveled with him like a spirit. Maggie steeled herself, in order to sustain her anger.

"What do I need to explain, Pa?" Fin asked his father.

"Show him, Maggie," Edward instructed. She stuck her arms out, watching as Fin took in her weeping sores. It was difficult to know what he thought. He wore his brows perpetually furrowed so that he appeared uneasy, even when relaxed.

"Looks like the pox to me," Fin said, his mouth set seriously.

"It isn't the pox," Edward scolded, "it's bed bugs, thanks to you."

"Me? What have I got to do with it?"

"Maggie slept with that bird she shot," Blythe told him. "Apparently it was riddled with lice."

Horror seized Fin's face. "You weren't supposed to do that," he told Maggie. "You were supposed to skin it and dry it and treat it with arsenic."

"How was I supposed to know?"

"I told you, that's how."

"Did not."

"Did too."

Perspiration glossed Edward's forehead. He cupped Blythe's elbow. "If you'll follow me," he said, "the unguents are this way." He led her down a long dark corridor, then turned to shout at Fin. "Let Maggie pick out some candy — anything she wants — and don't charge her for it, either."

Maggie followed Fin, her steps in synch with his. She surveyed six jars sitting atop a glass counter, each containing sweets: horehound and licorice drops, and a sugary concoction made from a secret Gilchrist family recipe. Mrs. Gilchrist was said to have inspired it, but it was Mr. Gilchrist who shaped the miniature hearts, then topped each one with a saying. Maggie stood eye-level with the jars, took her time as she shifted from one foot to the other and examined the contents.

"It ain't a spelling test," Fin chided. "Go on and pick one."

Maggie leaned in closer. "I'll take a bag of those," she said, pointing to the candy hearts. As an afterthought, she added, "But leave out the I LOVE YOUs, since clearly I don't."

"I don't love you either," he said, snatching a small metal dipper and jamming it into the hearts. "I never have loved you," he went on. "I'd love a frog before I'd love you, and kiss it first too."

Maggie's eyes grew moist, and her chin began to quiver. The sudden turn in her demeanor stunned Fin, and for the first time he understood how deeply her feelings ran. She'd pestered him plenty over the years and he'd treated her as a play toy—something to amuse him when he and Aiden took to the hills for adventure. And when she said she loved him, he took it for the ramblings of a schoolgirl, for plenty of others had said it too, girls of ten, eleven, and twelve. Yet in all this time he hadn't fully appreciated how hard a girl could fall in love.

"If I'd had any idea you'd sleep with that jaybird," he'd said, striving for kindness, "I'd have surely told you not to." He seemed on the verge of saying more, when there was a crash at the back of the store. Edward McFaddin had fainted. Even then, no one had the smallest clue he would live only a handful of years, then die of a heart ailment.

Now, as Maggie brushed her hair, Phoebe looked at her new friend in the mirror. "Fin McFaddin," she said, the name resonating on her tongue. She recollected aloud how he was once Aiden's best friend, how they'd had a falling out. "I don't remember the reason," she said. "All I know is that Aiden hasn't seen him for some time now."

Maggie gathered a handful of Phoebe's hair, hair so soft and slippery it was difficult to plait. "It's been nearly five years since we've seen Fin. He and Aiden were nineteen when they left for Malheur, and they had a good time, for a while. But then they got to arguing over Fin taking up plume hunting to earn money for his mother, and Aiden came home, while Fin stayed. It all but ruined their friendship."

"Yes," Phoebe said, nodding. "I remember that story now."

"Willa McFaddin does our laundry to earn extra money, although it shames me to admit it. I think we ought to do our own washing, so every now and then I stroll down to her place and lend what hand I can." Maggie sighed, and Phoebe's eyes met hers. "Every time I visit," Maggie went on, "I hope Willa's heard from him. He used to write once a month, send her money too. The letters quit coming some time ago, which means the money did too." She dropped a section of Phoebe's hair and then picked it up again, securing it with the little finger of her right hand. "Willa says he's too busy to write, and knowing Fin, that's probably true. According to Aiden, Fin's shooting all the birds from the skies, or at least he's hoping to."

"That's a dangerous profession, pluming. If something happened to him, how would you possibly know?"

Maggie tied a ribbon at the end of Phoebe's braid and gave it a tug. "Well, I wouldn't, but I try not to dwell on it. Willa says worry won't get us anywhere, because we can't control it, whereas thinking positive is completely within our power. So we think positive, and hope one day Fin will come home to us."

"Aiden mentioned you were close to him, like he might have been your beau."

"Oh, I wished it so. When I was a girl I loved him with everything I had, but he didn't love me back. I always thought he'd change his mind, but when he didn't come home, I figured it was because he didn't care enough to fetch me. It hit me hard, I'll admit. I swore I'd find some other man, but it hasn't happened yet. No one appeals the way Fin does. He's got a way about him."

Phoebe turned and gripped Maggie's hand. "I'm sorry," she said, her face pinched and hurting. That Phoebe had found sympathy for Maggie's heartbreak warmed Maggie greatly. She hugged Phoebe, and thanked her for her kindness.

"You've got the same goodness in your soul that Willa has in hers," Maggie told her. And then she had the notion that Phoebe might like Fin's mother as much as she did. "Willa will be here in the morning to pick up our laundry. Would you like to meet her?"

Phoebe said she'd be delighted to, although she slept too late and missed Willa's arrival, as well as her departure, by more than half an hour. Tula wasn't happy at having to make two breakfasts—three, if you counted the tray she'd hauled up to Blythe's bedroom, and propped on a mountain of books.

Phoebe wandered downstairs a little after nine wearing a walking skirt, a white shirtwaist, and laced, low-heeled boots. She'd arranged her hair in a complicated system of braids, which she'd piled atop her head. When Maggie told her Willa McFaddin had already come and gone, Phoebe sat at the table, her face folding in distress. "I'm sorry I missed her. I confess I overslept. Most nights I lie awake until two or three in the morning, and sometimes I'd swear I didn't sleep at all. It's a struggle to get up."

"Why can't you sleep?" Maggie asked.

"It's the curse of the Pembrokes," Phoebe told her. "My father doesn't sleep either." She looked around the kitchen, her gaze drifting toward the window. "Where's Aiden?" she asked. "I hope he didn't take to the forest without me."

"He's driving Willa home in Father's buggy," Maggie told her. "He asked me to tell you he'll be back in half an hour."

"It's a beautiful day for a buggy ride. I can smell the lilacs outside my bedroom window. We've got primroses at home, but they haven't the fragrance that lilacs do."

Tula turned from the stove with the one rubbery egg she'd cooked for Phoebe. When she caught sight of Phoebe's coiffure, the spectacle seemed to startle her and she stepped back. Regaining her composure, she flopped the egg onto Phoebe's plate. "Normally serve breakfast in the dining room," she said as firmly as the egg resting in front of Phoebe. "You git yoursef downstairs by eight o'clock, you'll get some bacon too."

"Oh, I don't need bacon, but thank you," Phoebe said, not wishing to be a bother.

"Aiden ate all but two sticks of it this morning," Tula went on, ignoring Phoebe's comment. "What was left, I fetched to Missus Elliott."

"Blythe takes breakfast in her bedroom," Maggie said by way of explanation. "I'll take you up to meet her after you've stuffed yourself with that one sorry egg there." She scorched Tula with a frown. "The least you can do is get her some toast to go with it, Tula."

"She come down at eight o'clock, she get toast too."

Phoebe fixed her eyes on Maggie, having no idea what to make of Aiden's sister and their housekeeper. Their banter verged on temperamental, yet they seemed fine with it. In fact, Tula had already turned to scour the pan, and Maggie was smiling again. As soon as Phoebe speared the last bite of egg and slipped it her mouth, Maggie grabbed her hand. "Come on," she said, while Phoebe was still chewing. "I'll introduce you to Blythe."

"Blythe's your mother?"

Maggie nodded.

"And she allows you to call her that?"

"I guess so," Maggie said, realizing she'd not thought on it since she was fourteen, and had tried her mother's name out for the first time. It was after helping Willa McFaddin with a load of laundry, when she'd poked her head into her mother's bedroom, thinking they'd have a chat.

"You want company?" she'd asked, forever hopeful, but Blythe acknowledged her with barely a murmur, and never once looked up from her book. She lay on her bed in a dressing gown, her back propped against two pillows. Her feet were bare, crossed at the ankles.

Maggie tiptoed in. "I thought I could read to you."

"I prefer to do my own reading, Margaret, but thank you," Blythe said, shifting. She glanced up then, and must have seen some flicker of disappointment in Maggie's eyes. She patted the bed. "You may lie next to me and rest a while, but you'll do it quietly."

Maggie was thrilled with that small permission, and hopped into bed at once. She tried not to move or breathe, or otherwise disturb her mother, but then her nose began to itch and she sneezed three times, the last one issuing forth like a shot from a cannon. Blythe glanced over and sighed.

"Sorry," Maggie whispered.

She lay as still as possible then, her hands folded beneath her cheek. She gazed at her mother, but Blythe took no notice. Maggie turned onto her back and let her eyes wander around the room. She took in the heavy curtains, draped across the windows, the books stacked on the built-in shelves. And then she looked across the way at her mother's armoire, its door flung open, its contents spilling to the floor. She sat up on one elbow, contemplating the pile of clothes heaped near the door, wondering how it was possible for one person to soil so many garments in so short a time. "I thought we just sent a load to

Willa McFaddin's," she said, knowing full they had, since she'd scrubbed a good many undergarments herself that afternoon.

Blythe slowly turned a page, her eyes never leaving her book.

"Mother?"

"Mmmm?"

"Why are those clothes piled beside the door?"

"They're dirty, and I'm sending them to Willa's."

Maggie picked a fingernail and got some blood going. "Don't you feel bad, asking Fin's mother to do our laundry?"

Blythe looked at Maggie at last, her eyes hovering just above her book. "Without us, and all the others like us, the woman would have no work. No income, you see? I'm sure she's glad of the employment."

"Fin's got money. He's shooting birds, collecting eggs, and selling everything he can."

"Evidently it's not enough, and Willa must work as well." Blythe's eyes drifted back to her book, and she resumed reading. When Maggie let go a boisterous sigh, her mother again looked up. "What is it, Margaret?"

"Nothing, Blythe," Maggie said, the words hot and accusing. But if Blythe took offense at Maggie's boldness, she gave no sign at all.

"She doesn't care what I call her," Maggie told Phoebe now, "and she won't care what you call her, either. Call her Blythe, or Mother, or whatever you choose. Because sure as the world, she'll be your mother and soon—as early as Christmas, I hear!" Maggie motioned at Phoebe to follow her up the stairs, then knocked on her mother's door.

"What is it, Tula?"

"It's me," Maggie chirped, propping the door open and sticking her head inside. "I've brought you a surprise."

She pulled Phoebe into the room and then stood beaming alongside her. "I want you to meet Phoebe Pembroke, Aiden's sweetheart from Berkeley." She turned toward Phoebe. "This is my mother, Blythe Elliott."

Blythe sat in bed, smoking a cigarette. The habit was not endorsed by her husband, who viewed smoking as unseemly. He had long since abandoned all attempts to get her to stop, however, as she was now addicted, requiring a puff or two, as she called it, to get her through the morning.

She wore a silver dressing gown with matching slippers. Her hair, which she'd gathered in a bundle and situated atop her head, leaned sideways and threatened to spill onto one shoulder. Her eyes sparking at the mention of Aiden's sweetheart, she rested her cigarette on a tray on the nightstand, set her book on her lap, and then extended her hand to Phoebe, a sapphire ring loose on one finger. "It's so nice to meet you," she said. "Aiden has told us so much about you."

Phoebe's eyes had been fixed on the cigarette, and for a moment she couldn't speak. She had never seen a woman smoking before, and thought perhaps Maggie's mother used tobacco as medication. She clasped Blythe's fingertips and gave her a small, sympathetic smile. "It's so nice to meet you, too, Mrs. Elliott. I'm sorry you're unwell."

Maggie was so used to seeing her mother in bed that she'd forgotten to warn Phoebe. "She's not sick, she's unsociable," Maggie said straight out. "And she defies all rules of propriety by smoking cigarettes."

"What I do in the privacy of my bedroom is strictly my business," Blythe told her. She turned to gaze at Phoebe. "Don't worry, dear, I feel fine. Truly, I do."

Maggie crossed the room and whipped open the drapes to reveal a patch of sunshine. "It's natural to assume Mother's ill, what with her lolling in bed all day."

"Oh, dear," said Phoebe, mortified. "It's just that I assumed—"

"Of course you did," said Maggie. "But Blythe's a reader, not a do-er, unlike Willa McFaddin."

"Who never read a book in her life," Blythe put in, ignoring Maggie's insult.

This banter, too, astonished Phoebe; just as Maggie spoke to Tula, she also spoke to Blythe. More astonishing than Maggie's impertinence was Blythe's lack of reproach. She seemed to accept without argument Maggie's assessment of her.

Phoebe dropped her gaze to the floor, uncomfortable with the conversation. It was one thing to speak similarly to a husband, after some twenty-odd years of marriage, but she couldn't imagine sparring so with her own mother, as the woman would scold her unmercifully, and as much as her father loved her, he wouldn't hesitate to clip her ear.

"Will you at least come down for supper?" Maggie said to Blythe. It wasn't a request so much as a summons. Blythe would have normally issued a sigh and begged some excuse, but being at least somewhat cognizant of her company's feelings, said, "Certainly. I want to hear all about Aiden's plans for Phoebe."

"Good," said Maggie, looping her arm through her future sister-in-law's.

On the way out the door, Phoebe whispered, "What plan is she referring to?"

"Oh, you know Aiden. As soon as possible, he'll want to trek you to New York City and parade you before Frank M. Chapman—"

"Why would he do that?"

"To show you off, of course. And why shouldn't he? You're

beautiful, and charming. Everything a politician could ask for."

Some realization must have sunk in then, as Phoebe smiled. "He's really doing it then? Throwing his hat into the ring?"

"You can count on it," Maggie told her. "And when he does, you'll be there as his partner, his teammate, as it were. If you truly aim to make a difference in this world, Aiden will show you precisely how it's done."

"All this time I thought my calling was a teacher," Phoebe marveled, "but maybe I've some other job, some task as Aiden's helper?"

"Likely he's already made a list," Maggie told her, "with tasks from A to Z. If I know Aiden, he'll open an office one of these days, then set you on a stool, and put you to work writing letters on behalf of the nation's birds."

"What a wonderful notion," Phoebe confessed. "All my life I've wished to work toward some cause. I just never knew what it would be, until I met your brother. You're absolutely right Maggie. Aiden and I *are* a team. While he endeavors to save the birds, I'll do all I can to help him."

Phoebe's mind instantly began spinning, as she organized her thoughts. Energized, she smiled broadly, wondering aloud where she'd find the time to plan a wedding, draft letters, and strive ardently for Aiden.

Maggie hardly knew what to say to that, since all she had was time. Which got her thinking about her own future, how empty it stood, and how she best might fill it.

Willa thought it wonderful to see Aiden again, although for a moment she hadn't known him. Had she not stood in the Elliott's kitchen and heard Maggie call his name, she would never have recognized him. He'd grown two inches since she'd last seen him, and he held the strong, firm features of his father, absent the belly of course. He carried new confidence, too, that he hadn't held before, and stood straighter, one hand in his pocket, like a businessman might do.

The moment he learned she had ridden Fin's bicycle, with its little cart, to the house to collect their laundry, he insisted on taking her home. She had objected, and he'd said he wouldn't hear it, but would fetch her home properly inside his father's buggy. Just like that, he loaded the clothes, hitched her bicycle to the back, then helped her up and hopped in beside her.

They traveled the same dusty road he and Fin had trod as youngsters, when they'd ambled barefoot past the McFaddin's, and then up into the forest—that land of toadstools and blackberries they'd loved so when they were boys.

Willa closed her eyes, breathing deeply as she rode. Aiden's scent lingered in the air and made her think of her husband. Edward's smell had been a manly one too, a combination of shaving soap and that savory tonic he splashed into his hair. She caught a whiff of it now, relishing not only Aiden's fragrance, but the strength he posed beside her.

Fin had stopped writing a handful of years ago, and Aiden's presence reminded her just how much she missed him. She had no notion why Fin's letters had quit coming, only that it pained her. She wanted to confide in Maggie, but held back, thinking it unfair to burden the girl. It was apparent how much Maggie still loved Fin, and how much she missed him too.

Willa recollected how she and Maggie had struck up a friendship after Edward had died. A few weeks after they'd buried him, Willa stood in the yard, bent over her washtub, scrubbing one of Owen Elliott's shirts. She had looked up to find Maggie striding confidently toward her, a length of fabric flung around her neck. A dinner bucket swung from one hand, like the one Fin used to carry. She sang a song Willa didn't recognize, a rhyme concerning itty-bitty urchins skipping two-by-two.

Willa stood and stretched her back, waving when Maggie looked up. Maggie's face lit up and Willa's heart went out to her. It seemed the girl had no real love in her life, and that her parents were only vaguely aware of her existence; as such, she clung to the slightest bit of kindness, even when it came from a stranger.

Maggie had followed Willa home the day of Edward's funeral, and situated herself on the sofa after everyone else had kissed Willa's cheek and said their sad goodbyes. Maggie's legs poked out from beneath her skirt, thin and supple as twigs. Something about those skinny legs gripped Willa's heart and squeezed it, since there was nothing sadder than a girl of skin and bones sitting alongside a fat woman.

"I'd be happy to spend the night if you'd like me to," Maggie had volunteered. But Willa declined, tired as she was, and brokenhearted too. She sent the girl home with Fin, who had balked, privately, when Willa asked him to escort her. "She'll talk my ear off," he'd complained, though he'd done it and returned, Willa noted, with his ear fully intact.

Willa recollected too how Maggie had set her dinner bucket on the porch that day, then tugged the length of fabric—a pair of Aiden's trousers—from her neck and flung it onto Willa's pile. "I hope you haven't already done the darks," she said, "my mother missed this pair." She plucked the bucket from the porch and handed it to Willa. "There's a slice of plum pie in there. Tula thought you'd like it, but if you ask me, it could use a pinch more sugar."

"Why, how thoughtful." Willa took the bucket, opened it and peeked inside. The smell of fruit filling and piecrust filled her nostrils, and got her stomach growling. Maggie's eyes grew wide at the sounds coming from Willa's insides. Laughing, Willa said, "I've been at this laundry most of the day—I guess I must be hungry. Will you sit here on the porch and have a taste with me?"

"Maybe just a bite," said Maggie. She sat down and scooted so close to Willa, their ankles knocked.

Willa broke off the tip of the flaky triangle, passed it to Maggie, and then bit into her pie. She brushed flecks of crust from her bosom and shrugged, not caring one lick about the mess she made. She grinned, her mouth full and her shoulders scrunched. She pointed to the well behind her right ear. "Sour," she said, wincing.

Maggie giggled. "I told you so."

Willa offered the last bite to Maggie. When Maggie said she didn't want it, Willa popped it into her mouth. "My," she said, wiping her lips with her thumb and forefinger, "that was delicious. Please thank Tula for me." She sat up straight and slapped her thighs. "It's back to work, I'm afraid. Your father's shirts won't wash themselves."

"I'll lend a hand, if you let me."

"Goodness, Maggie. I don't think your mother would appreciate that."

"She doesn't care what I do."

"She'd care plenty if she knew it was you washing her clothes and me she was paying."

"I won't tell, if you won't."

"All right then," Willa agreed, but only to appease the girl. She wasn't about to take advantage and only planned to let her rinse a stocking or two. But half an hour later, Maggie had helped finish the whites and then dug into the darks like they were presents from Santa Claus. Maggie's vitality impressed

Willa, as she worked quickly and competently, and seemed oblivious to the drudgery those piles represented, for she sang the entire while. Before Willa knew it, she herself had joined in, raising her voice and bobbing her head, singing of itty-bitty urchins marching two-by-two.

Maggie wrung out a sock, gave it a snap, then hung it to dry. "If I was my mother, I'd make Aiden wear his socks 'til they stood on their own," she said. "His drawers too. Why is it a girl's place to wash a boy's old stinky clothes?"

"Women care for the men in this world," Willa told her. "That's just the way it is."

Maggie said nothing for a moment, just rubbed another sock against the washboard, putting her whole body into it. "I wouldn't mind washing Fin's clothes, if ever he'd ask me to."

Willa had no idea the girl was sweet on her son. Fin hardly ever mentioned Maggie, aside from commenting now and then he wished she'd stay home for a change, not pester him and Aiden when they trekked up to the woods.

Over the years though, Willa had come to understand how much Maggie loved Fin, although she didn't believe her son's feelings had changed since he was a boy. Which is why she had no desire to bring up Fin in Maggie's presence; even now Maggie was still prone to ask questions to which Willa had no answers. "Do you suppose he's happy, Willa, in that basin by himself?"

Willa hoped he was. Heaven knew Aiden was happy, for all a body had to do was listen to the tune he whistled! He carried himself with such aplomb that Willa couldn't help but admire him. She thought it peculiar that he and Fin had taken such different paths, given they were all but inseparable as boys. Perhaps it was simply meant to be. Aiden was always the gregarious one, and Fin the far more serious. It was just like Fin to work as hard as a servant, saving every dime and sending it home — at least in those first few years he'd been gone. He wanted to give her a better life, and yet she hadn't lightened her load one bit since he'd left home. She was a worker, as much as he was, and though she'd spent a little money here and there, she'd stashed as much as she could. Every cent she saved would make it easier on Fin, when he at last came home from his travels. Oh, he'd fuss at her when he learned she'd never trotted the money to the bank, as he'd told her to. But then he'd laugh — of course he would! — to see that lump beneath her mattress, the size of a hearty potato. She smiled to think of it.

Aiden must have seen her grin, and guessed she was contemplating Fin. He asked after a moment if she'd recently heard from him.

"No, I've had no word from him for months and months now," she said, gazing at the horizon. "As much as I hate to dip beneath my mattress, I'm doing it more and more. I don't make enough to sustain myself — getting too old, I guess."

Hearing this, Aiden gripped the reins tightly. He looked over at Willa, realizing in years past she'd been invisible to him. Now, he truly saw her. Lines as fine as porcelain cracks formed at her mouth, and her face was darkly burnished. The sun had soaked up her youth, and played havoc with her skin. Her hands, chapped and raw from laundry soap, rested in her lap like worn-out bundles, sapped of all suppleness. She looked a woman of almost sixty, but was no more than forty-five.

"Perhaps I ought to set out for Malheur, see if I can find him."

"I'd never ask that of you, Aiden."

"I know you wouldn't, which is why I'm offering. Truly, Willa, I've been thinking of taking a trip to Malheur to take photographs. If Fin's still in Oregon, he's likely hunting herons in the rookeries there. I've got the entire summer to search for him. I can put together a trip in less than a week, and leave a few days after."

He sat straighter now, inspired by the prospect, for all he said was true. He'd recently been named secretary of the ornithological society in Berkeley, but wouldn't start working until early fall; it was no hardship to surrender a month in the middle of summer to look for Fin. Not only that, but he could take photos while he was there. He wanted more than ever to snap white herons before they too were gone.

Aiden glanced hopefully at Willa, but she seemed preoccupied. She was sitting forward now, clutching the rim of the buggy, gazing into the distance. Her brows were furrowed, and her mouth was still and puckered.

"Do you see that smoke," she said after a moment, "coming from beyond the ridge top?"

Aiden followed her gaze, and he too frowned with concern. "Likely it's a campfire," he said, although even he could see there was too much smoke for that.

"There were coals in my yard fire before I left for town," she confessed, gripping the buggy tighter. "If the wind picked up, it might have sailed a spark onto my rooftop."

Aiden sat straighter now. "You didn't douse it before you left?"

"I didn't want to drown it completely," she said, "it's too hard to get going again."

Aiden didn't say a word then, just flicked the reins hard and got the horse going.

Willa's eyes stung with tears as she thought on what she'd done. Her little house was all she had, and if it burned to the ground, Fin would have nothing to come home to. But as they rounded the corner, she saw it, charred and black and burning. "God in heaven, help us!"

When they came upon the house, Aiden brought the buggy to a rough halt. Willa leapt out, and landed crooked on one ankle. Her neighbors, Mr. and Mrs. Gary, were there, their faces red and shining. Mr. Gary dropped his water bucket and tossed Willa a burlap sack. Along with Mrs. Gary, she went at it, beating back flames while singing her eyebrows, and limping on her ankle.

Aiden too grabbed a sack. He gave it his all, before eventually falling back. The flames were too high, and the fire too hot, and they had to let it burn.

"Oh, Willa," Mrs. Gary cried, her sack dragging on the ground. "We came soon as we saw the smoke, but by the time we got here, the house was too far gone."

Willa stumbled back, praying it was untrue. And then it hit her, that thing she'd done, and her hands flew to her mouth. "Fin's money is under my mattress," she cried, and she took off. Aiden ran after her, grabbed her arm and yanked her to the ground. She wrenched away and shot back up, and when he reached for her a second time, she beat his chest and shrieked in wild torment.

"Willa!" Aiden hollered, shaking her now. "It's gone, you hear? The money's all burned up!"

Wailing, she threw her head back. Aiden wrapped his arms around her, but she pushed away and staggered toward the kettle. With everything she had, she pushed it violently from its stand. The little frame toppled over, and the kettle crashed atop it. "Fin's money, all for naught," she railed, her voice and body taut. And then she turned to Aiden. "He'll never forgive me, I know he won't—he'll hate me for what I've done."

Aiden walked up to her, took her in his arms. "He won't

hate you," he said, although it was true Fin could hold a grudge. Mr. and Mrs. Gary came up, and they too wrapped their arms around her. The little group stood as one, with Willa in the middle.

"You'll stay with us until Fin comes home," Mrs. Gary told her. "He'll get you on your feet again, just you wait and see."

Willa looked at Aiden, her eyes rimmed with tears. "Will you set out to find him, like you said you would?"

"I will, as soon as I pack my bags."

Willa turned to Mr. Gary, ashamed by the way she'd carried on, for even after Edward died, she'd kept herself composed. "I don't know what I'd do without you, and I want you to know I'm grateful."

"We know you are," Mr. Gary told her. He turned to gaze at her house. "Wisht we could of saved it. Edward built it not long after we built ours, and I know what it meant to you. I'm sorry we lost it."

Phoebe had never known Aiden to be so late, nor break a promise either. When he hadn't returned to take her to the forest, she knew something was wrong. As it happened, she was up in Maggie's bedroom conjuring all sorts of injuries when he tapped on the door. She jumped from the bed and ran to greet him, halting to see the state he was in, his shirt black with ashes, his hair tangled and filthy with gray soot. His cheeks and forehead were smudged.

"What on earth?" she said, just as Maggie stepped forward.

"McFaddin's house is gone," he said, "burnt entirely to the ground." He leaned against the door, told how Willa had left hot coals in the fire, how the wind had lifted the sparks that had burned the whole thing down.

Maggie's hand flew to her mouth. "Is Willa all right?"

Aiden nodded. "Mrs. Gary is putting her up until Fin comes home."

"Fin's coming home?"

"Not of his own accord. I've got to go and get him."

Aiden's tone was terse, although he hadn't meant it so. The strain of seeing Willa McFaddin with no husband and no home had taken its toll, as had the knowledge that Fin was nowhere to be found. To Aiden's way of thinking, Fin should have been there to protect Willa, and put the fire out. But off he was, same as always, his whereabouts unknown.

Phoebe's eyes went wide. "You'll fetch him, won't you, Aiden?" When Aiden said he would, she quickly added, "I'm going with you."

Aiden looked at Phoebe, then over to Maggie, then back at Phoebe again. He wondered how it was possible that in twelve hours' time, his sister's spirit had already infused his fiancée. "First, I don't know where Fin is," he told her plainly. "Might be to Malheur, might be down to Klamath. Second, he's caught up in the plume trade, and I won't expose you to it. It's an ugly business, Phoebe—ugly and dangerous."

"I told you before, Aiden, I'm a grown woman. If I'm to be your partner in business and in life, you best let me share the bad as well as the good." Her knees held stronger than ever before, and when she glanced at Maggie, it was with courage in her heart.

Aiden sighed, exhausted. "I haven't got it in me to deny you, although I suspect I'll regret it." Phoebe threw her arms around him, and kissed him on the mouth.

The sight of that kiss, and the love surging beneath it, stung Maggie's heart. "I want to go too," she said. "I want to go as badly as Phoebe does—I know you know that, Aiden."

With renewed energy, Aiden said, "No. You will not go." Gently, he extricated himself from Phoebe's grip. "I'll take Phoebe, because she's my fiancée, but there's no reason for you to go."

"I've got just as much right to look for Fin as you do."

In all this time, Aiden hadn't told her of his conversation with Fin, the one that fueled their argument all those years ago. He could end it now, if he wanted to, tell her straight out that Fin didn't love her. But when he saw her standing so tender and determined, he hadn't the heart to do it.

"Aiden, please," Phoebe pleaded, "let Maggie come with us."

Again, Maggie said, "Aiden, I want to go."

He tried reasoning with Maggie, telling her he thought she ought to stay. "Don't you think we owe it to Willa to help her out, seeing as it was our laundry she was keeping that fire for?"

"She's got Mrs. Gary to tend her, you said so yourself."

"Look," he said, his patience straining, "Fin's lived among plumers for five years now. We've no idea what state he's in. What if he's not the man we remember?" Aiden held up one hand, knowing Maggie would interrupt. "We've no idea how he'll react to our arrival, what sort of reception he'll give us. And the news we'll deliver is as rough as he's heard, apart from his father's passing. That's enough for him to deal with." Maggie had crossed her arms, and was regarding him with resentment. He took a breath, seeing he was getting nowhere, and that he should now strive for honesty. "As much as it pains you to hear it, Maggie, he doesn't love you—he said so in the marsh."

"Aiden!" Phoebe gasped. She embraced Maggie at once.

"She knows it's true," he countered gently, "yet she continues to hang on."

Tears welled in Maggie's eyes, and Phoebe held her tighter. "He doesn't mean it, Maggie," she insisted. "He's just not thinking straight, what with the fire and all."

"No," Maggie said softly. "He's thinking clear as he ever has." She pulled away, speaking earnestly to Phoebe. "I wish you would go to Malheur with Aiden, I do. He'll protect you as well as any sheriff, and oh, the birds you'll see there." Her mouth quivered. "Yes, go with him, and when you find Fin, don't mention my name. Just tell him his mother needs him. Will you do that for me, Phoebe?"

Phoebe agreed, having no alternative. By morning, she and Aiden were gone.

# CHAPTER FIVE

In 1897, when Fin was twenty-three, he thought he might leave Tule Lake. Malheur was on his mind again and the herons he might shoot there. He thought, too, he would depart without a word to Axel, having no desire to explain himself or discuss his departure; he had not, in fact, spoken more than a hundred words since he'd left LeGrande for good. But saying goodbye to Axel felt like something he should do, and so he mounted his horse and rode west to Lower Klamath.

"I wisht you'd stay," Axel said upon hearing Fin's news. "We ain't hardly seen one another of late."

It occurred to Fin to ask Axel to join him, but then LeGrande stepped forward and stuck his nose where it didn't belong. After all this time the marsh dweller still insisted Fin wouldn't be able to make a go of it, that he needed him and Axel to help with the shooting, and the skinning that went with it.

"I left you two years ago, LeGrande, and I been making out just fine. As would Axel, if he, too, was to venture out on his own." Fin glanced at Axel then, letting the comment dangle. He hoped Axel would put it together, the chance he'd just been given to pack his bag and get out of there, but the man held his pained expression and simply stared ahead.

"Was me and Axel taught you everything you know," LeGrande went on. "Least you can do is invite us to tag along, cut us in on your deal."

"Only deal you ever made me was stealing half my money."

"You warn't bright enough to keep it," jeered LeGrande. He kept his eyes on Fin, and smiled disdainfully.

Fin grabbed the red bandana hanging around LeGrande's neck. Jerked him over and held him close, so surprising the plumer that he lost his balance. LeGrande's hand closed atop Fin's, and they stalled, each grunting and straining until LeGrande stumbled backward and they both went down. Fin landed hard on the man's chest. They wrangled in the dirt then, one rolling atop the other, and stirring up the dust.

Axel scampered out of the way as the men spiraled toward him. "Hey now!" he cried. "You two knock that off!"

The men rocked to a halt. Fin lay sprawled on top of LeGrande, his legs splayed and his toes dug deep into the ground. His face was inches from LeGrande's, and he held a strong advantage, as he leaned against the man's throat. "I'm smarter now," he told LeGrande. "You won't steal from me again." LeGrande choked and sputtered, and Fin leaned harder still. The man's face began to turn the shade of a plum.

Axel lunged forward, grabbed Fin's coat. "That's enough, you hear? You got the best of him." When Fin didn't respond, Axel jerked his coat. "Get off, Fin. You've all but strangled him."

Fin let the man go. Pushing to his feet, he stood, breathing hard, and brushed himself off. LeGrande lay on the ground, gagging and spitting and carrying on, his hands held to his throat.

Fin strode past Axel, saying with one look he'd had all he would take from LeGrande. Axel's eyes held fast to Fin's. The young man might have said a small word, if it weren't for his uncle's glaring. LeGrande rose to one elbow, and with his small cat's eyes warned Axel not to make a sound.

Axel stood, his lips tight, his gaze boring into the ground.

Fin wasted no time putting the episode behind him. LeGrande could stew all he wanted to, but Fin had birds to shoot. It was the end of spring when he set out for Malheur, when the wild currant bloomed. The days were warm, the nights cold, and the world felt fine to him.

No sooner had he hit the trail than hummingbirds besieged him, little rufous ones called calliopes; Morris Kiff once told him that these were the smallest birds in North America. Fin thought the females prettier than the males, with their copper-colored bellies and lightly spotted throats. The males sported reddish-purple rays along their chins, resulting in a starburst effect when they lifted their feathers. Buzzing about, they zoomed passed his eyeballs like luminescent bullets, shooting high into the sky, and then falling with a *whoosh*. He estimated there might have been a thousand to the acre, and had they sat still for one minute, he would have tried to count them.

To his disappointment, he couldn't find their nests. He spent two full days looking, and finally concluded they didn't breed in the area, only visited, which got him thinking maybe he'd climb into the timber, take a look around. Josie followed, her nose snuffling the ground, her tail wagging, as he tracked one of the little birds to the edge of a mountain meadow. He lost it for a while, and so he sat, eating a biscuit and taking in the view. The ground was littered with forest debris: pine needles, branches, and twigs. In between, green grass and small spindly flowers sprouted. An orange butterfly floated by, and a big black ant scaled the trunk of a tree. Fin looked up, saw the sky painted a perfect blue, and then his hummingbird appeared. He watched it dip in and out of a conifer; the third time the creature zipped down from its tree, Fin headed over to inspect it. What he found so astonished him, that he could only stand and smile.

The little bird had built her nest on the base of a pinecone, camouflaging the cuplike structure so it seemed a part of the cone itself. In days past, he would have clipped it then and there, wrapped it in muslin and stuffed it into his satchel. But he so admired the calliope's cleverness that he left it untouched, bestowing upon the hummingbird a deference he'd declined to show his kingfisher all those years ago.

The incident stuck in his mind, even as he resumed his route to Malheur. Then, as soon as the flowers were gone, the birds were too, and this deflated him. The shimmering creatures had brought a pleasant diversion to his days, and now it was business as usual.

Wishing to save himself the trouble of hauling his boat across the rugged expanse of the desert, he'd left it at Klamath, figuring he'd rent what he needed at Malheur, as he and Aiden had done. He met up with a fellow named Ed Mott, who owned a duck boat suitable for navigating the tule-laden marshes. He rented it to Fin. Said the vessel had a leak here and there, and was in need of repair. Fin caulked the holes until it was solid and would easily hold a man.

Malheur country lay before him, a hazy apparition, silent and warm in the sun. Yellow-headed blackbirds called from the marshes, and all around him a dry alkaline breeze softly stirred the air. Fin expected the landscape to feel smaller somehow. He remembered how Gilchrist's Mercantile stood large and looming, when he and his father had worked there. How radically it seemed to have shrunk after his father died. He thought he'd find Malheur smaller too, yet now that he'd come upon it again, he had to acknowledge it was broader and more spectacular than he'd remembered.

He urged his horse toward a ridge top, and as he sat, scanning the ragged country, his heart began to tighten. It was an awkward sensation, strange and unfamiliar, and since he didn't know what to name it, he called it loneliness. The feeling took him aback, and he quickly brushed it aside, for lonely or not, he'd ponder no notion of going home to Portland. He'd go nowhere at all, in fact, until he'd shot the great and little herons he'd come for.

Unlike LeGrande's birds of Florida and Louisiana, which built their nests in trees, Malheur's birds built theirs among the tules. He knew he'd find herons among the islands in the middle of the lake. The next morning, when he and Josie set out from the Narrows in search of their goldmine, the sky teemed with birds. Fin sighted more terns, gulls, and white pelicans than most saw in a lifetime, all of them swirling and calling, and catching thermals from Heaven. It should have been a glorious day, an adventure like no other, but Fin knew there was something wrong when he noted that Josie held her ears back, and rested her tail near her rump. Every so often, she sniffed the air, then looked over her shoulder at Fin. Twice, that sixth sense she had kicked in, and she whined and licked her muzzle. That she was nervous made him nervous too, and he grew watchful, minding the buzzards that slowly dropped in and landed behind the tules.

The birds were thinning now. Fin sat taller and looked

around, drew the oars quietly through the water. Josie again whined, low this time, and he shushed her as he steadied his gun across his lap. Three more buzzards flew in, and dropped behind the bulrushes. He followed their shadows, veering slightly left and steering into a canebrake.

And then he saw it: the massacre. Hundreds of birds lay dead at their nests, their wings and skins hacked off. He gauged they'd been dead perhaps twenty-four hours, killed before his arrival. Frowsy-headed youngsters, wobbly and naked, clattered to be fed.

Fin's gaze locked on the carnage. He couldn't move, couldn't think—could barely take it in. His eyes drifted toward a splotch of red and his heart seized, for he knew it was LeGrande Sharp's bandana. The man had left it deliberately to send a hateful message.

His gaze drifted back to the baby birds. He'd seen plenty of massacres over the years, but nothing quite like this. Even that day at the grebe shack, when something indescribable had nudged him, he hadn't given a thought to the fate of any young ones—yet nothing but suffering surrounded him now, making him wonder who and what he was.

A lump seized his throat and his eyes welled. He glanced back, awkward and embarrassed, expecting to find a stranger there, shaking his head in shame. He fought his tears with all he had, but before long his shoulders began to shake and he started to sob. He cried for every hurt he'd never acknowledged. For Aiden and Maggie, and Willa too, whose back was no doubt breaking. Mostly, he cried for his father. Since Edward died, Fin had kept the memory of their last day together locked deep inside; now it consumed him with guilt and blinding pain.

His father had climbed from bed complaining of

heartburn and dizziness, yet he declined to ask, as most fathers would, if his son would kindly spell him. Instead, he demanded it. Ordered Fin to walk down to Gilchrist's, open the store, and fill the till with money. At eighteen, Fin had just sprouted his pinfeathers. He looked up from his oatmeal, told his father in a confident voice that he had other plans—that he'd open Gilchrist's after he had trekked to the forest and shot a few birds, when it better suited his schedule.

Edward's eyes had widened, and his face went red with rage. He strode over, snatched Fin's collar and jerked him from his chair. Fin flung one arm forward, cuffing his father's ear. Edward grabbed the side of his head and lurched back. Breathing hard, he spat, "You'll do what I tell you to, or I'll knock you to the ground."

"Excuse me, but you'll do no such thing. I'm my own man now."

His father stood—in shock, it seemed—one hand on his heart. The color left his face, and he said nothing more. Fin thought it a turning point, and all day long he delighted in his authority, and carried himself real tall. By evening, his father was dead.

Through a haze of hot tears, Fin remembered his mother's agony, how three days after his father's funeral, she had stood in the doorway of his bedroom, still wearing her funeral clothes: a black wool dress, absent embroidery, wrinkled and bunched at the hips. She hadn't slept in two days, and small violet moons glistened beneath her eyes. Her hair was clumped and tangled.

She leaned her cheek against the doorjamb. "You thinking on your father?"

Fin had been gnawing his lower lip, keeping at it until the flesh was raw and ragged. His blood was warm and tasted of tin, and though he knew the thing wouldn't heal unless he left it alone, the habit brought him comfort. "I'm figuring our future," he said, and let it go at that.

Willa walked over and lay beside him. Feeling the heat of her body through his blanket, he moved over, giving her more room. She had taken off her shoes and socks, and her feet were bare. Fin had never seen her feet before, not even in summer, and he averted his gaze, thinking he ought not see them now. Shifting, he looked at her face. Her eyes, brown and needful, welled to meet his own. She sucked in her breath, held it, then tucked her head into his shoulder. He wrapped his arm around her, and she cried until he thought she could cry no more. He himself had held his tears, but now he let them go.

After a long while he heaved a cleansing sigh, but his relief was slow to settle. The next week found him unwilling to rise to make a campfire or heat the smallest breakfast. He neither shaved nor bathed, but lay in his bedroll until his clothes grew stale and shabby. On the few occasions that he did get up, it was to toss a scrap to Josie. By the count of ten he had flopped down again, declining to rise until supper the next day, when he'd eat a bit of hardtack and sip from his canteen. All the while, Josie lay next to him, resting her chin on his stomach. Every now and then she lifted one eyebrow, and then dropped it again, resigned to Fin's indifference. When the biscuits and venison were gone, she left him. "Fine," he said, hollering after her, "leave, if you want to. You think I give a damn?"

After four days his back began to hurt. He got up, dragged himself to his blind in the tules and sat there a while. He spotted hundreds of birds within shooting distance but declined to take a shot, as the question of whether he was a hunter or a killer throbbed inside his head. That he couldn't put a name to what he was ate at him, so he sat in his blind with his gun in his lap, never once pulling the trigger.

It was eight days in all that he dwelled on his predicament. He had always been a loner, proud and independent. To see where all that self-sufficiency had gotten him made him feel miserly—so much so that he thought he'd gladly hug Maggie were she to reveal herself right now. Hug her and tell her how sorry he was for all the grief he'd caused her. But she did not appear, even in his dreams, and he was as alone as he'd ever been.

He slept most of that last day. When he awoke in early evening, he found Josie curled up beside him, her nose tucked into her paws. His eyes met hers and she whacked her tail, sending a bright hello. He tousled her fur, scratched her belly and hugged her head, understanding just how sorely he'd neglected her.

"Hey girl," he said, stroking her ears. "Where you been all this time?" Her muzzle was caked with dry mud, and he supposed she'd dug up some tubers somewhere and eaten them raw, despite their bitterness. His eyes welled in shame to think of what she'd been through, and he pulled her close, saying, "I oughtn't to have a dog." He told her he didn't deserve her devotion, since he hadn't begun to earn it. But she held no grudge at all. Day after day, from spring until summer, she stood beside him, nuzzling the palm of his hand. And when he was out, trudging the marshes, she served as his protector, watching for danger when he would not, and nudging him along.

Lost as he was, he willingly gave himself over. Let Josie tell him what to do and where to go; when she drank from a pool, he did too, and she sat and blinked at him. He glanced up at her, and then at himself, falling back at his reflection. His beard had grown in, thick and dusty, and his clothes all but hung on him. He looked every inch a marsh dweller, roaming the shoreline like some ragamuffin drifter, behaving like one too: rarely eating, hardly sleeping, hearing all sorts of things.

Voices, mostly.

The first time he heard them, it was almost eventide, the sun slung low in the sky. Redwings trilled from the cattails, and somewhere in the distance a lone marsh hawk called. Fin was gathering lattice at the time, and had just dropped a gnarled root into his pot when the low pitch of a man's voice carried across the water. He thought it LeGrande Sharp at first, and having no wish to spar again with the old-time plumer, he snatched up his pot and skittered back to camp. And then he heard a second voice, higher and lighter, with a lilt to it. It had been five years since he'd heard that timbre, yet there was no mistaking—a woman was in his country.

He stopped, turned one ear toward the sound. There was a clearing across the way, a stretch of grassland anchored to the shore. The voices came from there, he thought. And then the woman's laughter floated over the lake like some warm, magical wonder, and the hairs on his arms stood up. He longed to see the visitors, and so he set his pot on a rock and rushed toward his blind, bending back the tules and snatching his boat. Climbing quickly aboard, he grabbed the oars and gave them two quick licks, but no sooner had he got himself going than he braked hard, unsure what he'd find once he got there. What if they were outlaws, come all this way to rob him? He drifted a moment in his little boat, spun around and rowed back to shore.

He fetched his pot and strode toward camp. As he sat, grinding tubers to make flour, he gazed toward the laughter, pausing when he caught a word, leaning in to listen. Just after sundown, he fetched his boat a second time and turned to look at Josie. She stood, watching, her tail stirring the dark. Though it worried him to go off by himself, he couldn't take her with him, couldn't risk the ruckus she'd make if she disliked the people on the opposite shore. Gently, he grabbed her ears and kissed her head, told her to sit tight.

Hopping into his boat, he laid his gun in his lap and rowed across the water. Mosquitoes hummed in his ears and he longed to slap them, but restrained himself, as movement of any kind might alert the strangers.

In the distance a campfire glowed. Fin sidled over, letting the prow of the boat silently nudge the shore. Hunkered in the tules, he watched as a man and woman, their backs toward him, silently ate their supper. Neither looked a thief, nor much of a plumer either. The woman wore her hair in a loosely braided tail, which hung almost to her waist. She wore a traveling skirt with a belt around her middle, while the man sported a jacket and a hat, which hid everything about him. Both stretched their legs out long in front of the fire.

The woman set her bowl on the ground, turned toward the man and tweaked her mouth with her fingers. "I never thought I'd admit to loving beans, but I'll tell you they're delicious." She smiled, which Fin caught from afar. A moment later she leaned over and brushed something from the man's mouth, a gesture which nearly knocked Fin over, for he longed to be on the receiving end of the woman's velvet touch. There was her silhouette too, the swell of her breasts, the curve of her back, both of which ignited a spark he'd not felt since early manhood.

"If it weren't for you, Phoebe," said the man, "I suppose I'd look a fright."

Something about the stranger's tone sparked a dusky memory. When he said, "One of these days I'll sip my soup from the side of my spoon, just like the gents in Portland," Fin knew it was Aiden Elliott warming his feet by the fire.

He could barely breathe, so enormous was his shock. He hadn't seen or heard from his friend since he'd left Malheur, all those years ago. Yet here he was in the middle of the marsh, with a woman he called Phoebe.

Fin's mind reeled at the possibilities: Aiden had either come to collect eggs and had brought his sweetheart with him, or he'd arrived with the notion of finding Fin, but to what purpose, Fin couldn't imagine. As quickly as that thought came to him, he discounted it, since Aiden would have no idea in which county to start his search.

Still, there was no doubt about it, the man sitting before him was clearly his boyhood friend. He'd grown, to be sure, filled out as big as a stallion. All traces of his youth were gone, and he looked altogether accomplished. Fin's cheeks flamed to see how far Aiden had come, while he himself sat ragged in a boat. He shrank behind the tules, praying Aiden wouldn't spot him. Likely his friend would think him crazy, if he recognized him at all.

Fin might have rowed back to camp that very moment, but the woman wouldn't let him. He'd never seen a girl so lovely, yet she went about her business like she was nothing more than ordinary, carrying dishes to the lake and rinsing them, humming as she worked.

He felt the same tingling in his loins that he'd known as a boy in Portland. The sensation embarrassed him then, but now he saw it a consequence of falling in love, although he would have never believed in love at first sight had it not appeared to him.

His insides wilted when Phoebe ducked into the tent. He wondered if Aiden would follow, but his old friend did not get up. As was his habit, Aiden sat for a long while, writing in his notebook. When the air turned cold, Fin grew tired, shoved off from shore, and rowed back to camp. Climbing under his blanket without removing his shoes, he dreamed with his eyes wide open. It was Phoebe he imagined, the way the fire's glow danced on her hair and made her cheeks shine in the dark. He knew he had to see her again—commit her face to memory—before she left the Malheur region.

The stars were still gleaming in the morning's glow when he stirred beneath his covers. Even in sleep, Fin's body reacted to the notion a woman lay nearby. As he slowly came to wakefulness, he savored the sensation that had once shamed him as he hunted in the woods. The stirring beneath his blanket was keener and decidedly more painful than the stirring he'd felt for birds, and he took it as a sign he was coming around again.

He closed his eyes, letting the feeling linger. After a while, he sat up, surprised to see he'd slept with his shoes on, recollecting how distracted he'd been when he crawled into his bedroll. He'd spent a long while thinking about Phoebe, but once he'd finally fallen asleep, he'd hardly moved at all.

The morning had a bite to it. He built a fire, put coffee on and a pot of water, which he warmed to the touch for a shave. He'd camped at the mouth of the Silvies River, just like he'd done with Aiden, finding the water sweeter there than at the east side of the marsh. Low dunes covered with greasewood had built up during a dry spell, giving the place a moon-like appearance, as it held no trees at all.

For the first time in a long while Fin's stomach rumbled. He mixed a loaf of lattice bread and tucked it into his makeshift oven. While it baked, he wandered down to the lake with a bar of soap, thinking he'd take a bath.

Stripping off his clothes, he slapped his arms while he stood on the bank, steam rising around him. Stalling as long as he could, he at last strode in, the water stinging his skin. He sucked in his breath and quickly soaped up, lathering his arms and chest. Josie swam circles around him, a stick in her mouth, while he scrubbed the dirt from his hair. Holding his breath, he dipped below the water for a quick rinse, then shot up as fierce as a cannon. Josie thought it a game and swam up close, the twig locked between her jaws. Fin took it from her and tossed it. She fetched it gleefully. When he could no longer stand the cold, he got out and tender-footed it back to camp.

After he dried his arms and legs, and pulled on some trousers, he shaved his beard, an action which brought him wholly into the real world, for he understood he was shaving for a woman. Every now and then he had wondered if there was a girl out there who would ever measure up, tempt him to stay home when the forest was calling. Despite all the girls who had smiled at him and made their interests clear, his embers had never sparked. His lackadaisical attitude toward women had been a mystery to Aiden, and once, when they were younger, his friend had asked him, "How is it girls are drawn to you when you stand so cool against them?"

"Must be my good looks," Fin had teased, although even then he hadn't glanced in a mirror in a year or more, and had no earthly notion how he appeared to a woman. When he did stop to look, he saw some casual shape standing there and formed no opinion about it, for he'd never given so much as a cat's whisker what looked back at him. That was the difference between them. That Fin cared so little what the world thought of him gave him a confidence Aiden didn't possess, for Aiden cared with all his heart how he looked to others.

For the first time though, Fin wished to appear human again.

He ran his fingers through his hair, smoothed out the tangles and then dug into his saddlebags for a clean shirt. He found a worn white one without a collar and put it on, followed by a shabby black vest. Distracted by his endeavor to clean up, he forgot about his bread. He scurried over to the oven and pulled it out, but it had scorched a bit on top. Not waiting for it to cool, he sawed off a chunk and ate it, ensuring Josie got her share. But then his stomach did a flip-flop and he chided himself for eating his breakfast too fast. Underneath, he supposed he was just unsettled, unsure how he'd approach Phoebe and what news he'd give to Aiden. Likely, he'd tell him he'd made a fortune, just as he said he would. And then he'd ask after his mother, and how she was getting along. The truth was, Fin couldn't wait to pose this question and a hundred more, for now that he was among humans again he craved news of the outside world.

He hopped into his boat and rowed hard, wanting to get to the opposite shore as quickly as he could. Once again, he faltered. What if Aiden had risen high in some career, and now looked down on him? Although he himself had never possessed Aiden's ambition, he never considered himself less than his old friend's equal. Still, he would not turn back. He would approach Aiden as he planned to do, and say hello to Phoebe. Yet as soon as he hit the grassy flatland and looked around, his friend was nowhere to be found. The woman was there though, stirring a stick around the campfire.

Fin pulled his boat up to shore and hid it among the tall green reeds, then got out and ducked behind the cattails. Approaching the camp from where the tules grew thickest, he poked his way along, keeping an eye out for Aiden, and his ears open too. When he got within ten yards of camp, he stood quietly, listening to Phoebe hum, as she had done the night before. He had no real notion how he might approach her and so he held back, waiting for an opportunity to present itself. His heart beat as wildly as it ever had, though he held no gun in his hand. One minute passed, and then another, as he stared at her, his legs locked tight as a heron's.

Her hair fell loose beyond her waist, and if he were to name its color, he guessed he'd call it golden. She was the prettiest woman he'd ever seen, her skin as smooth as silk. He didn't have to touch it to know, he could tell just by looking; there wasn't a blemish on it, nor freckle nor mole to mar it.

As he stood, dizzy and breathless, his knees grew weak and then buckled. He jerked upright, cursing his carelessness.

"Aiden, is that you?" Phoebe called.

Fin held his breath.

"Aiden?" This time Fin heard her fear. She backed slowly toward the tent, then jutting quickly in the opposite direction, stumbled off to nowhere. Straining to see above the tules, she glanced back now and again just beyond her shoulder.

Fin hadn't intended to frighten her so, and couldn't say why he didn't step out and introduce himself once he saw she was scared. It wasn't like him to hold back, but then he hadn't expected her to startle. Revealing himself now would make him look foolish, or else suspicious, and that was worse than silly.

He skirted the camp's boundary, continuing to hide among the cattails as he followed her. She walked faster now. Her skirt snagged on the stubby stem of a bulrush, and she paused to yank the hem. She looked up, her face pale, and again called Aiden's name.

Fin imagined his friend had hiked off farther than he'd

intended, for as single-minded as Aiden was, he'd never leave a woman lost in the middle of the marshes.

Phoebe headed toward the lake, wandering deeper into the maze. Fin worried she'd fall in, that he couldn't let her go much farther without calling out. *Go back*, he willed her. *Go back right now*. But she possessed no intuition at all, no inclination of the trouble that lay ahead. A few more steps and in she tumbled, just as he predicted. Her skirt billowed up and around her waist, and floated in the water. Slapping her arms, she gasped for breath, sputtering as she went under. As soon as she bobbed up, Fin hitched one foot against the soil, where it was solid, leaned forward, and grabbed her arm. In one motion, he jerked her out. "You got to watch yourself," he said, setting her on the bank. "The shore drops off right quick there." He saw the terror in her eyes as she struggled to right herself. "Your camp is that way," he said. "I'll take you, if you like."

"If it's money you want," she clattered desperately, "I've got a wallet in the tent—go on and take it." Her cotton dress was soaked through, highlighting all that God created. She must have seen the look in Fin's eyes, for she covered her breasts with both arms as she slowly backed away.

Fin held his gaze. Never in his lifetime had he felt so strangled, so utterly consumed with desire. He met her eyes, saw her shame and quickly glanced away. He was aware quite suddenly that he stood ragged before her, even after his clean-up. "I ain't no robber," he told her gently, "nor man what's come to harm you." He began to unbutton his shirt, and she again stumbled backward. He held up one hand, told her softly *hold on now*, then slipped out of his sleeves and walked cautiously toward her. He draped his shirt around her shoulders, and she clutched it mightily.

"Who are you?" she demanded. "Why did you follow me here?"

"I wasn't following you so much as keeping an eye you. You were about to trot into the lake there, which I reckon you just did." He smiled, but she wouldn't have it, and so he introduced himself, thinking it might calm her. The realization must have set in who he was, as the pink returned to her cheekbones.

"Fin McFaddin? Aiden's Fin?" He nodded. "Why didn't you say so? You scared me half to death."

"I didn't mean to. It's just…well, I ain't seen Aiden in a few years now, and I wasn't certain of the welcome he'd offer. Until you got lost, I wasn't sure I'd show myself at all."

"What were you planning to do then? Watch us from afar?"

Fin didn't care to be made a fool of, yet fool was what he'd been. "More or less," he admitted, and to his surprise, she accepted this without judgment.

"Well, thank heaven you finally stepped forward. We've been looking for you for weeks now."

"Looking for me? Why?"

Phoebe opened her mouth to speak but quickly changed her mind. It was Aiden's place to tell Fin what had happened to his mother, and so she concocted a story she hoped Fin would believe. "Aiden and I, well, we're photographing the countryside. Aiden hoped you'd be our guide."

"Aiden don't need no guide. He knows Malheur as well as I do."

She nodded even as she realized her mistake. But she could think of nothing more to tell him. When she glanced up, she gave him a look that sliced deep into his heart.

"Is my mother dead?" he said, white-faced. "Is that what you come to tell me?" She shook her head. "Then come on out and say it."

"There was a fire," she began slowly. "Your mother is fine, I'll tell you now—but her house burned down and she's living with the Garys." Her gaze dropped and lingered on some weed, telling Fin there was more to the story. He waited for her to go on. "The money you sent," she said, looking at him now, "it all burned up in the fire."

"Now that's where you're wrong," Fin said straight out. "She put it in the bank, like I told her to."

"She meant to—she did. She just never got around to it."

Fin's brow furrowed. "Never got around to it?"

Phoebe shook her head.

"Never got *around* to it?" he repeated, going a little panicky now. "How much did she lose?"

"Three thousand dollars. All of it, I guess."

Fin clasped his head with both hands and walked a little circle. "God in heaven, don't say that." Halting, he looked straight at her, saw she spoke the truth. "*Three thousand dollars?*" She nodded, and his heart began to pound. "For two full years I sent her money, and for what? So she could waste my time and burn it up and—" He paused, struggling to take it in. "Where in hell did she stash it?"

"I don't know," Phoebe said, flinching, "but likely Aiden does. You can ask him when he gets back from the marsh."

Fin stood rigid, anger seeping from his soul. "Not once did she trot that money to the bank nor use it to help herself? Is that what you mean to tell me?"

"I'm sorry. You really need to—"

"I know," he said, cutting her off. "I need to ask Aiden."

Fin and Phoebe sat at camp, awaiting Aiden's return. Fin accepted a cup of coffee but wouldn't eat the biscuit Phoebe offered. His appetite had left him, and in its place anger churned. Never before had he felt anything but warmth and affection for his mother. The feelings he held for her now were dark and unfamiliar.

All this time he'd spent traipsing Oregon's high desert, the soles of his feet on fire in the summer, his fingers frozen in winter, to make something for her—something to look forward to. And now he'd learned she'd burned it up and lost her entire future.

He sat on a log, hunched over his cup. Phoebe disappeared into her tent, and when she returned, she carried with her the faintest scent of perfume. Lilac or lavender, perhaps, or something akin to rose. Fin didn't know his flowers, only that the smell of her made him a little woozy.

He saw she'd changed her clothes. Put her hair up too.

"You ought to of left it down," he said, speaking of the knot she'd crafted loosely on top of her head. The comment was forward and none of his business, but he could not help himself. Life seemed short, all at once, and he felt he ought to say the things that mattered most to him.

"It was only down in the first place because I wasn't expecting company," she said, her cheeks flushing. She hung his shirt on a branch to dry while he sat there, half-naked, save for his undershirt. She handed him an old broadcloth shirt of Aiden's. He set his coffee down, and accepted it, gratefully.

She wouldn't look at him then, so he tried to lighten the mood. "Aiden still wear a necktie?" he asked. Phoebe said he did. "Well, don't give me one of those," he added, chuckling, as he slipped into the shirt.

Phoebe sat on the opposite end of the log, putting distance between them. Twice her eyes drifted toward him, and twice she drew them back.

"I won't bite," he said. He tucked the shirt into his trousers, found it fit almost perfectly, save for the sleeves, which were an inch or two too short.

"I know you won't," Phoebe said, meeting his gaze full on. "Aiden wouldn't associate with anyone whose goal it was to hurt me."

"You didn't think that an hour ago."

"I didn't know who you were then."

She tugged absently at a loose thread on her skirt while Fin again took up his coffee cup. He studied the brew, letting the silence linger between them. And then he asked about Aiden, what he'd been up to, and his plans for the years ahead.

Phoebe sat at an angle then, her ankles together. "He just finished college down to Berkeley," she started slowly, "which is where I met him. We're engaged, you know."

Fin's insides went taut. "I figured," he said, holding back his congratulations. She must have picked up on some disappointment, and her cheeks flushed again. She told Fin of Aiden's upcoming job with the ornithological society, as well as his passion for photography. Said he was a first-class orator too. "You'd be impressed, Fin, you truly would—the way he conducts himself."

"He always was a talker," Fin said.

"Yes," Phoebe agreed, smiling, "although not always a polished one." She told Fin how Aiden had kept at it, practicing alone in his room and with other men in his debate club, until one day he invited her to one of his meetings to hear what he had to say. "I'll tell you, it was a powerful speech. He lay the blame of the plume-hunting trade squarely upon women. He told us we were responsible and could easily stop the cruelty by refusing to wear feathers on our hats."

Fin considered this. "That didn't put you off?"

"It might have, had he not argued his points so persuasively.

But I came away believing he was right. Milliners and hunters won't quit until women do, so it's my goal to assist Aiden in changing their minds." She sat a little taller and smoothed her skirt. "I'll do whatever I can to aid him. We've agreed I'll be his helpmate when he runs for office one day."

Fin stood. He walked a few steps toward the edge of camp, tossing what was left of his coffee. Turning, he looked at her. "You ought to know I'm a plumer, in case Aiden never told you."

Aiden had mentioned it, of course. While Phoebe herself held no understanding of what motivated a man to commit to such a career, beyond greed or ignorance, perhaps, she sensed there was something more to Fin and so she regretted saying all she had. "I shouldn't have gone on so — that was rude of me, and I apologize."

"No need," Fin said, shaking his head. "I am what I am, and the first to admit it. But those words Aiden spouted about women and all, they ain't entirely his. I suspect someone has put that notion into his head." He walked over to the log and sat down again. "I'll admit he had a few qualms, back in the day, but he wasn't as all-fired against it as that. When we were boys, all we did was hunt birds and collect eggs. Age of nineteen, we trekked to Malheur and spent a couple of months about a mile or two south of this very spot, camping under the stars. In the end I stayed, and Aiden returned to Portland, but we shot plenty of birds in those summer months. Even had us a skinning contest. He ever tell you that?"

Fin's mind went immediately back to Malheur a handful of years ago. He and Aiden weren't the only hunters on the marsh that afternoon; more than once they'd heard gunshots and hollering, a songfest now and then. "Likely they're plume hunters," Aiden had said, an edge to his voice. Most plume hunters preferred the company of garter snakes to humans, and as such were considered dangerous, as well as anti-social.

Fin suggested they sit a while, and see what the men were up to.

"You sit," Aiden said. "I've got birds to skin." He took up both oars and dipped them into the water, steering the boat toward home.

When they got back to camp, they spread their booty before them. That day's pile contained seven grebes, for which they would fetch seventy cents apiece; four white pelicans at one dollar each; four white herons at around the same price; and three avocets, which they anticipated would bring fifty cents or so. It was a good haul, for beginners. Fin held the notion he was the fastest skinner, so he divvied up the birds, and then bet Aiden he could beat him in a contest.

"What are you betting?" Aiden wanted to know.

"Loser puts supper together."

"I'll take that bet," Aiden said.

Fin readied his knife. "On your mark, get set—"

"Go!" hollered Aiden, and they were off.

Aiden had jumped the gun, and so held a slight lead. Fin called him on it, then seeing as how he'd lost a few seconds arguing, hunkered down in earnest. He flopped a pelican on its back and made an incision from the mid-point of the breastbone down to the vent. Pushing back the skin, he exposed the knee joints, severing each one and pulling back the legs, then cutting the tailbone and separating the body from its skin. Working toward the head, he glanced up, saw he'd not only caught up with Aiden, but passed him, although it was too soon to order supper, since they each had six more birds to tackle.

Picking up the pace, Fin sliced the carpal joints of the

wings and cut the neck at the base of the skull. He cut the ears and eyelids next, scooped out the brain and turned the entire skin right side out. Moving on to the next bird, he vigilantly kept at it, until he'd skinned everything in his pile.

"Done!" he rejoiced, sitting back on his haunches and flinging the last bird into his pile. Blood covered his hands and shirt, and the thighs of his trousers, and it looked as though he'd been in a battle.

Aiden swiped his forehead, knife in hand. He was disappointed, but he agreed that Fin was the skinning expert. "You won fair and square," he said, "though I hate to be the one to fix supper." While he finished skinning his last bird, Fin fetched the arsenical soap, a concoction of powdered white arsenic and other ingredients, meant to stave off insects. After treating the birds, they stretched the skins to dry. Aiden attached a tag to the left leg of each, detailing the species name and genus, date collected, gender, location, and name of the collector. Fin saw no need to bother, since he planned to sell his skins to middlemen and make himself some money. Aiden, however, thought he might one day wish to sell or trade his skins to museum curators, and so he kept meticulous records as to their origins and jotted notes inside his journal. Afterward, he whipped up supper.

Thinking on this now, Phoebe was quiet a long while. "No," she told Fin, "he never mentioned a skinning contest. But he's not that man anymore."

Fin nodded, and then carefully shaped his words. "I've had plenty of time to think, out here by my lonesome, and the truth is I questioned for a while exactly what I was. I confess I went a little sideways, trying to figure it out. Until this moment, I didn't know if I was a hunter or a killer, but I'll tell you now hunting is in my blood the way politics is in Aiden's.

If that makes me a killer, well, I guess that's what I am then."

He glanced up to see how Phoebe had taken the news.

"All that cruelty," she said, her voice almost a whisper. "How can you live with it?"

He might have told her there were a few others out there like him. Axel, for one. LeGrande though? He'd shoot a dandelion despite having no use for it at all. But neither Axel nor LeGrande fully illustrated who he himself was.

"I don't know that I can explain it, but it's the strongest urge I've known. Something that grabs hold of me and runs my life." He took a breath, hesitated, and then started again. "Stalking a bird gets my heart thumping, and though you won't like hearing it, I'll tell you there's an excitement in killing, not unlike the thrill a man feels when lying with a woman." He knew what that was too, for he had lain with a blonde-haired girl from Guthrie Park when he was no more than seventeen.

Phoebe's face flamed. In many ways she considered herself a modern woman, but never before had anyone spoken to her so directly, and she quickly stood and walked toward the tent, her gaze on the ground. Surely Fin sensed her embarrassment, yet he made no move to apologize, as she had apologized to him. She thought it likely he was testing her, as she had sensed his interest back at the tules, when his eyes had locked on hers. While she was frightened then, she wasn't now, for she could see that although Fin was raw and wild and rough at the edges, there was something good about him. Something kind and thoughtful. The way he'd saved his money and sent it to his mother. But when he learned their house had burned down, Phoebe saw his dark side too, and that left her feeling jagged. For who knew what else might set him off, how he'd react when he was angry? Would he hit a woman and knock her down, or kill a man, if he was able? She stopped, then turned to look at him.

"It's living in the marsh that's made me forget myself," he said, "and talk the way I do." He stood, and walked over to her. Reaching out, he gathered a tendril of her hair, kneading it with his fingers. He kept his eyes on her, still clutching that bit of hair. "If Aiden was a plumer, would you still love him?"

"He's not, so how can I possibly say?"

"It ain't that hard. A yes or no will do."

She fixed her mouth to speak, and her breath came in quick warm puffs. "I love Aiden, I do, but no. He'd have to hold a respectable job to capture my notice at all." She couldn't concentrate for the feel of Fin's hand in her hair. He wrapped a few strands around his finger, leaned slightly in to kiss her. But then the tules rustled and footsteps approached, and he stepped back just as Aiden burst through the weeds.

Aiden stopped short at the sight of a stranger in his camp. He stared a moment, as though Fin were a roustabout instead of a friend. It took several seconds for him to put it together, but once he had it, he pulled himself up and broke into a grin.

"Good God," he said, setting his tripod down. "I can't believe it's you." Without hesitation, he rushed forward and threw his arms around Fin, as if they'd never quarreled. The two men stood, locked in that embrace, not moving or saying a word, until Aiden demanded to know where Fin had stashed himself. He pulled away, punching Fin's shoulder in the way that friends do. "Phoebe and I have been looking for you for weeks now." Before Fin could speak, Aiden walked toward Phoebe and embraced her with one arm. "I take it the two of you have met," he went on, hugging her waist now.

"We have," Fin acknowledged, "and she's quite a charmer. You've done yourself proud, Aiden."

"Ha! You keep away from her, my friend. She'll have nothing to do with the likes of you." He squeezed Phoebe tighter and sighed happily. She didn't say a word, just stood with her face hot and flaming.

Fin half expected Aiden to stand back, take a good look at this woman he thought he knew, call her on her rosy cheeks and tease her with the comment she ought not to blush so, for everyone who'd ever met Fin McFaddin thought him too straightforward.

There was a confidence in Aiden that Fin hadn't seen before. Naivety too. Despite knowing Fin as he did, never in Aiden's imaginings would he guess his old friend had spoken so brazenly to his fiancée, nor that she in turn had stood so still to listen.

Fin felt a pang to know he'd been disloyal. While it was never his intention to antagonize Aiden, or cause him harm, he'd known full well when he'd plucked Phoebe from the marsh that he'd make her his own one day. But he wasn't about to let on just yet how he felt, so he slipped his hands into his pockets and let his voice go hard. "Phoebe told me Ma's house burned down. That the money's gone, and her future too, that it all went up in smoke."

Aiden's brow shot up and he leaned back, as if ruffled by a breeze. "I guess Phoebe's caught you up then," he said, his tone indicating his feelings had shifted some. "How long have you been here, Fin, working on that coffee?" He gazed at the empty cup in Fin's hand.

"An hour or so, I guess."

"He found me wandering in the weeds," Phoebe said brightly, seeing the change in Aiden, and wishing to reassure him. "I was looking for you when I got lost and tumbled into the lake. Fin pulled me out, wrapped his shirt around my shoulders and led me back to camp."

"Here we spent all this time looking for you," Aiden told Fin, "and what? You were our neighbor all along?" He was smiling but his tone was tight, and it was clear the warmth of their reunion had cooled, that Aiden had summoned some ancient insecurity.

"I didn't know you were here until yesterday," Fin said honestly. "I heard voices traveling over the water and I thought maybe it was LeGrande Sharp and his gang, come to cause me heartburn. I worked for him for a time, like I said I would. But you were right, Aiden, that man is bad news."

Aiden seemed not to have heard. "How'd you find us, then?"

"I set out in my boat after dark to have a look, and as soon as I heard your voice, I knew it was you."

"Why didn't you show yourself, let us know you were here?"

"I don't know," Fin confessed. "I wasn't ready, I guess." Just hearing the words made him sound off somehow, even to himself. "I didn't sleep all night for wondering about you, and as soon as I finished breakfast, I got on over here. Must have missed you by a while, though, for sure enough Phoebe was hollering your name, and you never even heard her."

Fin didn't mention he'd given Phoebe quite a scare, which prompted her to call for Aiden in the first place. And to Fin's surprise, Phoebe didn't bring it up. He looked over at her, kept the effort casual, and when he saw her looking back, something passed between them, some little current that sparked the air, some mutual understanding.

Aiden caught the exchange, but pretended he didn't. For what if he was wrong and simply oversensitive, which he was sometimes prone to be? "I was out beyond the canebrake, taking photographs," he said, gesturing toward the south. He turned to Phoebe. "What possessed you to paw through the tules, if you didn't know where you were going?"

Phoebe blinked, and by her hesitation both she and Fin knew she was about to lie. "I'd finished my chores and wandered off is all. I thought you were closer in, and maybe I could help you. Then just like that, I fell into the water."

"Well, don't go off like that again," Aiden said sharply. "I hate to think what I'd do if some plumer saw you in your apron and took you for a swan." He glanced at Fin, who understood the implication and resented it.

"I can't imagine I'd ever make a mistake such as that," Fin told him. He would have said more, if Phoebe hadn't stepped between them.

She turned to Aiden, promised to never act so carelessly again, and then kissed his cheek, excused herself, and walked quietly toward the tent. But there was no mistaking it, Aiden's words had stung her.

Fin shot Aiden a scornful look. "Why do you scold her so? All she was doing was searching the countryside for you."

"Why do you defend her?"

Fin thought about telling Aiden right then and there how he felt about Phoebe, but he glanced toward the tent, saw her looking back at him, biting her lower lip, and so he held off. He had no reason to believe she would leave Aiden to take up with him anyway, no matter how he wished it. "It's plain she loves you, and would do anything to please you," Fin quietly told him. "I'm just putting in a good word, is all."

Aiden thought his own judgment faulty then. "I'm sorry," he said. "I don't know what's got into me. My mind is swimming with all the goings on. As I said, we've been looking for you for weeks now, and just like that, here you are. I hardly know what to make of it."

Fin, too, softened. "I've been at Malheur a while now. Shot canvasbacks down to Klamath the last five winters, then grebes all spring and summer. Killed a good many terns too. I made my way north in April—thought I'd shoot some herons—but LeGrande Sharp beat me to it. Made the worst mess of a rookery I've ever seen. Pained my heart to see it."

Aiden's face lit up. "See now, that's what I've been saying. This whole damn business has got to end, Fin."

"I ain't leaving off it," Fin said, although he knew it wasn't what Aiden wanted to hear. He told him one of these days he'd find a new spot, one that wasn't shot out and filled with rotting corpses. "I won't leave no babies, either, crying for their mamas."

"How will you manage that?"

"I don't know, but I'll get it figured out. Maybe I'll find a spot where the young ones have sprouted all their feathers."

Aiden sucked in his breath, hesitated, let it go.

"Don't be holding your tongue now," Fin told him. "If you've got something to say, put it out there."

"What about your mother?" Aiden asked. "What's she to do while you're in the marshes, shooting the last of the birds?" Fin was about to tell him when Aiden again cut in. "She misses you something awful, you know. Since you've been gone, she's kept at it, night and day, just like she's always done. Both Maggie and I tried to get her to ease up some, but you know how she is." He shook his head. "And that money you sent? She was saving it for you, hoping you'd use it to build your own house when you finally came home again."

That his mother had saved her money for him was news to Fin, and when he heard it, he wandered back to the log and sat down again. He propped his elbows on his knees and rubbed his hands while he thought. "I can't go back to Portland," he said, his mind in a quandary. "The plume birds are in the marshes, and that's where I shoot them."

"Who says you've got to shoot anything at all? Why can't you find a different line of work? Something that takes advantage of your mindful abilities—a bookkeeper over to Gilchrist's, say, or some other shop in town."

"I ain't no bookkeeper," Fin muttered. He abruptly stood and walked another circle. Pausing, he looked at Aiden and flung one arm westward in a defiant gesture. "I go back, it'll kill me. Might as well return to Klamath, take my chances with LeGrande." He stared into the distance. "You know as well as anyone I'd rather spend the rest of my days in Satan's hell than two hours tending that store."

Aiden stood with one foot ahead of the other, his left knee locked tight as a bank vault. He regarded Fin coolly. "I didn't think I'd ever see the day when Fin McFaddin refused to help his mother. As much as she loves you, as long as she's awaited your return, you intend to stand there and tell me you won't come home?"

Fin looked over at Aiden, saw the harshness in his friend's eyes and hated him for it. Who was Aiden Elliott to tell him how to treat his mother? He turned and strode away, just as he had all those years ago, when they were boys on the cusp of manhood.

"That's right," Aiden called after him. "Get yourself off, like you always do."

Fin didn't say a word, just marched toward his boat. He crawled in, launched himself with a shove of one oar, and refused to look back to gauge Aiden's reaction. But then he didn't have to. From clear across the lake he felt the heat of his friend's disapproval, the sting of his disdain. Never before had Aiden's opinions meant that much to Fin, but now, as he rowed across the lake, remorse began to seize him. Regret for the man he'd become.

As much as it vexed him, Fin had to admit there was a pattern there, that Aiden might be right. He realized his reaction to the bloody rampage at the heron rookery was a sign he should go home, that the carnage at the grebe camp was a hint too, an indication of things to come. But he'd been too blind to see it. Well, he saw it now. So it was he headed home to make what life he could.

# CHAPTER SIX

Three miles from the southernmost shore of Malheur Lake, Fin stopped at Ed Mott's place to pay him the balance of what he owed on the boat, and to draw a map of the inlet where he'd tied the vessel to a log, then draped it with a canvas throw to hide it.

Ed asked him to sit a while, take a glass of buttermilk. The men each pulled up a chair on the porch, then sat back to watch clouds building in the east. Gray monsters with tails as frothy as cream danced on the horizon, while dust devils spooled and skipped on the wind. Yet it wasn't the earth that commanded Fin's attention so much as the blue-black sky.

He sipped his milk and breathed in the warm, dry air, enjoying the quiet comfort of Ed Mott's company. Josie lay at Fin's feet, gnawing a chicken bone. Every now and then, she looked up at him, and raised a knobby eyebrow. "Is it good?" he'd ask, and she'd whack her tail, then take to her bone again.

Lightning snapped in the distance. Ed counted to six before the thunder cracked, said the storm was getting closer.

He passed Fin a plate of Mrs. Mott's cinnamon bread, a ribbon of rust-colored sugar swirling loose inside it. It was still damp, steaming from the oven. Fin helped himself to a thick slice, and swallowed before he'd fully tasted it. After months of eating little more than lattice bread and frogs' legs, he'd forgotten the flavor of bread built with real flour, and to his embarrassment polished off four of the five pieces Ed placed before him.

"Oh my," said Mrs. Mott when she saw the hole he'd made there. Ignoring Fin's objections, she packed him a supper of their noontime leftovers, including fried chicken, a baked potato, and a hunk of apple pie. Into his satchel she also stuck a second loaf of bread and a small jar of apple butter. He was grateful as could be, and told her so, thinking if he was to see his mother soon, he'd best start thanking women again; he'd not done so in many years and was sorely out of practice.

Ed tried to talk him into staying the night, saying he hated to see a body get glued up in the mud. But the rain never came and then sun popped out, shifting the skies to cobalt. Fin bid Ed and his wife farewell. They didn't pester him for details as to where he was going, just watched as he gathered his gear and climbed onto his horse. Mrs. Mott waved when he turned in his saddle. She reminded him of his mother, her face bright and hopeful. He raised his hand too, and hollered his gratitude.

All the next day and the one after that, the wind scoured the landscape and blew the dirt around. Fin half expected to find LeGrande Sharp traipsing the same dusty trails that he himself crossed, but by the time he reached the country of tall grass and tules, nesting season was over. The grebes were all but gone. He had no notion where LeGrande had got to, and hoped he'd never see him again; likely he wouldn't, once he got to Portland.

The sky was orange and azure and the sun sinking low when he came upon the driver with the pinfeather whiskers. The back of the man's wagon was loaded with bird skins, and he said he was off to meet his middleman in Merrill. Fin asked if the fellow would like to buy his boat back, and the man said he would. He didn't want the trolley though, so Fin said he'd leave it, let the man do what he pleased with it.

"Where'd you park it?" asked the driver. Fin said it was over yonder, toward a stand of cottonwoods. The driver thought a moment. "Might could sell it to Axel Ambrose, if I happen to run into him."

"Axel Ambrose? LeGrande Sharp's nephew?"

"You know another?"

Fin shrugged. "I never knew his last name is all. Guess I don't know yours, either. Nor your first name, come to think of it."

"Cecil," said the driver. "Cecil Hammertoe." When Fin grinned, the man chuckled. "That's why I don't never tell it."

Cecil indicated Josie with a nod of his chin. "I see you still got that dog. Good one, is she?"

"Best there is," Fin told him, adding, "watch this." He whistled, and Josie trotted over. He told her to sit, and she did so on the spot. Fin sat on his haunches, pulled a strip of jerky from his pocket, and balanced it on her nose. She stayed right where she was, although her front legs quivered in expectation of the treat she'd receive. Cecil had a hard time watching and began squirming in his seat, insisting after a few seconds that Fin let her have it.

"She's good though, ain't she?" Fin said. Cecil nodded, agreed she surely was. Fin gave his tongue a click. Just like that, Josie tossed the strip into the air and snatched it in her mouth. Fin ruffled the fur behind her ears, told her she was clever. She was almost family to him now, standing beside him like a sibling. He'd not known a dog could be so constant, so loving, or so true.

Cecil stared admiringly. "Don't suppose you'd give her back to me?"

"No," Fin said, not even thinking on it. The men were quiet then, and Fin looked from Josie to Cecil, said he didn't expect he'd see him again. "I'm off to Portland tomorrow," he told the driver. "My ma's house burnt down, and I aim to build her a new one." He walked over to Cecil, extended his hand in farewell.

Cecil leaned forward to shake it. "I'd go too, if I had me a mother." He gazed into the distance, his face taking on a look of disappointment. "Pickings was slim this year," he sighed. "I reckon I got to quit soon."

"What will you get into?"

"Might could open a saloon over to Ashland, hire some dancing girls." He smiled, revealing a mouthful of yellow teeth.

Fin thought he'd miss this fellow, congenial as he was, although he didn't suppose he'd entice many women to come to work for him. "I'll camp here tonight, if you've no objection. It's a bit late in the day to take off for Portland."

"It's a free country," Cecil said, yawning. He shook his head as if to clear the cobwebs. "I'd throw my bedroll alongside yours, but I got to fetch these skins to Merrill."

"You best get started then."

Cecil slapped his reins, and without looking back raised one arm in farewell. Fin stood and watched the man until he was no more than a speck on the roadway. Dust roiled from under his wheels, then drifted toward the sunset. Everything looked hazy and green in the early evening light, and Fin couldn't help but admire it.

He was enjoying the twilight still, as he built a fire and made supper. He'd already eaten his chicken and his pie, but he'd saved some of Mrs. Mott's bread, which he now unwrapped from its tidy square of muslin. He spread a bit of apple butter on top, wishing he had jam instead—blackberry was his favorite—then opened a can of beans, which he set atop the coals and let cook until the juice began to boil. After the beans cooled, he spooned half onto a plate, which he set on the ground for Josie. The rest he ate directly from the can, mopping up the gravy with his bread and washing it down with the last of the water in his canteen. He had a hankering for a cup of coffee, but now had no liquid to make a pot, nor much coffee to put inside it.

Most men would light a match to a cigarette after supper, but he wasn't a smoker and disliked the smell of tobacco. Aiden had lit a pipe as early as seventeen. It was a habit Aiden's father Owen also found distasteful, in all probability because his wife Blythe so often smoked cigarettes in her bedroom. More than once, Owen had chided Aiden for stoking the dining room with smoke and ash and bits of stray tobacco. Fin remembered one such occasion, when Tula had invited him to stay for supper. Aiden pulled out his pipe after the meal, whereupon Owen excused himself, saying he had no wish to sit by and watch Aiden besmirch the house. The minute their father left the room, Maggie asked if she could smoke too.

"It's not womanly," Aiden told her.

"Blythe does it."

"She smokes cigarettes, and in her bedroom where no one can see her."

"If you won't let me, I'll talk that good old boy from Seattle into giving me a taste. He'll do it in an instant, likely behind some barn."

Aiden clucked his tongue, passed her his pipe, and told her to sip it as she might hot tea. But Maggie being Maggie, sucked as hard as she pleased. She sputtered and spit and slapped her tongue, crying, "Jumpin Jehosophat, Aiden! A dirt pancake tastes better than that old thing."

Fin chuckled, thinking back on it now. He found himself remembering Maggie more fondly these days, likely because he was going home and missed humanity some. And then his thoughts drifted to Phoebe. Truth told, they'd lingered on her since he'd left her at the tent that day, the lie she'd told Aiden hot and alive on her lips.

He'd wondered about that lie since the moment it had left her mouth. She'd glanced over at him before she'd told it, and he'd looked back at her, telling her with his eyes it was their secret if she wished it so. He wondered too if she'd seen him as he'd seen her, if she'd felt the same jolt inside her belly that spoke of mutual attraction.

As indifferent as he'd been about making love to a woman—reserving all that heat and energy for hunting birds—lying next to Phoebe was all he thought of now. For the first time he saw clearly what he had missed, all that he'd postponed, until the flames of his desire scorched the boundaries of decency.

He didn't relish the confrontation he would one day have with Aiden over the woman they both loved. He had gotten a taste of his old friend's jealousy at Malheur, and expected Aiden might even take a swing at him, for if the tables were turned, he would likely hit Aiden. Even so, Fin went to bed with a heavy heart, for of all the things he was in this life, a thief wasn't among them. How he'd reconcile the theft of his best-friend's sweetheart, he'd not yet figured out.

It was a long while that night before sleep overtook him.

A little after dawn, when the sky was as gray as flannel, a low guttural rumbling seeped into his brain. He lay, resisting, warm beneath his blanket, until the noise exploded and drove him to sit up. It took a moment to fix his eyes, groggy as he was. He realized Josie was making the racket. He expected she was chewing out some coyote, but as soon as he turned, he saw LeGrande Sharp, standing two feet from him. The man held a shotgun loosely at one hip. Axel stood nearby.

Josie bared her teeth and kicked the dirt, her saliva flying.

"Shut her up," LeGrande warned. His voice was calm, but his pupils were dark and popping.

Fin hollered at Josie to hush, but she wouldn't have it. She barked harder still, carrying on until LeGrande lifted his gun, pulled the trigger, and shot her in the head.

Fin recoiled from the blast. Twisting sideways, he scrabbled against his blanket, caught sight of his dead dog, and released his breath in a gasp. He threw his covers back.

LeGrande took a step forward, steadied the barrel of his gun against Fin's chest. Fin froze, his heart thumping. LeGrande smiled a bit. "Guess I'm the one whipped you after all, wasn't I, boy? Had to hustle to do it, but Axel and me, we got to Malheur the day before you and licked them herons good." He turned toward his nephew, grinning like a mad man. "Reckon Fin found my bandana, too, wouldn't you say, Axel?"

Axel gazed at the tops of his boots, refusing to look at his uncle. Nor would he look at Fin. His face held a look of anguish, of wishing he were gone. He sported a cut above his eyebrow, which could have used some stitches. But he'd let it go too long now, and it hung slack and oozing. LeGrande wore his own damage. A yellow moon hung beneath one eye and a thin red line slashed his upper lip. His tongue flicked out to lick at the rawness there.

Fin slowly reached up. With two fingers, he shoved the gun's barrel from his chest. "I didn't need no bandana to tell me — the minute I saw that mess at Malheur, I knew you were responsible."

LeGrande propped his shotgun on the ground with the butt against the dirt. He gripped the barrel in one hand. "Seeing as how you know it all, I guess I don't need to tell you that me and Axel was just passing through when we come across your camp. I spotted you before Axel did, seen you wrapped up in your blanket."

"So you thought you'd mosey over, maybe shoot my dog?"

"That's payback, what it is. You mess with me, I mess with you. That's the way it works." LeGrande again looked over at Axel, his gaze lingering a moment. Looking back at Fin, he said, "You had a chat with my nephew here a while ago. You and him set out to shoot grebes, and you filled his head with the notion he could fend for hisself. Stick up for hisself too, if he'd a mind to. Then you wrestled me to the dirt. That give Axel the idea he could get me down, and he tried, not long ago. But you can see how far it got him." He was speaking of the damage he'd done to Axel's festering eye.

"I see you took a lick or two yourself," Fin pointed out.

"I did, I did," LeGrande acknowledged. It was as if the marrow in his bones was filled with reason rather than rancor. But then he clenched his gun barrel with that one gnarled hand and told Axel to tell Fin why he'd clobbered his uncle. Axel didn't speak. "Go on," LeGrande insisted. "Tell Fin how I shot your girlfriend — that crane you tamed at Malheur. How you thrashed me for it."

"Weren't my girlfriend," Axel objected, glaring at his uncle.

LeGrande spat on the ground, wiped his chin with the

back of his hand. "I shot the bird with the red topknot to teach the boy a lesson. Impress on him that no plumer worth his salt would go around throwing cornbread crumbs to a stilt bird to make hisself a friend."

"It was no more than a baby," Axel cried. He stepped forward with his face set hard. "You had no right to kill him."

LeGrande gripped his gun barrel so tight the color left his knuckles. "We going at it again?" Axel took a breath, his nostrils flaring. Fin knew if the boy put everything he had into whooping his uncle, he'd come out the victor; he was quicker and taller and twice as strong, yet loyalty held him back. It made no sense to Fin.

"I shot Axel's bird," LeGrande said, "and damn, that boy went crazy. Come runnin with his arms twirlin and his eyes flashin—I saw he aimed to lick me. We went at it, but he took the worst of it. His eye is rank as a stinkbug, while mine ain't even puffy."

Fin's heart seized anew. "You ought not go around, shooting a man's best friend."

"And you ought not stick your nose where it don't belong."

Fin sagged, exhausted all at once. "Or what? You'll tear into me like you did Axel?"

"Naw, I won't tear into you," LeGrande said congenially. "I'll break your head is all." With that, he swung his gun up, snatched its butt in both hands, and smashed it hard into Fin's face.

Fin's eyes rolled up into his head, and he keeled backward, collapsing on his blanket. Blood gushed from his nose.

LeGrande gave him the once-over, before glancing over at Axel. "Looks like Fin McFaddin won't have no more advice for you."

"I didn't ask for none."

LeGrande walked past his nephew, gruffly bumping his shoulder. He paused, letting the message sink in. "That's advice of my own."

Aiden hadn't said ten words to Phoebe since they'd headed back to Portland. Normally, he hung back to see her safely through, but now he nudged his horse forward, without glancing to either side. Every now and then she looked over at him, knew he sensed the same turmoil she did, as he dipped his fedora to shade his eyes and the anger brewing behind them. She noticed too how he raised his chin, as a prideful man would do. She opened her mouth to speak, wanting to expose the awkwardness between them, but doing so might reveal her lie, and so she kept quiet, telling herself she'd discuss it with him later.

Not since she was a child could she remember having told a single untruth. Yet here it was, not four days since she'd met Fin McFaddin, and she'd deceived the man she loved. Not in a literal sense, of course, for she hadn't kissed Fin or encouraged him at all. But she'd not been forthright when she should have been, and that made her a liar.

Again, she looked at Aiden. It was no easy thing, watching his back, and she knew she stood a chance of losing him, if she couldn't bring him closer. As difficult as it was to admit the truth, Fin had not done anything she hadn't wanted him to. She had liked the way he'd looked at her, and had wanted him to kiss her, although it shamed her to admit it. She wasn't a schoolgirl but a full-grown woman, and she should have behaved like one. She should have heeded her intuition — not just her moral compass, but the inner knowledge Fin was too unlike her. He had no plans to build a future, nor desire to leave the marsh, while she and Aiden had mutual goals and would make a difference. Hadn't Frank M. Chapman said so?

Aiden's horse fell back. He turned in his saddle to look at her.

"I love you," Phoebe said. He said he loved her too. They rode a while in silence. "You're not still mad at me, are you, Aiden? For wandering into the marsh?"

He didn't know what to say to that, and for a while didn't answer. He'd slept little the night before, thinking on Fin and Phoebe. It was foolish to jump the gun. After all, Phoebe was his fiancée. Still, he'd only known her but a few short months, so how could he know, deep down, what went on inside her head?

Aiden supposed it should be Fin he stewed on. The marsh had turned his old friend inside out, and played havoc with his head. He wasn't the best influence, willful as he was, and stubborn too, unwilling to face his problems. But that wasn't Aiden's only concern. No matter what he told himself, or what he tried to deny, he had sensed a spark between Fin and Phoebe. Yet if he accused Fin of ignoring his problems, he himself could not ignore what he suspected was the truth.

"Do I have reason to believe you'd leave me for Fin McFaddin?" he asked Phoebe now.

She reached over instantly, grasped his hand in hers. "I love *you*," she insisted. "I want to marry *you*. You're an angel in my heart, and all I've ever wanted." She leaned in sideways and tilted her head just so, waiting for him to kiss her, wanting him to kiss her, for tenderness on Aiden's part meant he could forgive her.

He did kiss her. But instead of airing his concerns as he should have done, he saved them for Portland.

Maggie was sitting in the parlor when they stepped into the house. She screeched when she saw them, jumped up at once, and ran into the foyer to greet Aiden and his fiancée. Though Phoebe was covered with traveling dust, Maggie threw her arms around her and hugged her with all she had. Aiden kissed his sister on the cheek, and when she stood back to glance over his shoulder—not even trying to hide her hopefulness—he told her she needn't bother.

Maggie's face folded. "Don't tell me you couldn't find Fin."

"Oh, we found him, or rather Phoebe did." Aiden's tone was accusatory, and all he'd held back since they departed camp spilled freely now. "Thick-headed as he is, however, he refused to come home."

Stricken, Maggie slumped at the bottom of the stairs.

"I don't know why any of us thought he'd listen to reason," Aiden went on, "why we believed he'd come to help his mother. The man is morally bankrupt, Maggie, and the sooner you accept it, the better off you'll be."

Maggie buried her head in her arms. Phoebe stood in such surprise at Aiden's outburst that for a moment she couldn't move. And then she strode to Maggie's side, and sat beside her on the stairs. Phoebe looked sharply at Aiden, told him he might employ an ounce of kindness, given Maggie was his sister. "We don't know yet what Fin will do," she went on, and rather sternly too. "Give him time. He may yet come around."

"He hasn't the capacity to come around," Aiden snapped. "It's one thing for Maggie to live in denial, and quite another for you to do so, Phoebe."

Phoebe saw at once where he was going. "Aiden, please. Don't say something you'll regret."

He worked his mouth convulsively. "He's an eye for you, and you for him. Why don't you just admit it? I saw the way you looked at each other. Had I not arrived when I did, who knows what might have happened."

Phoebe stood, regretting the guilt she'd endured so profoundly, given Aiden's indictment. "I've not broken one promise to you," she chided, "and I won't be punished for a sin I didn't commit. If you've no more compassion for me than you've exhibited for your sister, we'll both thank you to take your leave, and sleep in a barn somewhere."

"Leave?" he stammered, in part to Phoebe's back, for she'd taken Maggie's arm and started up the stairs. "Unless you've forgotten, this is my house, Phoebe."

"The sooner the better, Aiden."

"What's he talking about?" Maggie asked, stumbling clumsily along. "And why is Fin involved?"

"He's not involved," Phoebe insisted. "Neither of us is, Maggie, and that is God's honest truth."

"That's not the truth!" Aiden thundered. "Fin's inserted himself between Phoebe and me. Just ask her, Maggie. Ask Phoebe if I'm wrong."

Maggie halted, then looked at Phoebe. "Is Aiden wrong?"

Blythe appeared at the top of the stairs, her hair tumbling over one shoulder. Her eyes went to her son, and widened in surprise. "Why, Aiden, you're home. How was the trip, dear?"

"Ask Phoebe," he spat, turning on one heel. He strode toward the door and then tromped through it, slamming it firmly behind him. Just then, Owen walked out of the kitchen, a slice of Tula's apricot pie in hand. He stood in his stocking feet, a hole in the big toe, looking more the servant than someone remotely regal. No one made a comment, however, as they turned to gaze at Phoebe.

"It's not what it seems," she said, insistent. "Aiden has accused Fin of garnering my affection, which isn't true at all."

Maggie slowly dropped her arm from Phoebe's. "Why would Aiden lie?"

"He's rousted some false idea based on what he *thought* he saw. But you've got to believe me, Maggie, I would never do anything to hurt you or Aiden. Not in this lifetime or any other."

Maggie took this in, and then her face turned dark. "No, you wouldn't, Phoebe. But Fin would."

Owen slipped the pie into his mouth. Chewing thoughtfully, he gazed at his daughter, and then glanced up at his wife. Blythe stood with her hand on the banister, but she too kept silent. If any human in the Elliott family were to offer Maggie the smallest bit of comfort, this was the time to do so.

Blythe opened her mouth, but never having practiced a word of consolation, exhaled without uttering a sound. It was Owen who finally spoke. "Fin's been on his own too long, Maggie," he said. "It's possible he's traveled to some gloomy side. Best let him go while you can, while you've the wherewithal to steel yourself against him. He isn't marriage material, that much has long been clear."

Never before had Maggie's father demonstrated he understood a single thing about her, yet there he stood, pretending that he knew her. He didn't know her. She hardly knew herself. She didn't know if she loved Fin or hated him, and so she turned her back on the lot of them, and made her way upstairs.

The next morning Phoebe was gone, as were her belongings.

She left a note for Maggie, setting passionate words to paper, telling of her love for her and Aiden, and disclaiming affection for Fin. "Though Aiden would dismiss any good Fin has done, it's true he rescued me in the marsh. You should know I'm grateful, and unlike your father, I pray you'll not give up on him. He is a man in need of solace, although I suspect he'll work like the devil to hide it—and you are the one to provide it, Maggie. If he's to be redeemed, it's you who must save him, for you are as good a soul as I've ever met, and as much in need of Fin's love as he is of yours. Do not abandon him, Maggie."

Maggie choked on Phoebe's plea. Despite their earlier discussions, the woman had no real understanding of the effort she'd made over the years to bring Fin around. Yet not once had he demonstrated he'd have her. Reading Phoebe's words, seeing them on paper, made Maggie realize she'd been living in a dream world, that it was time she forgot Fin and found a man willing to love her as much as she wished to be loved, for she'd proven herself faithful, if far too patient. And much too persistent too.

Aiden slipped into the house sometime after midnight. He'd spent two hours walking the streets, three more sipping beer. He'd had plenty of time to sort out his feelings and had come to no new conclusion; it wasn't just Fin that perturbed him, but the aura that had emanated from Phoebe in the marshes. The sense that she had changed somehow, that some ghostly specter had enveloped her, and she'd fallen victim to its spell.

When he came downstairs before breakfast, Maggie showed him the note. "She never said goodbye," he cried, "just packed her bags and trekked back to Berkeley?"

"What did you expect?" Maggie scolded. "You all but called her a liar, and in front of the family too."

"I did no such thing. I merely pointed out that Fin had come between us, and I assure you, there was no misstatement there."

"Fin comes between everybody," Maggie snapped. "But it was you Phoebe came home with, and you she loves." Her tone softened then. "The two of you were meant to be together, Aiden. Can't you see? She's a politician's wife, if ever there was one. Her only goal is to find good in this world, and help you all she can. Who could ask for more than that?"

"It's true our goals are similar."

"If you were ever inclined to take my advice, brother, listen to me now: climb down from that high horse you're riding. Reclaim Phoebe as your own, for if you let her go, some other man will snatch her up, and marry her quick as you please."

"Fin, you mean."

Maggie might have scorched him with words as hot as flat irons; instead, she spoke evenly. "I imagine right now you wish you'd never met Fin, but the fact is you have. All your life he's been your hero, and your biggest competitor too. But only because you've made him so. He's got no hold on Phoebe, and she's promised to marry you. Fetch her now before Fin gets back, and muddies up the waters."

"What if he does come back?" Aiden asked. "What will *you* do, Maggie?"

"I'll never set my mind completely against him, much as you'd like me to. It simply isn't in me."

"Have you no pride at all?"

Maggie glanced at her shoe tops, then looked again at Aiden. "Fin needs my support, and if I can't give it as his wife, I'll give it as a friend. It's what I want to do. What I have to do. I won't abandon him."

"Do as you please then. God knows we've never been able to stop you."

## CHAPTER SEVEN

Fin could have used a friend, and a hand upon his forehead. When he came to, a fierce throbbing commenced between his eyes and echoed beneath his nose. He knew at once it was broken. He brought his fingers to his lips, feeling for damage. Dabbing lightly at the space above his mouth, he found that the blood had begun to congeal—so much so, in fact, he had a little trouble breathing. He rolled slowly to one side. Stars skittered across his eyes like snowflakes, and he lay still a moment, panting until the sunflash subsided.

His gaze went to Josie, and his eyes welled to see her so stiff and straight. She'd been a good dog, a friend when he'd had no one. She'd had no expectations, but had simply shown up when he'd needed her, and had stuck steadfast to his side. He reached over and rested his hand on her belly; it was soft where the fur was sparse, but her flesh was cool now. The ache in his heart was as severe as he'd known, and he lay quietly, accepting this pain, until the sun went slowly down.

Tugging a handkerchief from his pocket, he blew the clot from his nose, gagging as old blood slid down his throat. He had begun to shiver, and knew he needed a fire and a nap inside his tent. He hadn't the strength to pitch it, however, and so he let the tent go and gathered a bit of kindling. After he got a fire going, he warmed a can of beans and gingerly ate two spoonsful. His lips were swollen and tender to the touch, but his heart hurt more than his injuries, for he had no dog to share his meal with, nor head to pat goodnight.

After supper, the wind picked up and blew his fire out. He gave up on the day then, and crawled into his bedroll. Despite the burning of his body and the fever in his head, he quickly fell asleep. His rest was fitful, however, punctuated by dreams of baby herons, plucked of all their feathers. Three times he awoke with a start, his right hand groping for his gun. Twice, he aimed it at the shadows, threatening to shoot whoever stood there. When no one stepped forward, he understood it was pain making him hallucinate, and he lay down and fell asleep again.

The next morning was much the same. He felt as if he'd tumbled from a rim rock and landed on his face. His mouth pounded in rhythm with the blood rushing through his veins, and his nose continued to throb. He thought he'd never move again, but thirst overcame him and he was forced to get up and fetch water. He drank long and deep from the creek. Once he'd had his fill, he dipped his head beneath the surface. The cleansing helped. This time, when he fell back onto his blanket, he felt considerably better.

With the sun beating warm on his skin, he again thought of Josie, how her head should be resting on his belly. He didn't want to look at her, and hadn't the strength to bury her, so he covered her with brush and a few nice rocks, diverting his gaze while he did so. He said a few kind words when he'd finished, telling her how much she'd meant to him, although he hadn't properly shown his appreciation. "I hope I see you in Heaven," he told her, then rested his cap on her headstone.

Around noon, he ate another spoonful of beans, and one more after that. His stomach groaned with its effort to digest, but he kept the food down, and the water too, and by evening of the second day, he sat upright and properly tended his fire.

While he mended, his thoughts turned to LeGrande Sharp. Whether he should track him down and kill him. Despite those dark ruminations, he realized if he again started something with LeGrande and *didn't* kill him, the man would never let it go; the two of them would hash it out until one of them lay bleeding and dying on some mossy waterway. What's more, LeGrande had the help of his young nephew Axel, where Fin had only himself.

When he thought on it, it was hard to say what kept him going, exactly. It might have been his mother, the knowing, deep down, that he wouldn't let her suffer, despite his bitterness. Or it might have been the memory of his sickness in the marsh. Whatever it was, he knew he'd had his fill of sadness, and that he desperately needed rest.

Willa didn't know him. There wasn't an inch of his face that wasn't bruised or swollen, and to make him stranger still, his frame stood gaunt and his hair hung long, now three inches past his shoulders.

She stood tense on the Garys' porch when she first saw him. Folding her arms across her chest, she held her chin high. "I've got no cash here," she called, like he was a vagrant come to rob her. But the more she stared, the more she saw him, and she soon realized who he was. "Stars in heaven," she cried, drawing her hands to her mouth.

He hardly knew her either. She stood in her worn cotton wrapper and long white apron, sleeves pushed to her elbows. The dress had a little pointed collar and was belted in, showing how thin she was—he guessed she'd dropped forty pounds and shrunk three sizes. Her hair was mostly silver.

"I heard you burned our house down."

She rushed toward him and hugged him hard. After a moment, she leaned back to study him, then pulled him close and sobbed into his shoulder.

His grip was loose and awkward, and he wasn't of a mind to hug her like she wanted. Willa understood, and instantly took the blame. "I ought to have done what you told me to," she cried, her cheeks wet with tears. "Believe me, I regret it."

"I done things I regret too," he said, not saying what they were. Nor did he discuss how he'd lost his mind in the marshes of Malheur. Looking around the Garys' place, he sighed.

Willa took his hand and led him into the house. He sat at the table while she fussed over him, sawed him a chunk of sourdough, then slathered it with honey. She brewed him a cup of chamomile tea, telling him it was what the doctor ordered. He sipped it, though he didn't touch the bread. She sat next to him then, speaking intently but quietly of the years that had passed between them. "Five, it's been," she pointed out, in case he hadn't counted.

The truth was, he hadn't counted, not until recently. He opened up, as much as he was able to, telling his mother of the birds he'd hunted, leaving out the sad parts. He told her too it was LeGrande Sharp who'd beaten him, how he himself considered taking retribution.

"Why'd he light into you in the first place?"

"I stuck my nose where it don't belong—tried to encourage his nephew to step away from him and make a life of his own. LeGrande didn't take kindly to it. Least that's what he told me."

"But to beat a man so? Over such a middling thing?"

Fin sipped his tea. "Goes deeper than that, I guess. We'd tussled before. I put him in his place, which irked him, so he wanted to get even. And he was aiming to nip the competition too, for that's the way he viewed me. Things are tight in Oregon, just like the rest of the world. Only so many birds to go around, and he wanted them for himself."

He sat quietly, his fingers wrapped around the teacup. After a while, he told his mother that while he hadn't a lot of money, he did have some, and would do his best to get another house going as soon as he could. The announcement surprised him, since he hadn't known until that moment he was ready to help her again.

"I'll strike a tent near the burned-out house. The two of us can move into it, so as not to take advantage of the Garys." His mother clasped his hand, thanked him with all her heart. He smiled despite himself, touched by her gratitude.

She took his face into her hands. "You look a sight," she said, reaching up to smooth his hair. "Have you seen yourself of late?"

"I ain't pretty, I know. My nose feels swollen as a tree stump, and I still have trouble breathing."

Willa got up and walked into the little storage room that served as her bedroom. She brought back the hand mirror Edward had given her for her birthday the year before he died. It was the one treasure she'd salvaged from the fire, although it didn't look much like its former self; its handle was scuffed, its glass stained and broken. She handed it to Fin.

He stared into it. It wasn't so much the bruises that startled him, but the gaunt figure beneath them. His cheekbones jutted fiercely from beneath his skin, and his eyes seemed sunken in their sockets. It wasn't his face at all, but the face of a cadaver. He'd lost ten pounds, he guessed, since he'd met Phoebe in the marsh, and was skinny even then. He wondered what she had seen in him and moaned, forgetting for a moment his mother stood beside him.

"Don't fret," she softly told him. "We'll get you looking like your old self in no time at all." She hugged him, told him again how glad she was to have home, even if home was now the Garys'.

He looked around the cabin, realizing just then that there was no sign of the couple who lived there. "Where'd they get off to so early in the day?"

"They're picking blackberries in the valley. Mister helps his missus, and as soon as they get home, she makes gel and he puts it up in jars. They sell it to Gilchrist's, if you can believe it. Folks pay good money for it too."

Fin leaned back, astonished. "People pay for something that grows wild in the hills?"

"Not so different from folks in New York City, is it? Buying feathers for their hats?"

She had a point, although Fin didn't wish to get into it. His nose was starting to throb again, and his head too. Willa must have seen he was hurting, as she told him to lay down on the cot in her bedroom. He hadn't the wherewithal to argue, feeling weak throughout his bones, and so settled in and shut his eyes, intending only to doze. He slept two hours. When he awoke, the shadows washing the walls told him it was evening.

He stayed in bed a while, listening to the Garys murmuring in the kitchen. Every now and then his mother chimed in. What they spoke of, Fin couldn't say, nor did he really care; it was enough to know he could sleep all night if he wanted to, without fear of waking to a gun. He might have slept another hour had the scent of fried chicken not fired his brain and jostled his stomach. The smell of cornbread too.

He was hungry now, and so he got up. After exchanging proper hellos, he ate supper, and plenty of it. Afterward, Mrs. Gary broke open a jar of blackberry jam, lobbed a tablespoonful onto a warm biscuit, and soaked it all in cream. Fin gobbled that one and quickly accepted another. Blackberry jam was his favorite, and he'd not had so much as a thimbleful since he'd left Portland. He got a dab on his finger and was about to lick it, when his eyes traveled to his mother and settled on her napkin. She dotted her mouth with it, and so he took his up too, and swiped it across his mouth. His manners were poor and embarrassed him, but now that he was among the civilized, he'd start practicing again.

He started by paying a compliment to Mrs. Gary. "Best jam I ever tasted," he told her, "and if don't offend you, I'll gladly give you a dollar for a jar to take to my tent."

Mrs. Gary hooted. "No one in his right mind would pay more than fifty cents, and that's twice what it's worth."

"I never claimed to be right in the head," he said, smiling. And with that he laid a dollar on the table.

Mrs. Gary gently pushed the money toward him. "You needn't make amends, Fin. We've loved caring for your mother, and she's more than earned her keep here."

Willa blushed, the kindness pleasing her.

Mr. Gary fingered the strap of his dungarees. "Not another woman in Oregon can do a wash as bright as Willa's."

Willa reached over and patted Mr. Gary's hand. "It's to your credit, and Mrs. Gary's too. I don't know another couple as willing as the two of you to let me stoke a fire — not after what I did to my own house. Mine and Fin's, that is."

It was an awkward admission, but honest, and everyone went quiet.

After supper, Willa helped Mrs. Gary clear the table and wash the dishes while Fin rode out to the old house with Mr. Gary. The men pitched a tent just beyond the heap of burned-out timber, and then Fin took a good look around, saw firsthand the work that lay before him. He figured he was up to it, if he paced himself and bit off just a little at a time. The sleep he'd gotten at the Garys' had done him good, and so he said out loud he'd get started as early as tomorrow. He wanted to get the house up before winter set in, which, if he'd calculated correctly, would be just about the time his money ran out. What he'd do to earn another dollar he couldn't yet say, but he supposed it would have something to do with Gilchrist's.

He tried not to dwell on those bleak months in the future, but on the work now at hand. By morning of the next day, when the air smelled as sweet as cider, he brought his mother out and the two of them worked together. Fin hitched a three-sided travois to his horse, and then filled the cart with ash and charcoal, emptying the rubble in a field. Willa, in the meantime, filled a wheelbarrow with broken nails, dumping them in a pile at the far end of the yard. When she came upon the kettle she'd toppled all those months ago, a flood of memories washed over her. She recollected how she'd chugged the streets of Portland on Fin's bicycle, just weeks after Edward had died, a little wooden cart hitched to the back wheel, wobbling behind her.

How she managed to cycle those many miles was still a mystery, since in those days she was a good deal heavier. Fin's bicycle had no skirt guard either, and more than once, when she was learning to ride it, a chunk of fabric worked around the chain that made the contraption go. How she had wished she could wear a pair of Edward's trousers instead of a troublesome dress, yet a woman on a bicycle was peculiar enough, and so she compromised, arranging a series of clothespins around the hem so that she pedaled easily and rode with confidence.

Mostly, folks reacted well to her comings and goings. Asa Collins, the butcher, hollered hello when she rode past, as did a woman named Mrs. Cotley, who owned the bakery. Even now, Willa remembered the smell of peach pie and cinnamon bread wafting from the store and how her mouth had watered.

To Willa's surprise, Fin had put his foot down when he learned she'd first taken up laundry. "I'd sooner see you work at Gilchrist's than take in dirty clothes," he'd scolded. "If you don't break your back leaning over a washboard, you'll crack your head for sure. You got no idea how to ride a wheel."

"Do too," she had said, holding herself up proud. "I've been practicing while you're up to the woods, and I've almost got it down."

He hadn't known what to say to that, and when he spoke at last, it was to ask in a pinched voice if she feared he couldn't support them.

"You can support us, of course you can," she reassured him. "But I know how desperately you want to get to Malheur, and I just figured the sooner you get going, the sooner you'll get home. Why shouldn't I do what I can to help you along?"

"Well, I don't like it and neither would Pa, were he alive to see it."

Now, that grated. Of all the people in the world to take Edward's side, the last would be her Fin. When Edward was alive, father and son had fought like badgers and rarely seen eye to eye. Yet how many times had she defended Fin, when Edward had gone too far?

She ripped a page from Fin's old book, and gave as good as she'd got. "It's the right thing to do, whether you like it or not," she had told him. And then she turned from him and smiled, for it felt good to stand up for herself and make her own decisions.

Once Fin accepted the notion that his mother would work as a laundress—with or without his blessing—he was up every morning at five o'clock, lighting the range and stoking the fire. Each Tuesday morning he filled her washtubs with water, and as often as not, made his own breakfast too—a slice of bread and pat of butter—and a bite for her as well. Afterward, he set out to shoot birds and collect eggs, which he later sold to Morris Kiff. Fin gave Willa sixty cents on every dollar, and always straight from his pocket. It was nice while it lasted. Soon, he'd left for Malheur.

Now, Willa leaned down and plucked a few more nails from the dirt. Those, too, she threw into the wheelbarrow. She stood, breathing in the cool air—which still had a bite of smoke to it—and thought how much this morning was like the one four years ago, when she had first bicycled to the Elliotts'. She'd climbed the steps and pulled off her mourning bonnet, its long crape veil clinging to the sweat on her back. She'd dabbed her throat with a handkerchief, and bravely knocked on the door.

A dark-skinned woman poked her head out, regarding Willa with one eyebrow raised. "You Miz McFaddin?" the woman asked in a deeply languid tone. Willa nodded. "I'm Tula, Miz Elliott's housekeeper." She stepped outside rather than inviting Willa in. "Laundry's over there," she said, pointing to one corner, "separate, like you ast. Aiden bundled each one and fixed it with a string, so's you could manage it better." She walked over to the tidy piles, regarding them disdainfully. "Happy to say I seen the last of Mister Elliott's drawers. Missus' too." She chuckled, and gave Willa a wide white smile. She must have seen some parched potato there, for she asked Willa if she could use some refreshment.

"I surely could, thank you," Willa said, the notion of a cool drink reviving her altogether.

Willa followed Tula into the house. The place was cool and quiet as a tomb—fitting for the proprietor of a funeral home, Willa thought. Other than a clock ticking on a wall above the mantle there was no sound at all. Everything within the place shone, from the wooden banister to the hardwood floor to the hulking furniture. Willa couldn't imagine cleaning a house so large, and tackling the cooking and laundry besides. It was a testament to Tula, and Willa admired her at once. She asked in low tones if the Elliotts were out, since it seemed quite possible her voice would carry to the rooftop, if she spoke any louder.

"Oh, they home," Tula said, swaying into the kitchen. "Mister's to the parlor, putting the sheen on a baby what died in her sleep last night. Missus up to her bedroom. She won't come down 'til suppertime."

"Has Mrs. Elliott taken ill?"

"No, she ain't ill. She readin." Tula's tone held judgment, as if there were no explaining why anyone would spend the day in bed, unless her legs were broken. "She won't come out 'less it's to lean over that staircase and tell me what to do, even when she see I got my hands full. Last time she done it, I said, 'I ain't your slave, you know,' and you know what she did? Laughed. Said, '*Slave?* A slave is someone who, when you tell 'em to do something, they do it.' So I guess she right. That ain't exactly me."

"No," Willa agreed. "You're no slave at all."

"I free, so to speak," Tula went on, "but then I ain't. Jes you wait and see—you'll get it figured out." She handed Willa a glass of water, watched her drink half of it in four swift swallows.

Thanking Tula, Willa dabbed her mouth, then set her glass in the sink. She had a notion of what it was to work for someone other than her husband, to toil at the beck and call of someone outside her family. Oh, she'd never once told herself it would be easy, yet she'd imagined her employers would treat her fairly, refusing to ask for no more than they were willing to pay. Now she realized that wasn't necessarily so.

Thinking back to the pile of clothes on the porch, it occurred to Willa she should have charged by the hour as opposed to the load, since some folks would dump molehills on their porch steps while others heaped mountains. It was a lesson well learned, although a tad too late, and one she committed to memory.

Tula nodded with her chin toward the porch. "I'll hep you hoist your bundles on your cart," she said. While they loaded the piles, Tula told Willa she was sorry to hear of Mister McFaddin's passing. "I know what it is to be a woman alone."

"I've got my son to help me," Willa said proudly.

"My husband run off years ago. I wisht he'd died—no disrespect intended. It's jes I don't need him comin back one day, holdin out his hand, thinking I got money to throw in it."

"Heavens," Willa said. "I'd give everything I owned to have my Edward back."

"Likely he never took one thing that didn't belong to him, is why."

"That's true," Willa admitted. "Edward was an honest man."

"Be glad of it," Tula told her, patting the bundles into place. "And pray your boy's jes like him."

Now, Willa looked over at Fin as he shoveled ash onto the travois. Yes, in some ways Fin was better than his father was, and in other ways far worse. Here it was, a lifetime since he'd taken off, and she could fool herself no longer. She could no longer say, as she once had, that he was right to take his path, for the trail he'd forged was dark and lonely, and had gotten him in serious trouble.

He still wouldn't speak of it. Oh, he'd given her those few details about the birds he'd shot, and that fellow LeGrande Sharp. But there was more to his story that he wouldn't share, specifics that aggrieved him. She could tell by the way he twitched in his sleep and sometimes cried out loud. She had no notion whether it was something he would eventually overcome, but she'd give him what help he'd allow her to and aid him in moving on.

So it was they worked side by side, toiling until the trees lost their leaves and the air turned brisk, until frost overtook the meadows. By Christmas, the house was up. It was rough and nothing fancy, and Willa hadn't yet hung a curtain—a length of fabric cost more than they could afford—but wood was free as long as a man was willing to cut it, and Fin had built a table, setting it off with two long benches, and then carved them each a bed. Mrs. Gary made a gift of two fine quilts; the newest she had stitched especially for Willa, the older she had pulled from a closet and kindly given to Fin.

Cookware was something else. Willa had salvaged what she could from her burned-out house, finding a few sprightly treasures. She unearthed a teapot and a fry pan, which she stored in the Gary's barn. Stored her washtubs and kettles too, which, as ironies go, the fire hadn't ruined. Now she carted the entire lot from the barn and set it up while Fin whittled three stirring spoons and two supper plates, which he later sanded smooth. His last few dollars he spent on a mirror for his mother. She cried when she saw it, and hugged him.

By New Year's the flour was gone, as well as the beans and sugar.

Willa stood before her son, insisting she'd take in laundry. Fin refused to allow it. "I'm walking up to Gilchrist's and asking for a job." Her mouth puckered at the news, and she glanced at her shoes, her brows staunchly furrowed. "It ain't my first choice," he went on, "but it won't hurt me, either."

She shook her head. "I won't be the one holding you back. You want to return to Malheur, you head on out and go."

"I'm of no mind to leave," he said, which was the truth as best he knew it. "LeGrande Sharp soured me, and my heart just isn't in it." But it was more than that. He could not get Phoebe out of his mind, nor keep from wondering what she was up to. Wondering too whether she thought of him, and if she wished to see him. Aiden more or less indicated with his put-out attitude that he'd caught the look she and Fin had shared that day at the marsh. And while Aiden wasn't the cruel sort, he was surely known to panic; if he didn't suffocate Phoebe with some cloak of suspicion, he'd smother her with questions, wear her down until she confessed to sins she'd never once committed. He was smart that way. Fin held no doubt Aiden would use his cleverness to get her to marry him.

Fin wished he possessed even an ounce of Aiden's shrewdness. As it was, he couldn't think of a single way to inquire about Phoebe without arousing suspicion. And if she'd already married Aiden, well, it did no good to bring her up one way or another. Still, he found himself dreaming about the possibilities, fantasizing she was free for the taking, and imagining he'd be the one to brush her arms with his fingertips, and persuade her to go with him.

He might have talked himself into earnestly searching for her, had Maggie Elliott not walked into Gilchrist's three days after he started stocking shelves there. Her silhouette was unfamiliar, but a beam of sunshine angled softly behind her, illuminating a mass of red, unruly hair. He knew her by her curls. Had most women possessed Maggie's halo, they would have called it into submission, believing those loose spirals a reflection of their character. Not Maggie. Even now, it seemed nothing would contain her.

"They told me it was you," she said, "but I told them the Fin McFaddin I know would never work at Gilchrist's."

It touched him to see her now. Ever since that day at the rookery, when he'd gone so all-fired crazy, it seemed his emotions got the best of him, that his eyes watered as easily as rain on a blustery day. He clenched his jaw and checked himself, not wanting Maggie to see a side of him he could no longer quite control. Yet if there was a woman alive who knew him—who wouldn't care if he teared up or cried out loud—it was surely Maggie Elliott.

He softly smiled. "We do what we got to, I guess."

"You don't miss hunting your birds in Klamath?"

"That ain't my life now, Maggie."

Until that moment, she had held herself tall. Now she sagged a little. Walking over to Fin, she wrapped her arms around him, and laid her head on his shoulder. "I've missed you so, I can't begin to tell you."

He held her in his arms. It felt good to hold a friend, to know that he still had one. She looked up after a while, and with one finger caressed the crease across his nose; the butt of LeGrande's gun had left a fine white scar there, and it had yet to fully heal.

"I heard about your beating," she said. "You might have

survived it, but this place—" she looked around the store, frowning—"will suck your life away."

Fin let her go. He walked over to the window, slipped his hands into his pockets, and looked out. "My mother thinks so too, although it's you who actually said so." When she did not reply, he turned to look at her. "What would you have me do, Maggie? I haven't Aiden's education, or a lick of his smarts. Aside from shooting birds, Gilchrist's is all I know."

"You can take up a camera, like Aiden did, if you'd a mind to."

"That's your brother's hobby, not mine." He again turned, and now gazed at the street. A horse plodded by, pulling a wagonload of boxes. Dust roiled everywhere, and all at once the air felt hot and stifling. Fin longed for a little rain.

"Phoebe's left town," Maggie said, "in case you're wondering."

He turned, his forehead taking on its old familiar furrow. "What do you know about it?"

She told him her story, how Aiden suspected something had happened between them that day at Malheur, how he and Phoebe had argued in front of the family. She told him too how Phoebe must have thought Aiden might never believe or forgive her, and so she'd slipped away in the middle of the night and taken the train to Berkeley. "I told Aiden to fetch her before he lost her for good," Maggie said, leaving out the part about Fin doing the fetching if her brother waited too long.

"Well, there you have it," Fin said. "He's done just that, I reckon."

"He did," Maggie said. "That very morning, in fact." She watched closely for some hint of Fin's true feelings, although so far it was only his tone that hinted at how he felt. She reached into her purse and pulled out a folded piece of paper. "Phoebe wrote me a note before she left. I thought you might like to see it." She held it out to him.

"Why?" he asked. "She married Aiden, didn't she? Took him for her husband?"

Oh, how she wanted to say it was so, to bring Fin around to her. She still loved him as much as she ever had, and wanted him to know it. But she couldn't claim what wasn't true, and so she told him Aiden and Phoebe weren't married yet. "It took longer than any of us thought it would for Aiden to win her back. But win her, he did. The wedding's three weeks from now."

Fin glanced up. After a moment, he held out his hand, and Maggie dropped the note into it. He unfolded it, and read it slowly. His chest went tight when he got to the part about Phoebe loving Aiden, how she never felt so much as the slightest flame for Fin. He looked at Maggie.

"Go on," she said. "Read what else it says."

He read and then reread the note three times, lingering on Phoebe's claim that he was a man in need of solace, and Maggie the one to provide it. He looked at her again, understanding now what she wanted from him.

She walked up to him, grasped his hands, and brought them to her breast. "It's no secret I've loved you as long as I've known you, and wished you loved me too. It's no secret, either, that you've withheld your love, saved it for some other—"

"Maggie—"

"I tried to let you go, I did. But I couldn't do it, Fin. And now here you are, and here I am, and it seems we need each other. I know I can make you happy, if only you'll let me try. Will you, please? Let me try?" She brought his hands to her mouth and kissed them.

He dug deep to find the words, for with all that was

in him, he wanted to get this right. "Maggie," he said softly, "you've been a friend to me my whole life. Aside from my mother, there hasn't been a being on this planet who knows me better than you. I'm sorry I've hurt you and wasted your life. Sorry, too, I can't give you what you want—what you've waited for and maybe even prayed for. I hope you'll forgive me that." Gently, he pulled his hands away. Maggie's face folded, but he pressed on, knowing if he paused, she'd fill that space with hope. "I know you want me to come around, but it isn't going to happen. I love Phoebe, and if she'll have me, I'll take her from Aiden, as soon as I'm able to."

"You don't even know her—I'm the one you know." Maggie turned from him, making no sound at all. Fin came up behind her, and for one moment steadied his hands above her shoulders, as though he'd rest them there and offer some small condolence—but then thought better of it.

"Aiden won't forgive me," he said, "and likely you won't either. Maybe it's best if you don't come around again, Maggie. I'm not the friend you deserve."

She turned to look at him, her face twisted, and then composed herself. "Aiden's coming up from Berkeley on Friday," she said stiffly, "with a man named Frank M. Chapman. Chapman's throwing Aiden a party, and I'm certain Phoebe will be there. If you've a mind to steal her, do it then, you hear?" She walked toward the door, stopped, and turned toward him. "And if you do take her, take her as far as possible, for neither my brother nor I will see you again, nor call you friend *or* lover." With that grim reprimand, she strode out the door.

Just as Berkeley belonged to Aiden, Chapman claimed New York City. The man would not live elsewhere, for he was as wedded to New York as he was to his job, which kept him running eighteen hours a day. It wasn't just the museum he toiled for, but for birds across the nation. Their protection was his crusade and his calling, the thing he truly lived for.

Since he'd spoken in Portland, at the meeting of the Oregon Öology Society, he had labored to promote the Model Bird Protection Law, as set forth by the American Ornithologists' Union — the AOU, it was called. The law would prevent the killing of birds for commerce, since as many as five million of them were slaughtered annually for the fashion industry in the United States alone. The law was also designed to head off bitter battles over the hunting of game birds, and as such exempted waterfowl, pheasant, turkey, grouse, and quail. But all other birds were protected.

The AOU was founded for the stated purpose of furthering the study and knowledge of birds, and it was the group's goal to get the law passed in every state. But while some states stepped forward and offered their cooperation, others refused to do so. So Chapman and his cohorts kept at it, gathering supporters where they could and working toward passage of a national law that would prevent interstate shipment of birds and other animals killed in violation of state laws.

The effort was complicated and exhausting. But one supporter, in particular, was especially enthusiastic. Theodore Roosevelt, a naturalist and conservationist, assisted Chapman in organizing the New York Audubon Society; in turn, Chapman intended to help Aiden Elliott do the same in Portland. Chapman greatly admired Aiden. It was his personal duty, he believed, to champion Aiden's work and to coach him along. Occasionally, he even assisted Aiden with his more demanding speeches.

Aiden considered moving to New York City in order to absorb all that surrounded Frank M. Chapman. But Chapman talked him out of it, telling him Berkeley suited him better, that he was needed in the West. "Anyway," he said as an afterthought, "it's time you fledged the nest, young man. When you do, I'll be there to cheer you."

And so that time had come.

The party would be held in Portland rather than Berkeley so Aiden's friends and family might attend, and perhaps donate a dollar or two to help get a local Audubon Society started. Maggie had originally planned to go, but had changed her mind, standing hard against Fin now. She had no choice really; he might well show up at Aiden's party, make some sordid scene while claiming Phoebe as his own. She decided to stay home, feigning blight or illness, or indifference, as her mother so often did.

She took to her bed around noontime, complaining of a fever. Yet when Blythe came in to feel her forehead, she found Maggie's face cool, her complexion robust and glowing. There was no hot flush to be found at all, and her eyes were bright and lucid. And when Phoebe came in and sat beside her, she too was mystified. "Your mother says you haven't a fever," she said to Maggie, her hand on her forehead. "Is it your stomach that's besieged you?"

"Isn't always a fever that makes a body sick," Maggie told her, her tone hot where her face was not. She looked at Phoebe, felt a spiteful chastisement rising up inside her. She thought for a moment she might just tell Phoebe what all she knew, but then she held back, knowing in her heart Fin was the culprit, and the cruel one too, the one she ought to despise. Even so, she couldn't abide Phoebe just then, and so she pulled the covers around her neck and asked to be left alone.

"Aiden will be disappointed," Phoebe said, patting Maggie's back now, "but I'm sure he'll understand."

*That's what you think,* Maggie wanted to say, but didn't, for she wasn't as cruel as Fin.

It had crossed Aiden's mind that Fin might attend the party. He'd known for some time Fin was back in Portland, yet he himself had not stepped foot into Gilchrist's during his brief visits to town. He had not welcomed Fin home, nor had Fin sought Aiden's presence. Phoebe, too, knew Fin was home. Aiden told her, testing her, to see her reaction. It was a risky game, and he'd pushed it only so far, putting it to her mildly. "Fin is back," he'd said one day, as if the news were uneventful.

"Is he?" she'd said, skipping an unintended beat, as the news surprised her. This might have worried Aiden had she not added, and quickly too, "Next time you're in town, you should stop in and say hello." That she hadn't tried to interject herself in some get-together with Fin was a good sign, he thought, an indication she loved him just like she said she did. He berated himself for needing that reassurance, for hadn't she done everything possible to demonstrate her love since they'd gotten back together? Worked as hard as he did and campaigned on his behalf? Hadn't she enlisted Chapman and his colleagues in building his own reputation, insisting that one day he'd be known not only as a statesman, but perhaps a governor?

She was a gift to him, a blessing and an inspiration. When he grew weary, it was she who kept him going, she who sang his praises, and believed in him wholeheartedly. It shamed him now that he'd ever accused her, and so he ignored the signs he might have seen, had he otherwise been watchful: the skill she'd acquired at changing the subject whenever Fin's name came up, the telltale blush on her neck. That she'd worked like the devil to keep Fin from her mind never occurred to Aiden, for his focus was on his success, and the party soon at hand.

The event started at seven-thirty. The hall — not two miles from the Elliotts' house — was bigger and more festively decorated than the one Aiden rented the first time Chapman spoke. When Aiden strolled inside, Phoebe on his arm, he glanced with satisfaction over the crowd that had gathered there.

That so many people had turned out to congratulate him delighted him completely. Phoebe was equally pleased; she blushed and beamed and greeted every visitor, repeating their names and then employing small tricks to ensure she remembered them. There was Elizabeth Hyatt, for example, whose last name rhymed with riot — and whose incessant chattering might well incite one — as well as Bishop Jacoby, a kindly man who could have been a preacher. There was Thelma Cotley too, who was the owner of Cotley's bake shop and whose last name brought to mind an apricot, the essential ingredient in Phoebe's favorite pie. And then there was the woman whose name Phoebe didn't catch, but who had marched boldly forward and announced, "I've every confidence your Aiden will get Portland's Audubon Society going one day very soon, dear."

Drawing herself taller, the woman went on to explain she'd been following Aiden's career since she'd heard Frank Chapman speak at an OOS meeting several years before. Chapman had told a story, she said, regarding his friend Harriet Hemenway, the woman who had maintained that women looked silly in hats decorated with birds, and as long as they looked silly, they'd be perceived as silly, and never acquire the right to vote. "I handed my plumed hat to my husband right then and there," the woman told her, "and to this day I've worn nothing but ribbons on my bonnets. The one I'm wearing today, in fact, they call an *Audubonnet*."

Phoebe smiled, wide-eyed, for this stranger was both articulate and clever—in short, the perfect candidate to assist in garnering additional support for Aiden. "Perhaps you'll help us gather a list of potential members then, for a society here in Portland."

The woman said she'd gladly do so, starting with herself.

Phoebe was in the midst of recruiting the help of several other women when Frank Chapman approached, asking that she and Aiden make their way up to the platform. The makeshift stage stood at the front of the room, a burgundy skirt with gold trim secured around its edges. Some considerate soul had strung a blue sash across the wall behind it, attaching it at both ends with a length of gold braid. Someone else had hung a butcher-paper banner proclaiming AIDEN ELLIOTT, OUR BIRDS' MOST ARDENT SAVIOR, and painted it red, white, and blue.

Chapman's presence lent an air of formality to the event. He stood in the middle of the stage, Aiden at his left, Phoebe just beyond. He cleared his throat and raised both arms, calling the room to order. As soon as he'd gotten everyone's attention, he thanked them for their support.

"Some of you I recognize and others I do not," he went on. "However, if I've not yet had the pleasure of making your acquaintance, please introduce yourselves afterward, during the reception. Until then, allow me to present to you Miss Phoebe Pembroke, who will no doubt assign you a task before the night is over." The remark was a reference to the bit of work she'd done just before the meeting, and everyone laughed.

Phoebe blushed and Aiden grinned, and Chapman moved graciously onward.

"The last time we met," he said, "it was under darker

circumstances. I'm pleased to report this evening that since that time, my sometime-birding companion, Harriet Hemenway, took up George Bird Grinnell's former mission and formed the Massachusetts Audubon Society. Others have since followed suit, and formed societies in their own states—Maine, New Hampshire, New Jersey, and Connecticut, to name just a few, and, of course, my own beloved New York. Much work remains to be done, but I'm delighted to say we've made substantial progress and are fully on our way to forming societies in Oregon and California."

Applause again broke out, and someone toward the back of the room whistled enthusiastically. Chapman waited for the guests to grow quiet again before continuing. "It is my opinion that much of Oregon's progress is owed to Aiden Elliott, for it is his work—his illumination upon the field of ornithology—that first acquainted your citizens with western birds and their habitats. A good many of his papers have dealt with his observations here in Oregon, but he's also reported from San Francisco, the Farallon Islands, and as far south as Monterey. His stories, accompanied by an array of brilliant photographs, have inspired a generation of future naturalists, and it is to him we owe our gratitude, respect, and admiration.

"And so it is with great pleasure that I introduce to you this evening Aiden Elliott, who has not only placed Portland in the ornithological spotlight, but is well on his way to bringing similar recognition to Berkeley."

Chapman turned, stepped aside, and indicated Aiden with a flourish.

Aiden sighed a sigh of happy nerves, took a breath and then a step forward. He bowed in acknowledgment, lingering a moment in that bent-spine position, as he absorbed the crowd's warmth and recognition.

Standing straight, he intoned, "I would not be here today save the exuberance of my friend and mentor, Frank M. Chapman. I owe him a great deal, for not only has he overseen the process of my learning, but introduced to me those who've taken an interest in ensuring my success, men who've shown me the way by virtue of their own exemplary careers.

"To demonstrate my appreciation, I will continue to work diligently to inform an uneducated public on the perils facing our birds—most obviously, working toward legislation to protect plume birds—and to encourage my fiancée, Miss Phoebe Pembroke, to work alongside me, sharing her learned abilities, intelligence, and keen moral insight."

Phoebe smiled gratefully, and when Aiden stepped back and circled his arm around her, the crowd again issued a robust cheer. Chapman stepped forward, encouraging the revelers to celebrate with a cup or two of cider as well as a few of Tula's cookies, while reviewing Aiden's photographs of hawks and owls and hummingbirds. The room filled with chatter then, and in sets of twos and threes, the partygoers filed toward the photographs, and then wandered toward the refreshments.

Phoebe worked her way through the throng, wishing to fill a cup for Aiden. She shuffled sideways to better navigate the crowd, pausing to chat with a redheaded woman and to share a humorous story.

Fin watched her from the shadows of the cloakroom door, his heart throbbing in his chest. Not only was Phoebe beautiful, but she had a knack for drawing people in. Had he not discovered for himself the influence of Phoebe Pembroke in the wilds of southeast Oregon?

No sooner had she broken from conversation with the redheaded woman than Blythe and Owen appeared. Blythe glided over, stately as a swan, and kissed Phoebe's cheek. Owen patted her hand, rousting from her a warm, contented smile.

Fin kept his eyes on her, watching as keenly as he ever had, shifting to see her better as she pressed onward through the crowd. Every so often she glanced down, and then up again, as though ensuring her path was clear. Her eyes traveled to one corner of the room and then the other, as she inspected the revelers. Her gaze skimmed past Fin, casually, unseeing, and then froze, her whole body stiffening. She looked slowly back, her eyes anchoring on his. Her mouth, closed until that moment, parted slightly, and it seemed she stood breathless.

He took it all in, the workings of her mind, the inner struggle to escape while her legs would still carry her. He took in the glance over one shoulder, as she debated what to do and where to go, before she looked at him again.

He beckoned her with his being, the man he simply was, and saw in her face the yearning he had hoped for. She took one tentative step forward. Paused. Took another, and one more after that, slowly pressing forward until she was with him at the door. In one fluid motion he took her hand, twining his fingers through hers, and led her into the cloakroom. He quietly shut the door. The same dark flame that fueled his need to hunt also fanned his hunger, and so he disregarded all that was right or wrong or hurtful to another, and reached up with one hand and gently clasped her neck. Drawing her in, he kissed the edge of her mouth, and then took the whole of it, persisting until she kissed him back. She stood taller to reach him, buried her face into his shoulder, and then quickly broke away. Breathing hard, she held one hand against him. "We can't do this, Fin, we can't. It will kill Aiden and Maggie."

He pulled her in, kissing her once more, and then opened the cloakroom door and swept the room with his gaze. Ensuring no one was watching, he pulled her through and headed brusquely toward a back door. Phoebe stuck to his side, her head down, and so missed the shock on Aiden's face when he glanced up and saw her leaving with Fin.

He strode across the street toward Gilchrist's, Phoebe's hand in his. The store was dark and empty, and no one would see them there. He unlocked the door and stood a moment, letting Phoebe decide whether she would come, or go. She turned to look at him.

"You all right?" he said.

She shook her head. Said *no*. But she stayed with him, and so he took her hand, led her inside and through a door at the back of the store, where a yellow curtain hung. They stood, each gazing at the other. Fin stepped closer, placed his hands on Phoebe's waist, and gently pulled her in. Her heart next to his made him almost dizzy, and he lifted her, sat her on a desk, and undressed her, peeling off her stockings. Her thin white petticoat too. He hadn't realized until that moment just how small she was; she didn't weigh more than a hundred pounds, or stand as tall as Maggie.

He too began to undress, wanting her to see him. But then her eyes welled and her forehead folded, and he was afraid he was losing her. He moved quickly, kissed her eyes and her mouth, insinuated himself between her thighs, and buried his face in her neck. "Do you love me?" he asked, holding her tighter, desperately wanting an answer. He clung to her, kissed her face repeatedly, and as she held him, he let himself go, let himself drift like a leaf in a spiral, until his head was spinning.

When he was spent, he raised himself to look at her. Smoothed her hair and wiped her tears. "We've got nothing to be ashamed of."

"What will I tell Aiden?"

"Why would you tell him anything? I'm the one who loves you, more than life itself. I'll marry you now, in fact—pack your bags and we'll go."

"I can't marry you, Fin," she said quietly. "In two weeks I'm marrying Aiden."

Fin stiffened. "Why are you here then? Making love to me?"

"I shouldn't be here at all," she said, and then nearly whispered, "I don't know why I came."

"That's a lie, Phoebe. You know exactly why you came."

She was trembling, and it was a moment before she could speak. She wouldn't look at him. "I didn't think it through."

"That's a lie, too."

Now she looked at him. "I never thought I'd see you again—I trained myself to believe it. And then there you were, standing at the back of the room. When I saw you, all I wanted was to be with you, to feel your mouth on mine. But Aiden has proposed, Fin, and I've accepted. I've promised to be his wife."

Fin grabbed her wrist. "You love *me*," he insisted, his voice wracked with pain. "I saw it that day at Malheur, and again just now, when you stood there in the hall—"

"I love Aiden."

"I got that job at Gilchrist's," he went on, "a respectable job, which makes me respectable, just like you claimed you wanted."

"I want what Aiden wants," she said. "I've never held differently, Fin. *That's* what I said in the marsh."

"Then by all means marry him," he said, stepping back, "for you'll garner no accolades married to the likes of me."

"Don't, Fin—please. Don't let it end like this."

"End? Hell, Phoebe, we ain't even half begun!"

But she'd said all she intended to say, and she slipped

down from the table, silently dressed, and walked out the door.

Fin sat for a long while after that, seething with all she'd told him. All that night and half the next, he berated her under his breath, thinking her some cruel heart to taunt him so unjustly. He'd given her too much credit, bestowed on the devil the persona of an angel, for only a woman as cunning as Satan would marry a man she didn't love.

He stewed for six days, and then having cooled by the seventh, regretted the things he had thought. Phoebe was no devil. She was torn, drawn to Aiden for his predictable ways and stalwart stance at living. Fin understood that. But clear as the world she'd wanted him as much as he'd wanted her, and had he taken a different tack, she might have come around. As it was, he'd scared her off with his pleading and his anger, and now he'd have to prove himself and show his reasonable side.

The next day, shortly after breakfast, he practiced his speech on the way to the Elliotts' house. He hoped Aiden was off in the woods, as he didn't want to fight him. But fight him he would, if he had to. Phoebe was worth that much.

He strode up to the front door, removed his cap and knocked. Tula answered. She raised both eyebrows when she saw him. "Didn't 'spect to see you anytime soon," she said, "the trouble you brewed last week."

"I'd like to speak to Phoebe, please, if you wouldn't mind, Tula."

"Cain't. She ain't here."

Fin hadn't anticipated Phoebe might be gone, and he frowned as he thought. "Is she off to town then, with Maggie and Mrs. Elliott?"

"No, she ain't to town," Tula said, her expression softening now. "She married. Phoebe and Mister Aiden stood before the Justice of the Peace three nights ago, and said their wedding vows. Next morning they took off, got themselves to Berkeley."

Fin didn't speak or move, but stood, dazed. "The wedding's not for another week yet," he said, not sure he'd heard her right.

"Something happened to hurry things along, but I suppose you know more 'bout that than I do."

"But I've got things I need to tell her."

"You done missed that boat, young man. Best find you a raft to paddle."

# CHAPTER EIGHT

It took some women longer than others to leave their father's houses. Maggie was one of the slow ones. She conjured a plan to save her dignity and reputation, since there would be plenty to criticize her decision and say a woman had no call to take a job in town. But Maggie had never been one to travel a clear-cut route. All her life she'd walked a crooked path, a trail of stubbornness and determination. It hadn't gotten her far, but she wasn't done yet, and so she sat down and took a look at her life, viewed honestly what that perseverance had got her. Not very much, it seemed. When she looked around her bedroom, she saw very little there. All she owned in the entire world were the few knickknacks she'd collected as a girl, traipsing the forest with her brother. Yet nothing in the room spoke of who *she* was and what she wanted, and where her life might go.

Now that she thought on it, she couldn't say what all she represented, or believed in. But when she thought back on the events that made her happiest, she recollected they were the times she'd pleased another: those days in the woods, when she'd fetched Fin a snack, or when she'd surprised Willa McFaddin with a homemade treat of Tula's. She remembered well the look on Willa's face the first time she had arrived at the woman's house with a slice of plum pie, how Willa's pink tongue had darted to capture every morsel. Maggie was proud too of the help she'd given Willa, washing shirts and trousers, and her father's underclothes. Yet a life of scrubbing laundry held no appeal at all, and so she sidled up to Tula the very next day, saying, "I need to learn how to bake a pie."

"Why?" Tula sprinkled a handful of flour on a sticky lump of dough, then whopped it hard on the table. The kitchen was warm and steamy, enticing the coils around her forehead to spring up and dance.

"I'm thinking of opening a bake shop, right around the corner."

"Town's already got one. Cotley's place, in case you don't remember."

"But you ever notice how her shelves are always empty? Half the time she's out of this and that, and the last time I was there, I overheard a customer complaining. Mrs. Cotley said it's her rheumatism keeps her from baking what she needs to, and sure enough, you look at her hands and they're gnarled as ginger root. It's an opportunity, Tula, and I aim to take advantage."

"Where you get the money to get started?"

"I asked Father for a loan."

"Well, who gonna run it?"

"I am, at least until I can afford to hire a helper."

"And do the baking too?"

Maggie nodded. "Which is why I need you to show me how to make sweet goods—like the pie you're making there."

She nipped off a thumbful of dough and popped it into her mouth. "Maybe dumplings too, and I suppose customers will want a slice of cake now and then—"

"Angel is good," Tula put in, "though Devil's is my favorite." She'd gotten the recipe for the rich, dark cake from a relative a number of years before; its ingredients consisted of butter, sugar, eggs, sour cream, flour, unsweetened chocolate, a pinch of salt, and the smallest splash of vanilla. "Secret is to underbake it jes the slightest bit, test it with a broom straw 'fore you pull it from the oven."

"You'll help me then? Teach me what you know?"

Tula kept her mouth hard while she whipped a cup of sugar into sliced plums.

"You'll turn those plums to pudding, if you don't slow down," Maggie told her.

Tula tapped the spoon against the edge of the bowl, then set it on the table. "What's in it for me? I teach you my secrets, what you give me in return?"

Maggie blinked. "What do you want?"

"Take me with you—let me be your helper."

"And pay you with what? I doubt I'll have enough money—at least in the beginning—to pay myself."

"Will, if you charge extra. Folks be glad to lay their money down."

"You do have a reputation," Maggie admitted, recalling the lemon-custard meringue that everyone was so enthralled with at the OOS meeting a few years ago. The word had gotten out that Tula was an exemplary baker, and a woman named Beatrice Hutto once tried to steal her from Blythe. Tula squashed the offer though, saying she wouldn't work for a woman who allowed her children to run wild in the streets. Maggie had laughed when she'd heard that—as if she herself hadn't grown up some forest urchin, just as Fin had claimed.

It was a daring venture, two women running a bake shop, one of them a maid and a dark-skinned one at that. But in the end Maggie decided Tula was right, and with her father's money opened her door six weeks later with Tula as her helper.

Maggie hadn't yet decided on a name for her business. When her first customer stepped inside the shop and looked at the dessert menu, he expressed shock at the cost of an apricot pie. Maggie didn't apologize, but decided then and there to call her place the SIMPLY WORTH IT BAKE SHOP, telling customers if they weren't completely satisfied she'd return their money in full.

"What if I eat half the pie, *then* tell you I don't like it?" asked the man, who looked as doubtful as the woman standing behind him.

"If you're unhappy for any reason at all," Maggie repeated, "I'll refund your money." But Tula's pies were wildly popular, as were her tarts, cakes, and cobblers, and not once was Maggie required to make good on her promise.

That she'd stolen her parents' housekeeper didn't seem to matter; Owen had no interest in household affairs and Blythe simply hired Tula's cousin and worked her just as hard. The first month after Owen set his money down, he told himself Maggie's loan was more an indulgence than any real investment. But by the beginning of her eighteenth month in business, she'd not only shown a profit, but the capacity to expand, and so he offered her a second loan before she'd fully repaid the first.

Maggie's customers were loyal, but none more so than Willa McFaddin. At least twice a week she stepped into the sweet-smelling shop and inhaled its rich aroma. Chocolate cakes, buttercreams, and all manner of pies lined the wooden shelves behind the counter. And there was a glass case filled with "pretties," as Maggie called them: miniature white cakes decorated with marzipan frosting and topped with pink roses. Willa's purchases were generally modest, however, since she made it a habit to select only what she and Fin would eat that day after supper. She often trotted a slice of apple or peach pie down to Gilchrist's, so Fin could eat it warm. Maggie never pressed Willa to buy more than she'd selected, but Tula wasn't as shy. "Your boy earns as good as his pa once did—why don't you take him a whole pie every now and then? Invite him to dig in?"

Maggie clucked her tongue. "Fin can't eat a whole pie," she'd chided, not wishing to pressure Willa into buying more than she needed.

Willa chuckled. "No, he can't," she said, "but I can, which is why I don't dare." When Fin started working again at Gilchrist's Mercantile, Willa quit the laundry business and was once again the little doughnut that her son had long admired.

In all that time, Maggie didn't once ask about Fin. Every now and then Willa shared news of him, how it seemed he'd lost the weight she'd gained, how he hardly said a word. Still, Maggie stood true to the promise she'd made; she steeled her heart and stayed away from Gilchrist's, and not just for her sake, but for her brother's.

Phoebe had crushed them all when she'd taken up with Fin. None more so than Aiden. He strode back to the house that night after the party, furious at having seen Phoebe leave with another man, and his former best friend at that. Not two hours later she had come home, seeking forgiveness. What a row they'd had. Aiden hollered while Phoebe cried, and all the while Maggie stood at the top of the stairs, watching from the shadows. She might have taken the news as hard as Aiden had, except she'd had warning. She had, in fact, resigned herself to the notion Fin *intended* to steal Phoebe, and so she'd stood astonished when Phoebe told Aiden she loved him more than she loved Fin. That she was sorry she had hurt him. Maggie had stepped quietly forward then, angling for a better view.

Aiden looked Phoebe over from head to toe, and by the state of her dress and crush of her hair had known exactly what she'd done. "You've lain with him," he accused, his suspicion a bitter accusation.

"But it's you I've come home to." She rushed toward him, grabbed his arms, and clung to him.

"Goddamn you," he cried, flinging her away.

"I love you, Aiden, and I'll do whatever you want."

He stepped back, his face cracking. He might have wished to inflict one-tenth the pain on Phoebe that she had cast on him, but he could find no words harsh enough to sufficiently punish her. He turned on one heel and strode through the door, slamming it behind him.

Phoebe sucked in her breath. Paced the floor and cried into her kerchief. Time and again she knocked on Maggie's door, pleading for Maggie to come out and talk to her. But Maggie sat tight, as did Aiden, until two full days had passed. On the morning of the third day, Aiden walked into the house, his face pale and his tie askew, his chin dark with stubble.

Phoebe was there at once, standing in front of him.

"If you love me as much as you say you do," Aiden said, glaring, "you'll never see Fin again."

"Never," she said. "I promise."

"Then get upstairs and pack your bags, for you'll marry me tomorrow. On Wednesday, we'll leave for Berkeley."

Maggie had again stepped from her room to better hear it all. She leaned against the wall, sick inside. Hurt and angry as she was, this didn't feel the answer. As things stood now, Aiden had to forgive Fin and Phoebe, Phoebe had to forgive herself, and Maggie had to forgive the whole lot of them.

Things got easier in time. Working in the bake shop helped, keeping her too busy to worry about the things she couldn't change. All she really thought about was the work at hand, and Willa arriving twice a week to collect small cuts of pie.

And then one late September morning, when the sandhill cranes flew overhead as they made their way south, Willa's smile was gone. Maggie knew at once something was amiss. "What is it?" she asked, disregarding her vow to distance herself from Willa's problems, for she knew almost certainly they'd somehow involve Fin.

Willa's eyes grew moist. "I know you don't want to hear it, Maggie, but I've got no one to turn to."

Maggie cupped the woman's elbow and led her to a table. She sat Willa down and settled in beside her. "I'll help however I can. You know I will."

Willa hesitated. "It's Fin," she confided after a moment, "as you might well have known. He gets gloomier by the day and nothing I do will cheer him. Some days I can hardly roust him from bed, and now that the cranes are flying, he fixes his eyes on the ceiling and hardly moves at all." She leaned in and lowered her voice. "He hears them clacking, Maggie, and goes into his dreamworld."

The last thing Maggie needed was word of Fin's despair; she had amassed enough of her own over the years, and had only recently recovered. Yet Willa was her friend — sometimes her only one. And so she sat back, and asked Tula to bring a pot of tea.

Tula took one look at Willa and issued no complaint, just

appeared with a porcelain teapot and a treat she called a scone. "Dot of raspberry jam to go with it," she said. Willa gave no sign she'd heard. She sipped the steaming brew, and in time told Maggie that Fin was as low as she'd ever seen him. "When he came back from Malheur after my house burned down, he told himself he could work in that store and make a go of it, though I never once believed it. I knew in time it would eat at him, gnaw at his insides, you know? He's lasted longer than I imagined he would, but he's taken a turn of late, like his life is upside down."

"Have you talked to him about it?"

"He won't talk. Some days it takes all I've got to get him out of bed. And when I do, the first thing he does is look out the window, dips low to see high. It's birds he's looking for, and each time he hears them, oh! It all but eats him alive. He wants to go again, I feel it in my bones, but he stays because of me. I guess he thinks he's got to."

"He stays because he loves you," Maggie told her. "And because he promised you he would. Don't be fussing at him now, telling him he should go, when you really want him to stay." Maggie saw that Willa wasn't listening. She was in some faraway land, wringing her hands over Fin.

Though there was a time Maggie would have run circles to help Fin, he had long ago used her up. It was Willa she wished to help now. "What do you want me to do?"

"Talk to him? He'll confide in you, I know he will, where with me he'll tell some lie."

"Fin wouldn't lie," Maggie put in softly. "Give him that, at least." They sat quietly a moment, and then Maggie asked what she should say to him.

"Tell him to get on with his life. Tell him as much as I hate to see him go, it's far worse to see him unhappy."

"It's not just birds he's pining over. You know that, don't you?" It was a reference to Phoebe, and Willa said she knew. She said too it didn't matter if it was a woman or a warbler he was heartsick over, since it was his way to take to the woods whenever he felt down.

"He's never learned to cope," said Willa, "the way most people do."

Maggie wondered what it was: coping. She hadn't learned it either, for if she had, she would possess a normal life, like half the world around her. But she had no wish to bring up her own deficiencies, nor discuss them with Willa, and so she told the woman she'd stop by her house after supper one day, and do what she could to help Fin.

The sun was low and the air cool when Maggie walked to Willa's. The country smelled of autumn. Maggie had always embraced the fall, and as a child had looked forward to collecting acorns and pinecones, filling her baskets with them. She likened the acorns to Chinamen's heads, and drew little faces on them. Many had names, like Wing and Tang, and there was a fellow she called So. Having no one to play with, she plucked their hats off and glued on little braids of yarn, then devised scenarios in which the acorns were her children, babies that she loved. They slept in matchboxes with cotton coverlets, and she kissed them each goodnight. In the morning, when they awoke, she read to them, and they to her, and not once did they ignore her.

Aiden, on one occasion, gathered acorns with her. He might have gone along a second time, had he not met Fin and begun collecting eggs instead.

Maggie glanced up, toward Willa's house. She hadn't yet seen the new structure, and when she came upon it, she eyed it fairly. It stood strong, with a good-looking porch and an overhang to stave off heavy rain. Curtains trimmed the windows, and gold and burgundy chrysanthemums bloomed in pots out front. Maggie's tension began to melt, knowing Fin had made this house; it told of his affection for his mother, and that something good lay inside him still, dormant as it was.

Willa must have been leaning on the door, for as soon as Maggie knocked the woman stood to greet her. "Come in, come in," she sang, beaming like a flower. Willa's neck bloomed crimson when she glanced toward Fin, worried, apparently, he'd cipher her deception. He sat hunkered at the table, busy with a project. When Maggie walked through the door, he glanced up.

"Well," Willa spouted awkwardly. "No doubt you've come to see Fin, Maggie. I'll leave the two of you to visit." She grabbed an apron hanging on a hook and scooted out the door.

Maggie smiled, finding Willa humorously transparent. Fin must have seen through her too, although he didn't say a word, just sat in his chair, a coal-oil lamp on the fireplace mantel illuminating his profile. Maggie stood, her hands clasped loosely, willing for the first time to view him as he was. He had lost weight, as Willa said, and he did indeed appear defeated, beaten down by a life he didn't love. Beyond that, she saw the same dark hero she'd always seen, as much as she preferred not to. She wished to see some devil there, and call him what he was.

"Hello, Fin," she said.

He studied her. She wondered if he saw some difference in her too, the serene self-confidence of a Gibson Girl, whose look she'd recently acquired: the shirtwaist blouse and vase-shaped skirt, a simple hat dipped toward her forehead. But if he saw a change, he said nothing, and if he had two words to tell her, he kept them to himself. He dropped his chin to his chest, and concentrated on the tools on the table.

She set her purse down, pulled up a chair, and sat across from him, watched as he selected a short wispy feather from a pile, then deftly lashed it to a hook. "I didn't know you were a fisherman," she said, striving for conversation.

"I enjoy tying flies. It gives me something to do."

"Why not carve a duck whistle? Something you'll actually use?"

He twirled the thread around the hook and feather, and it seemed to Maggie his face softened as he thought about her question. He made a knot, nipped it with his teeth, and then set the hook down in a box with separate little slots. "Call," he said, looking up at her. "If I was to whittle anything at all it would be a duck call, not a whistle." When Maggie only nodded, he looked down again. "My mother put you up to coming here today?"

Maggie exhaled, not realizing until then she'd been holding her breath. "Willa was in the shop a few days ago, and we got to talking, is all. I told her you hadn't once come to see me, and she invited me to stop by and say hello."

"See how I was doing?"

Maggie followed Fin's eyes as his gaze traveled beyond the window and settled on Willa as she walked along the garden. The woman bent to pluck a weed, and then a carrot, which she swiped clean with one hand and stuck into the pocket of her apron.

"If you've stopped for just a visit, why isn't my mother in here instead of out there, pulling carrots from the dirt?"

"She's worried you're unhappy. As much as she wishes you would stay in Portland, she can't stand to see you wallowing in misery."

Fin picked up the hook and fingered it, pressing it hard against his thumb. The point made an indentation there, but didn't break the skin. Just when Maggie thought he might pinch it tighter, draw a little blood, he set it down and looked at her. "She thinks I'm going crazy."

"Are you?"

"If I ain't turning cartwheels, maybe I got my reasons." He flushed a bit, his mouth firm. "When you're out there in the wilderness as long as I was, your mind plays tricks on you. One minute you're a hunter, the next you're cryin over everything you killed." He shook his head. "Now that I'm home, I tell myself every day I ain't inclined to go back, yet when I look up at the stars, see them gleaming, I hear the killdeer calling…I don't know. Maybe they're not birds at all, but demons. You think it could be so?" He looked at her now as if he almost believed it, and while in days past the gesture might have moved Maggie, now it irritated.

"Those aren't demons," she scolded. "They're voices of your own making. You've got them arguing with each other—one saying 'stay,' the other saying 'go'—all because you've never talked to people. You don't know how to talk to people." She didn't want to get sucked in, yet here she was, swirling down some sink hole. "In the end, your heart will tell you what to do, if for once you'd only listen."

"I have listened," he objected, his tone defensive now. "I don't see where my heart gave me no good advice at all."

Maggie guessed he was talking about Phoebe, which irked her further still. "I'm not talking about your love life," she huffed. "I'm talking about Lower Klamath. Get yourself down there, if you're so all-fired determined."

"I can't shoot a bird now—I'll get arrested if I do."

That much was true. Aiden and his cohorts had worked

diligently to guarantee passage of the Lacey Act, the first federal conservation measure that prohibited the interstate shipment of wild species killed in violation of state laws. If Fin shot a grebe or heron, and in turn that bird was shipped to a milliner in New York City, he'd be fined and maybe jailed. But it wasn't only the Lacey Act that would set him back; it was the pressure of the new Oregon laws — laws allowing hunters to shoot only fifty game birds a week, when just a few miles away in California hunters were permitted fifty birds a *day*. Then there was the law requiring each hunter to take out a hunting license.

It hardly seemed worth a man's while to aim his gun these days, what with the laws and competition, although Fin understood there were plenty out there willing to take that risk. His own pluming days were over, but he himself might be persuaded to shoot a duck again one day. He badly missed the Klamath Basin, as well as the creatures in it. Despite that, he had no taste for jail, and so kept his longing to himself.

That Phoebe Pembroke's hand was in these changes confounded Fin. Willa occasionally mentioned the woman, after hearing through the grapevine in town about the afternoon teas she was hosting, a la Harriet Hemenway. "It's her plan to mobilize and excite American women," Willa reported, adding that Phoebe had persuaded friends and acquaintances not to wear feathered hats, but ribbons and bows instead. "She's working toward the promotion of bird protection, at least in the western states."

"Guess you best stay then," Maggie told Fin now. "That's right," she repeated when he looked up. "Stay — and end up hating every one of us for trying to make you happy, for loving you more than we ever had a right to." She snatched her purse and stood. "There was a time I lived for you Fin," she said bitterly, "but now I live in spite of you, just like everyone else." She paused, and drew her lips tighter. "By the way, you don't have to *shoot* birds to kill them—your outlook alone will slaughter them just fine."

"I don't reckon an outlook can kill a bird," he said sharply.

Maggie glared at him, turned on her heels, and stepped solidly out the door. She clomped past Willa, where the woman stood in her garden, gnawing on a carrot. "What'd he say?" she wanted to know.

"He said he's a numskull," Maggie reported, "without a brain in his head."

Maggie might have stayed mad at Fin forever, but she wasn't a cranky soul any more than he was a tender one. She went about her business, making coffee and wiping tables, filling orders when folks wandered in off the street or sent a note by messenger. That morning alone Morris Kiff had sent in an order requesting two Deil's cakes, as he called them, thinking it unlucky to write or say the word Devil. He needed the cakes for a get-together on Friday, the note said, and he wondered if Maggie would bring them by, saying he'd gladly pay extra.

Bring them by? She'd never thought of offering such a service, and yet why couldn't she? Fin had delivered groceries as a boy on his bicycle, just as Willa had trucked her laundry. Logistics were the challenge. How would she balance two fresh cakes in the basket of a bicycle while navigating the rutted streets of Portland?

"Tula," she hollered into the kitchen. "Morris Kiff wants two cakes delivered to his shop on Friday. How will we get them there?"

Tula emerged from the kitchen, flour smudging her nose. "Kiff ought to fetch 'em hisself, he wants 'em so bad."

"He can't get away," Maggie said, eyeing the note again.

Tula sighed. "I can't hardly keep up now, and here you 'spect me to bake Kiff's cakes, then trot on over to his place and drop 'em off too?"

"Diel's cakes, he calls them," Maggie said, ignoring Tula's rant. "He says they're his favorite."

"'Course they are," Tula said with more irritation than pride. "Why don't he send his missus?"

"I don't believe he's married."

"Well, I ain't cartin 'em over. You can take 'em if you like." She walked back into the kitchen.

Tula's testiness demonstrated just how tired she was. Maggie's business had grown more successful than she ever dreamed it could be, and she supposed she'd have to hire a helper soon, since she herself was inept in the kitchen, burning the custards and over-whipping the cream, often until it turned to butter. And she hadn't come close to mastering Tula's recipe for lemon icing, which is why she spent her time up front, and left the baking to her partner.

Still, Maggie had a knack for numbers and an innate understanding of which services would attract customers. The shop wasn't technically a café, yet she offered coffee and tea, and individual slices of pie, so that a customer could sit at a table, if she wanted to, and satisfy a sweet tooth.

Although it was Morris Kiff who actually came up with the notion of offering a delivery service—albeit indirectly—she recognized the possibilities at once. It was on the way to Kiff's shop, in fact, that Maggie decided the next hire she'd make was a delivery boy—or perhaps a girl, if such a creature inquired, seeing as how girls were apt to care for a cake just as they would a baby. She'd limit the delivery area, of course, unless she bought a buggy, in which case deliveries could be made clear to the edge of town. The question was what to charge. Or whether to charge at all. On that point she would decide after she dropped the cakes at Kiff's and saw what he offered in the way of additional payment.

Morris spotted her from the window, and stepped outside to greet her. "Well, if it isn't Maggie Elliott," he chirped. She stood before him, the handle of a wooden wagon in hand, two boxed cakes sitting pert inside it. "Have you brought my Diel's cake?" he asked, eyeing the boxes. She said she'd brought him two, and he snatched them up and drifted inside the store. "Come in, come in," he called over one shoulder. "You can leave your wagon parked outside the door there."

Maggie stepped in, took in the flavor of the store, its musky scent of books and oiled furniture. She hadn't been in the curio shop since she and Aiden were children, and she found it cozy as always. When Morris set the boxes down, he caught her looking around. "Haven't got but a handful of birds' eggs these days," he told her, "and not a skin at all. Sell mostly stamps and postcards of late, and relics from the Civil War." He nodded toward a sword hanging on the wall, claimed it belonged to George Armstrong Custer.

"How did you come across it?" Maggie asked, not that she held any particular interest in or esteem for the army general; there was a rumor he had graduated last in his class at West Point, which explained why he'd lost the battle at Little Big Horn. If he'd paid attention to his studies, the way that Aiden had, he might have devised some strategy to spare his hide and the hides of all his cohorts.

Morris said he'd bought it from the friend of a friend of a cousin. "I'll sell it to you, if you like."

"I'm not in the market for a sword, but thank you just the same."

"Maybe you'd like a globe to hold colored water?" He set the cakes on a shelf, then clasped her elbow and steered her toward a display of crystal bowls; one held azure liquid while another held amber; the one on the end swirled with a concoction that looked suspiciously like pond weed.

"I'm not in the market for a globe, either," she told him. "I just came to drop off your cakes."

"So you did," he said, smiling broadly. "And seeing you, it's come to me that I've got an item that might mean something to you." He guided her toward the back of the store, and from a dark and dusty corner produced a box with a lid. He held it out, both eyebrows raised, awaiting her reaction. When Maggie merely stood, displaying no recognition at all, Morris blew the dust from the lid and pried it open. Inside, four buff eggs lay nestled in a nest. He reached in, took up a note, and squinted as he read it; satisfied he had what he was looking for, he handed the card to Maggie. "What do you think of that?"

Maggie read the card, looked up at Morris. "These are Fin's old eggs."

"They belong to the mate of that jay you shot," he said, beaming. "Fin told me all about it—how you couldn't bear to part with that bird. Said you took it to bed with you too. Got a mess of bug bites out of the deal, if I recollect."

Maggie took the box from Morris. She remembered well how she and the boys had traipsed the forest, so many years ago. My, how the world had changed. She smiled at the memory and told Morris about the rash the bird had given her, saying when Fin first saw her bug-bitten arms, he thought she'd rolled in nettles. "He had no idea I'd slept with that bird, at least 'til my mother told him."

Morris shook his head; the notion anyone would sleep with a bird was beyond his comprehension. He plucked one of the eggs from the box. "Fin didn't blow even one of these correctly, but he was a boy then, and didn't know no better. I set him straight after I bought this set, and in years to come, well...he was the best that ever was. Best egg collector, best egg blower—best skinner too." He sighed at the memory. "Days of collecting like we used to are over, I'm afraid. Shame too. If ever a body was meant to scour the great outdoors, it was surely Fin McFaddin."

They both stood a while, lost in their reveries. And then Morris rallied and gave Maggie's back a pat. "Keep the eggs, if you want to—give them to Fin. He'll have himself a chuckle, seeing what a mess he made of them."

Maggie nodded, her mind still in the forest. When she left Morris's shop, it was without having uttered one word regarding payment for her delivery. He had to run down the block and catch her, just to hand her fifteen cents.

That evening, she set the eggs on the kitchen table, pulled up a chair and sat until the room grew dark and chilly. Drawing a shawl around her shoulders, she again thought on those old memories, how furious she was with Fin after those bugs had eaten her so, how she'd trained her mind against him, claiming it was his fault her arms were stout and swollen. She had sworn then that she would never marry him, even if he begged to be *her* slave and baked her a mountain of sweet plum dumplings—although she herself preferred peaches, baked in a cinnamon pie.

Despite herself, she smiled. She wanted Fin to have the eggs, and the memories that went with them. Yet she wasn't of a mind to visit him at Gilchrist's—he'd worn her out with his prideful ways. And so she decided to send Tula.

# CHAPTER NINE

Tula screwed up her face. "What he want with those smelly old things?" she clucked, leaning over to inspect the contents of Maggie's box.

Maggie explained how Fin had collected the eggs all those years ago, how he'd blown them incorrectly and Morris had docked him for it. "They're souvenirs from his boyhood," she said. "I imagine he'd like to keep them, and put them on some shelf."

"Uh huh," Tula said, seeing now where Maggie was going with her story. "And I 'spose you 'spect me to trot 'em over."

"I'll wash the dishes if you do." Maggie knew how much Tula hated washing dishes; it was a carryover from the days she'd worked for Blythe, when the family ate at eight o'clock and Blythe no earlier than nine. All day long there were dishes to wash, but no trolls appearing from beneath some toadstool to help her scrub them.

It didn't take Tula two seconds to snatch the box from Maggie. She tucked it under one arm, said she'd be back in the shake of a stick. Then she headed down to Gilchrist's.

Fin didn't see her come in. He was standing behind the cash register, waiting on a man. The customer had a backside as big as a barrel, and wore his trousers low. The loose flesh of his stomach spilled over his pants in a waterfall, and his nose stuck out like a snout. He tossed a pair of suspenders onto the counter. "How much for them there 'spenders?" he wanted to know.

Even Tula could see from her dark spot in the corner that the suspenders had a small white tag attached with a string. Fin frowned slightly, leaned forward to look at the price. "Seventy-five cents," he said.

"Johnson's don't charge but fifty."

The Fin Tula knew would have coolly told the customer to go on then, buy his suspenders at Johnson's. Except Johnson's wouldn't have them, as any fool would know. The owner of that store didn't carry half the stock that Gilchrist's did, and if a fellow complained about a lack of this or a lack of that, Johnson would say, "I order it, you'll just buy it, I'll have to order it again."

The man slapped a handful of coins on the counter. "Why don't I just give you fifty?"

"Because the tag says seventy-five."

The man worked his mouth. "You Edward McFaddin's boy?"

"I'm his son, yes — or was. He's been dead for years now."

"Too bad you ain't more like him."

Tula scowled. It was cruel to suggest Fin was anything less than his father had been, for Edward McFaddin had an ornery side. At this very minute he was likely walking some line between heaven and hell, waiting, as a dead man would, to see which side he fell on.

Tula had spent plenty of time and money over the years in Gilchrist's, charging to her various employers' accounts coffee beans, sacks of sugar, and the smallest tins of tobacco—which Blythe had asked her to buy on the sly.

Tula had often arrived a few minutes before the store opened, and waited for Edward to get there. He'd come a short while later, greeting her with a nod but no smile. To the store each day he wore dark trousers, a white shirt, and a gray flannel vest. As soon as he entered the mercantile, he hung his hat on the same hook on the same coat rack, before slipping on an apron and securing its ties around his belly. It was clear to anyone who thought to look that work was his ethic, his pride and joy, and that he'd never understand why Fin didn't see the world as he did, as a box of sorts with a hundred compartments, each serving some pointed purpose. There were squares for sweeping and squares for dusting and squares for stocking shelves. It drove Edward mad that Fin fit no box, a fact Tula discovered when she'd overheard them arguing one day at the back of the store.

"When you planning to make those deliveries?" Edward had brusquely asked.

"Sometime later this morning, I guess." Tula couldn't see Fin, but recognized his voice, since he was Aiden's best friend and had often been to the house.

"Don't think for one minute you'll head to the forest before your work is done."

"Pa—I'll take care of it. I ain't a child, you know."

There was the sound of a slap, and then a scuffle: metal tins and wooden buckets cascading to the floor.

"I hate you," Fin shouted. "I hate you and this goddamn store." A door slammed, and it was quiet a long moment then. Edward yanked the curtain aside to find Tula standing there.

His face glowed hot as an ember, and his forehead was bathed in sweat. He strode forward, his head down while he adjusted his apron, and asked what he could do for her.

The moment was charged with electricity. She had no wish to invite a shock by saying something foolish. "Just browsin," she replied innocently, as if she had heard nothing more unusual than a rooster's call. In a moment, she too was gone.

If the fat man in the store right now reminded Fin of the incident with his father, he showed no sign at all. With his shoulders low and his head down, Fin reached out, raked up the money, and dropped it into the till. "Go on then," he said quietly. "Take them."

The fat man snatched up his purchase, and strode handily from the store.

If Tula herself hadn't witnessed Fin's complacency, she never would have believed it. She stood a moment longer, wondering how she'd slip from the store unnoticed. She shifted as quietly as possible, but Fin must have caught the movement, as his eyes drifted her way. He ducked a bit to see her.

"Tula? Is that you?"

She stepped from behind the bookrack. "Why didn't you give that man what-for? Tell him to jump in the lake?"

Fin smiled benignly. "Don't got a lake," he said, "at least that I'm aware of."

"You can play fun all you want, but you know what I mean."

Fin slid his hands into his pockets. "It's not that hard to figure," he said. "Maggie come to see me a while ago. She'd got her feathers up, said I could kill a bird with my spirit alone—tons of birds, I reckon. I gave it some thought, and decided she was right. I'm tired of fighting, is all."

"I knowed Maggie Elliott to kill a bird in her day, too, you know. You ain't entirely alone."

"Except she's never been one to wallow in pity. She makes the best of things. I let them drag me down. It's high time I made my way here at Gilchrist's, found some satisfaction."

"Satisfaction," said Tula. "So that's it."

Fin dropped his gaze to the floor.

It was this silence that pinched Tula's heart. She had no notion to give Fin his eggs then; it seemed a cruel thing to do. He needed no reminder of the boy he'd been and the life he'd lived, after his pa had died. This wasn't the Fin she'd known of old, but some oddly fragile stranger.

She pretended she'd come on some other mission, a headache known as Maggie. "Boss lady sent me to fetch a treat to satisfy her sweet tooth," she said. "Candies with sprightly sayings."

"We don't carry those no more."

"Then pick me out some favorites. I'll fetch her those instead."

He couldn't seem to make a decision, however, and in the end Tula made her own selection, choosing a dozen assorted chocolates. She asked him to box them, if he would, and then she carted them to Maggie.

When she got back to the bake shop, she told Maggie what she'd seen. "I didn't know that man, Mister Down with the World. He's give up, is what he's done, and all because of you."

"Me?"

"Was something you told him about his attitude. You don't set him straight, he'll stay at Gilchrist's, die inside that store."

All this time Maggie had thought Fin was simply

prideful. But to hear he'd truly changed dredged up her old despair. Morris Kiff had called it: if ever a body was meant to scour the woods, it was surely Fin McFaddin.

She took the chocolates from Tula, saying she had a notion how she could help Fin, and then rode the train to Berkeley. It would be the first time she had seen Aiden since he'd left the house with Phoebe that day so dark and ugly, tears falling all around. Before she'd left, Phoebe had twice knocked on Maggie's door, and Maggie had refused to see her. Well, she'd see her now. Speak a few kind words, for her anger had diminished. Her enthusiasm too. She was tired of the arguments and accusations, and assumed Aiden was, as well.

The house was her brother's, and so she didn't knock, but walked quietly through the door. She found him sitting in what looked like an office. The room was filled with dark, heavy furniture, and a lamp on the desk threw off a golden glow. He was leaning toward the light, flipping through a magazine, a journal called *Bird-Lore*.

He looked up and nearly fell backward in his chair when he saw her; he'd been expecting Phoebe to walk into the room. "Good heavens, Maggie! What are you doing here?" He tossed the pamphlet down, strode over, and took her in his arms; it was the first time they had embraced, at least that Maggie could recall. They held one another the longest time, a surge of affection between them.

Aiden kissed her forehead, held her at arm's length to have a look at her. She was a woman now, fully grown, and appeared to have come alone. He glanced into the hallway, saw just one bag sitting there. "Why didn't you call to say you were coming? We might have arranged a social."

"Because I've a favor to ask. If you say no, I'll leave on the train this evening."

He sat down then, seeing how serious she was. He bade her sit too, and so she did, in a chair across from him. When she told him of Fin's circumstance, Aiden's good mood evaporated. "I don't know what you want me to do about it," he groused. "Even if I could help, I don't know why I would, after all he's done to me."

"And me," Maggie pointed out.

"Well, there you have it," he said. He gazed out the window, conjuring some hurtful memory. All Maggie had to do was look at his face—his furrowed brow and puckered mouth—to know which one he'd chosen.

"You've every right to cling to your resentments, Aiden," she said. "I don't blame you. But when it's said and done, what will those hard feelings get you, except grief and unhappiness?" Aiden looked at her with narrowed eyes, but made no comment.

"Fin's been your best friend since you were ten years old," Maggie continued. "I'd think you'd want to help him."

"If you call a thief a friend."

"I don't know what all he stole," Maggie said gently. "You're the man that Phoebe married."

To Aiden's way of thinking Fin had stolen plenty—that which he himself so ardently desired in the snows of the Tahoe mountains, and which Phoebe had denied him. He might have gone ahead and said it, had Phoebe not walked into the room.

She was carrying a large gilt tray, a wedding gift from Frank M. Chapman, which held Aiden's sandwich on a white china plate, a small glass of milk, and a slice of butter cake. She'd cut a rose from the garden, a yellow one, no more than a bud, and placed it in a vase. It rested just above a silver fork, which sat on a linen napkin.

Phoebe halted at the sight of Maggie, her green eyes blinking.

"Hello, Phoebe," said Maggie. She stood, looking at the woman. Phoebe was as lovely as she had ever been, her hair a pale yellow. But she was thinner too, the events of the last few years taking their toll. Her eyes appeared tired and puffy, which meant she wasn't sleeping.

Phoebe set the tray down on a parlor stand, then strode over and embraced Maggie. She held her with all she had. And when she wouldn't let go, Maggie knew she couldn't, for Phoebe was weeping into her shoulder, shedding her pent-up guilt.

All this time, Maggie had thought she'd relish Phoebe's pain, let her cry her whole life through, if she'd had a mind to. But her heart was no longer in it. No harsh words from Maggie would make Phoebe's anguish keener, for the woman's pain was so pronounced, so difficult to endure, even Aiden looked away.

Maggie pulled back. Looking into Phoebe's eyes, she said, "Don't cry. I mean it now. I forgave you years ago." In truth, forgiveness had only come that moment. She turned to speak to Aiden. "I'll forgive you, too, brother, if you'll offer Fin a hand."

"What have I done that needs forgiving?" Aiden wanted to know. "I haven't harmed a soul."

"You've held yourself higher than a body has a right to," Maggie told him. "Come down a notch, and make yourself more human."

Aiden pursed his lips as he considered Maggie's statement. She'd hit some sore spot, for it was true he lacked humility. It was something of a paradox since so much of his life he'd lacked true confidence. But as soon as he got it, it went straight to his head. Now, instead of holding his chin up, he dipped it somewhat, for a man couldn't conjure humbleness simply by wishing it so; he had to practice it too. "What do you propose?"

"Get Fin out of Gilchrist's. It shouldn't be that difficult, with your connections. But if you succeed in helping him, I don't want him to know, ever, that I asked you to lend a hand. I'd just as soon he believed you offered it of your own volition, because you're his lifelong friend."

"He'll never believe it, not after what we've been through."

"Yes, he will. He's tired. We're all tired. Why wouldn't he believe you've exhausted your anger, just as we all have?"

The truth was, now that he'd moved to Berkeley, Aiden feared Fin less; it wasn't likely Fin would appear again and threaten his happiness. To please his sister, Aiden acquiesced. He did, however, allow two months to slip by before packing his bag for Portland.

Fin stood stiff when he saw him, assuming Aiden had finally come to swag him. He supposed he'd fight Aiden if he had to, although he dreaded the notion; even after all this time his nose still ached, mostly when he awoke at night, following a nightmare concerning LeGrande. So there was that, and the fact Fin hated to hit a friend, especially one he had wronged.

"What brings you to Portland, Aiden?" he asked instead. He curled his fingers into a loose fist, in the event he'd need to defend himself.

Aiden eyed Fin's posture. "It's just like you to stand ready for a fight," he said, not having entirely spent his anger, the way his sister had. "Why must you always assume the worst?"

"I don't know," Fin said. "I just do, I guess."

"I'm not here to plug you, but to offer a proposition."

"And what would that be, exactly?"

"I was hoping we could discuss it over supper."

Fin thought a moment. "Maggie's ain't open after two o'clock, but we could walk on down to Remy's, though their pie ain't half as good."

"I guess Maggie has Tula to thank for that."

"Don't sell Maggie short," said Fin. "It's her cleverness that makes that bake shop go. You know she's the only one in town to charge for deliveries?" He shook his head at that. "No one else would dare try such a thing, but she's got a product folks want, and a way to get it to them. That they're willing to pay extra for it—and for delivery too—says a lot about her."

"I'm surprised to hear you say so, considering your history with Maggie."

"Maggie's never been one to brag on herself. I guess I'll do it for her."

"Well," said Aiden, "I'll be sure to stop by her place tomorrow, see for myself this venture she's created."

"I'll join you," Fin quickly put in, though he'd never once set foot in Maggie's café. He didn't completely trust Aiden—nor would Aiden have trusted him, were the tables turned—and he didn't want his former friend claiming an advantage. Even more, he didn't want Aiden to speak ill of him to Maggie, now that he was struggling to be a better person.

Aiden looked around the store while Fin locked up. It hadn't changed much since Edward McFaddin had died. The shelves were leaner, perhaps, and the floor a little dusty. He now saw that Maggie was right; Fin had not found his calling here and likely never would. The realization touched him, which he found somewhat annoying.

The two of them walked over to Remy's. Aiden requested a seat near the window, saying it would be nice to watch passersby. More likely, he wanted to be seen by them, Fin thought, since it seemed true that some things never changed, and Aiden was one of them.

The men ordered steak and green beans and mashed potatoes, a spoonful of gravy on top. While they waited for their food, they talked of Aiden's life and the politico he'd become. Fin had heard that Aiden was one of Teddy Roosevelt's cronies now, serving as a mouthpiece for birdlife in the West. It meant something, Fin knew, to rub elbows with Roosevelt, for the man was president now, promoted from vice-president after McKinley's assassination in 1901. No doubt, Roosevelt's elevation would give the nation's conservation movement a boost, not to mention Aiden's career.

Aiden sipped some water. He told how he was working toward passage of the Oregon Model Bird Law. It was known, even as far east as Washington, D.C., that thousands of grebes, terns, and other non-game species were still being killed in Oregon for the feather trade. "Thirty-thousand dollars' worth of grebe skins were shipped to milliners this year alone," Aiden told him, "and that takes only Tule and Klamath into account. We've got no idea how much blood was spilled at Lost River and Clear Lake, or from areas where a man can hardly get to."

Those figures seemed high to Fin, and he asked Aiden how he'd arrived at them. Aiden told him they had a contact in San Francisco, a fellow who worked in the millinery trade. "Of course, knowing the numbers isn't the same as acting on them. What we need is a game warden, someone to enforce the Bird Law — once it passes — at Klamath and Malheur."

Fin sat back in his chair, grasping all at once the purpose of Aiden's visit. Aiden didn't give him but a second to consider the ramifications of what was clearly an offer, since Fin was likely to summon a problem where none existed. Leaning forward, Aiden took up the empty space on the table with his forearms. "I recommended you for the position," he said.

"Why would you, after what I done to you?"

Aiden pursed his lips. He thought he might tell Fin after all that Maggie asked him to. But then he said, "No one knows the marshes quite as well as you do."

"Why would they have me, when I was once a plumer? Likely I've killed enough birds in my lifetime to fill the entire White House."

"Likely you have," Aiden agreed, "but they need you. They're aware of your history, yes, just as they're aware you're out of it now, toiling at Gilchrist's and wasting what is otherwise valuable knowledge. We need an insider, Fin, someone who has worked the marshes and knows its trespassers by heart."

"I know its trespassers, all right." Fin stared out the window, the old familiar furrow creasing his brow. "How much does it pay?"

"Thirty dollars a month."

Fin nodded, and then sly as a jaybird said, "It's a dangerous job, and no plumer I know will go quiet if caught in the act."

Aiden again bit his tongue. Here he was, doing Fin a favor and the man didn't even appreciate it. "We'd pull your wages from the Thayer Fund, money which goes to wardens to enforce bird laws." He hesitated. "I'm authorized to offer as much as thirty-five," he said, his tone tight, "but that's it, Fin. I can't go higher than that."

"No need to. You knew the minute you saw me in Gilchrist's I'd take the job."

"I suppose I did," Aiden said, relaxing now.

"I guess you know, too, I'm deeply grateful." Fin rested his gaze on Aiden, took in the slick wave of his old friend's hair, how he'd likely worked as hard as a madman to drench his curls with sweet-smelling tonic, then squash them 'til they lay flat as a broom on a table. The look didn't suit him. Fin supposed it fitting, however, that Aiden should appear a gentleman now, with his boyhood days behind him. "Remember that story you made up for yourself when you were a boy in the woods?" he asked. "The one with the Argonaut?"

"How do you know about that?"

"Maggie told me—you can't keep a secret from her."

"An adventurer engaged in a quest," Aiden said, recollecting the event. He smiled. "That was a long time ago."

"I got to hand it to you," Fin told him. "You've embraced that quest, and made a difference in this world."

Aiden started to object, but Fin wouldn't hear it. "I owe you an apology," he said, "for all those times I doubted you, and all the wrongs I done."

Aiden had never known Fin to say he was sorry for anything, and the comment came as a shock. He stared at Fin, saw there was truth in his eyes, and sadness too, something akin to heartache. "I accept your apology and thank you for it," Aiden told him. He reached over and grasped Fin's forearm, gripping it sincerely.

Fin's eyes welled, and he looked away. There was so much he wished he'd done differently, but the fact was he'd made his choices, good and bad, and now had to live with them.

Aiden was in town just long enough to meet Fin at Maggie's bake shop the next morning for coffee and a scone. Maggie threw her arms around him, acting as if she hadn't a clue as to the reason for his visit. Aiden put on a show too, saying he'd come on business, and to offer Fin a job. Aiden stayed only long enough to eat breakfast, and then excused himself to stop in and say hello to their parents.

Maggie stood alongside Fin. For the first time in a long while she thought he looked right again, carrying the confidence of the man she once knew, which is exactly what she told him.

He looked up at her, perplexed. "I guess I'm the same as I always was."

"No," she said. "You're content now, happier than I've seen you in a while. It does my heart good to know you're satisfied."

"It's a weight off to be done with Gilchrist's, I'll tell you that. Though I never imagined myself a game warden."

"Maybe you weren't imagining hard enough," she said. She poured him a little more coffee and it seemed he was watching her in a way he never had before. For a moment she worried he'd found her out, figured she was the one who'd gotten Aiden to come to town. But then he dropped his gaze. "I wish you'd sit a minute," he said. "There's something I'd like to ask you."

She set the pot on the table and sat beside him, uncertain where he was going with his desire for small talk. He fidgeted with his scone, stabbing his fork here and there, trying to gather words that were struggling to come. She glanced around the shop with a nervous eye; it was beginning to fill with customers, and she needed to get back to work. Yet she hated to rush Fin, since it was a rare day that he asked for anything, let alone serious conversation.

It was another moment before he found his words. "Were you the one got Aiden to offer me that job?"

So he had guessed, after all. She was about to lie, then found she couldn't do it; it was this hesitation that told him exactly what she'd done.

"That's what I thought," he said. He sipped his coffee, then set his cup down on its saucer, missing the little indentation there so it sat half-cockamamie.

"I know I shouldn't have interfered," she said. "But Willa was worried about you, and when she came into the shop one day and asked if I could help, I had no idea what to tell you. I went out to your place thinking I might lend a hand, but then we had that tiff, like we always do. For a while I didn't care what all became of you."

"That was my fault," Fin told her. "It was easier to sit around boo-hooin than it was to hear the hard stuff. But I pulled myself together, put on my big-boy britches, and made myself a man." He smiled at that, and Maggie did too; it was such an earnest confession and so very unlike him.

"The truth is," she said, striving for the honesty Fin had just put forth, "a little bit of me died to hear Tula tell of seeing you in the store, taking that fat man's guff. I wanted to help you get out of Gilchrist's, but I knew I couldn't do it alone. It's Aiden you need to thank, Fin. He's the one who made it happen."

Fin stroked one finger along the teacup's handle. "Time was, I wouldn't think to thank either of you for anything you'd done, but I want you to know I'm thinking now, and I appreciate it, Maggie."

"I know you do," she said. "I know too that your departure to Klamath will be hard on Willa, but I don't doubt for one minute she'd rather live alone than see you suffer so. She'll be as happy as the rest of us to see your heart so glad."

"Miss Elliott," a customer called from the counter. "You've got a pecan pie on the shelf there that my Joe would simply love. I wonder if you'd box it for me?"

"Be right with you, Mrs. Westman," Maggie called. She pushed back from the table, telling Fin she had to go.

He gently clasped her wrist. "I know I got no right to, but I got one other thing to ask."

She waited patiently, though from the corner of one eye she saw Mrs. Westman staring, and it made her feet twitch. Fin let Maggie go, then scratched his eyebrow and grinned. It was an awkward moment, and it seemed to Maggie he had kindness in him yet. It so warmed her heart that she gave him her full attention. She sat down again. "Go on," she said quietly. "We've got no secrets now. Say what's on your mind."

"I was just wondering," he started, and then hesitated again. "I was hoping…well…that you'd take supper with me sometime. I know you don't know what to make of that, and I'm not sure I do either. But I want to thank you proper for the things you've done, and supper seems a start."

"You don't have to thank me, Fin. For all that's come between us, I'll always be your friend."

"Is that a yes, then?"

"Miss Elliott," called Mrs. Westman again. Maggie looked over to find a whole line of customers staring at her.

"I've got to go," she told Fin, standing again. Hurrying toward the counter, she turned, and in a voice loud enough for everyone to hear, said, "But yes, I'll take supper with you tomorrow."

The entire store went quiet. Every person present knew of Fin McFaddin's history, knew how Maggie had stuck steadfast to him, and how resoundingly he'd rebuked her. Mrs. Westman scowled. Anyone seeing her expression knew she thought Fin a pitiful choice for a supper date, while Tula smiled and held her tongue in check.

But Maggie was no fool. She wasn't a girl anymore either. She'd never had much interest in trying to charm a man, and over time had come to understand it wasn't charm that would attract a mate, but the woman underneath. It was with a relaxed air then, that she met with Fin the next night, expecting nothing from him and asking nothing in return.

He picked her up at her own little house, the one she'd bought with the earnings from her shop. Before stepping inside, he stood a moment, enjoying the sight that was Maggie Elliott. She was fully a woman now, dressed in a rust skirt with matching jacket, and a hat of dark brown straw. Her shoes, too, were brown, with high tongues and miniature bows. Fin told her she looked lovely, and she thanked him. He stepped inside and looked around, taking in all that told of Maggie: the lichen-wrapped branches she'd plucked from the woods and set upon her bookshelves, the nests she posed on top. A robin's nest in particular caught Fin's eye, and he walked over to investigate it. Constructed of dried grass and mud, it held three azure eggs, blown professionally. Fin knew as soon as he picked up one of the eggs it was Aiden's work—on the egg's underside Aiden had written all its details, including what it was and where he'd found it, with a special postscript to his sister: *Happy Birthday Maggie*. His penmanship was fine.

Fin replaced the egg and took another look around. The room had the feel of a forest dwelling, and it seemed in perfect keeping with Maggie. The history of their childhood, really, and the people they'd become.

Spying more birds' eggs, he walked over to another shelf. They struck him as oddly familiar, and he frowned, some vague memory coming to him. "What are you doing with these?" he asked, reaching to pick one up.

"They're the jay's eggs you gathered that day, back when you were a boy. Remember? Morris gave them to me and I gave them to Tula. She was planning to give them to you that day at the store, and then, well…"

"We've pretty much covered that, haven't we?" Fin said, and she said yes, she thought they had.

He turned the egg over in his hand, studying it a moment. "I made a mess of this one, I'll tell you that right now."

"That's what Morris said too." Maggie laughed, as did he, and then a silence settled between them. For a moment she worried Fin's mood had tumbled, but then he looked at her and smiled. "I don't know why you keep them. Was me, I'd toss them out right now." He made a move like he was headed toward the door. Maggie rushed toward him, one arm flailing as she tried to tried to grab the egg. "Don't you dare," she cried, but he held it just beyond her reach, laughing as she swiped her hand through the air, trying to get at it. She punched his arm and he brought it down, handing it over at last.

"I wasn't really going to toss it," he said. "Just wanted to see you jump a little."

"Don't poke fun at me," she said, and he saw he'd embarrassed her.

"I ain't poking fun," he said, but then he couldn't help himself and he chuckled again. "Well, maybe just a little." He kept his eyes on her, for she appeared an angel to him now. In the past, he'd never seen her as anything more than a child gone wild in the woods, but now she was pretty; perhaps she'd been pretty all along, and he'd been too dense to see it.

He took one step toward her, and just like that she pulled back. "I ain't gonna hurt you," he said, defensive.

"No, but you were going to kiss me, and I'm not about to let you."

"Why not?"

"Because you should have kissed me years ago, and now I don't want you to."

He stood quietly, remembering how she had indeed made it clear, so many times, that she was in love with him. The way she stared at him with dream-filled eyes and ran after him too, waving goodbye like a crazy girl when he first took off for Malheur. "I guess I got that coming," he said.

"I guess you do," she said.

They stood, awkwardly. "We're not gonna let this spoil our evening now, are we?" he asked. "A little joshing with each other?"

"I don't want it to."

"I don't want it to either. Why don't you get your wrap and we'll get ourselves some supper."

He took her to Remy's, the same place he and Aiden had gone, and they sat at a table in the corner. The scent of a roast browning in the kitchen's oven made their mouths water. "Meatloaf is good here," Fin told her, "and their roast is too, but their pie don't hold a candle to Tula's." Maggie said she'd heard those rumors, but had never personally put them to the test; he told her not to bother, then thought Maggie might not want to be bossed around, and quickly amended his remark. "'Course, you might want to try it for yourself," he added, "seeing as you're the expert."

And so she did, as soon as she'd finished supper. "You're right," she told him, setting her fork aside after only two bites of a peach cobbler. "They sat this on the sill too long, and it's gone a little soggy. No one can top Tula's pastries."

Fin sat back, taking satisfaction in that. Maggie sat back too. She couldn't get over the change in him. Ever since Aiden had offered up the job, Fin had switched from glum to giddy almost overnight. It was good to see him so—wonderful, in fact—and she cocked her head a bit, wanting to take it in.

"What?" he said, watching her smile at him.

"I'm happy for you, is all."

His face turned solemn, and Maggie wondered if the man could sustain a minute's worth of pleasure. He looked at her much as he had earlier in the bake shop, and again told her he wished to talk seriously. He took her hand and leaned in, chewing his lip a bit.

"I'm no orator, Maggie, you know that as well as anyone. But when I speak, it comes out true, and I guess you know that too."

"I do," she told him. "Of course I do."

"I won't waste time then, trying to make this fancy. I just want you to know how much I appreciate your being my friend, for there were times I had no friends at all." He paused, thinking back on that awful time in the marsh, when he had gone nearly mad. He quickly spoke again, before Maggie could interrupt and tell him of course he had friends, and how dearly they all loved him. "I know that was my own doing," he went on, "that I should have seen a long time ago the ones that would stick by me. But I didn't. I was prideful and stupid, and it seems I made more than my share of mistakes."

"Fin—"

"Let me finish now." Maggie clamped her mouth, and Fin went on. "I can't undo the things I done, but I can start anew right now. I want to do that, Maggie—start again with you by my side, acting as wife and partner."

It was all Maggie could do to breathe, so terrific was her shock. When she'd caught her breath, she shook her head, for a proposal was the last thing she expected. "What am I supposed to say to that?"

"Say yes," he said. "It ain't that hard to do."

A dozen thoughts crossed her mind, but still she couldn't speak. When her heart had slowed and she had gathered herself, she said, "I swear, since I was five years old I've waited to hear you say that—all those times I pestered you, you said you'd never take a tomboy for a wife. What made you change your mind?"

He hesitated, and in that instant Maggie's lifeblood left her. As much as she needed an answer, she didn't want to hear it. He sensed her discomfort and said, "You once told me that as much as Aiden and Phoebe are alike, so are you and me. It took a long time for that to settle in, but for a while now I've believed it and known it to be true." Maggie opened her mouth to speak, and he again called on her patience. "Hear me out," he said. She quietly waited.

"I don't know if you can love a man who's put you off like I have. I don't even know if it's right to ask you to. But it seems there's a reason you haven't married another, like maybe you've waited for me, knowing I'd come around one day. And since I have, I surely wish you'd accept my proposal and take me for your husband."

"I thought Phoebe was the love of your life. Have you forgotten her so quickly?"

"Phoebe married Aiden — that should be your answer."

"But it's not what I asked."

"No, I don't love her. And it makes no difference anyway, for if you take my hand I'll never pull away. I'll never hurt you again. That's God's honest truth, Maggie."

Her lips had gone bone dry. She licked them. "I've spent years training my heart against you, fighting my desires. After you left for Oregon that first time, I knew you'd come back for me. When you didn't, it almost killed me. Loving you has made me old, Fin — old, and frankly exhausted."

"Give me one last chance, Maggie," he said earnestly. "I promise I won't disappoint you."

She shook her head. "I'm sorry, I can't do it, Fin."

Her refusal stunned him, but set him on fire too: all at once he had a bird to pursue, a songbird he called Maggie. The thrill of that opportunity so invigorated him that he did everything he could to prove himself worthy. Every evening after he'd closed the store, he called on her, bringing her bachelor's buttons and foxglove and dahlias from Willa's garden. And when he wasn't working, he was at her house, making small repairs, fixing the fence where the gate scraped the ground, and patching holes in the roof. Once in a while he prepared a meal too, supper mostly; three times now he'd burnt the chicken, saying, "I ain't used to a cook stove. A spit's what I need, in the middle of the floor, and some coals to boil the coffee."

Maggie laughed at that. When he suggested they take their party outside, where he could cook a proper meal, she joined him, sat on a log he'd dragged over to the fire, as if they were camping in the marshes. He got the coals going just the way he wanted, then set up a small Dutch oven and got some biscuits baking too. They ate their meal out-of-doors, plates resting on their laps, the scent of roasted chicken and biscuits wafting in the air. Maggie's neighbors walked over and hung on her fence to comment on all the doings.

"What's going on over there?" called a man named Jasper. When he saw that Fin was cooking in the yard, he exclaimed, "If that don't beat all!"

"Smells like heaven, whatever it is," put in Jasper's wife, Onetta.

"Fin has cooked a chicken and baked us some biscuits," Maggie called back. "We'd be happy to have you join us."

The man looked at the woman and she at him, and they hurried over. Fin handed each of them a biscuit slathered in butter, and Maggie passed the honey. Jasper bit into one, closed his eyes, and let go a wide smile. His wife did the same, inhaling as she did so. "You ought to put these on your menu at the bake shop," Onetta said to Maggie.

"Except you can't cook them in no wood stove," Fin informed the woman. "Got to have a Dutch oven, and cook them on a fire."

"I don't suppose Tula would go for that," said Onetta. Maggie agreed no, she likely wouldn't.

When the sun dipped behind a copse of Douglas firs, Fin put on a pot of coffee and asked Jasper and Onetta would they stay and have a cup? In the old days he might have sat apart from Maggie's visitors, but now he wished to show his better side, and so he joined them as they sat back with their legs stretched out, their feet crossed at the ankles. He participated in the conversation too, putting in a word here and there, where normally he'd sit silent.

Maggie looked at him and smiled. She must have noticed how hard he was trying. He smiled back in a shy, surprising way, and for the first time in a long while, Maggie let her defenses down. It felt good, too, since it was more like Maggie to say what she thought and how she felt, to let it out in the open.

After the couple had left, Fin helped Maggie carry the dishes into the house. He dried while she washed, watching as she did so. She felt his gaze, and turned slightly, saying, "What?" as he'd once said to her. Her eyes misted as the realization sunk in that not six weeks after he had first tried to kiss her, he was going to try again. And that this time she would let him.

He set his towel down, walked over, and pressed his mouth to hers.

In all her imaginings, she'd never dreamed of anything quite as tender as this. He seemed to melt into her, telling her with his languid form that she was all he wanted now. By the time he dropped to one knee and asked for her hand, he'd won her heart completely.

There were plenty who thought her crazy, and who frankly told her so. They wondered out loud why Fin had rallied now after sitting idle all those years. When Maggie came out with her announcement, Owen stood torn before her; on one hand his daughter had found a suitor at last, while on the other it was Fin McFaddin, the least suitable prospect in all of Oregon. It struck him as an unlucky turn of events.

Blythe, despite her previous indifference, weighed in with surprising conviction. "I'm not sure you've thought this through, Margaret," she said, setting down her book. "You've worked hard to make a name for yourself, to establish your reputation. Here you've got a marvelous shop, and Tula as your baker. Why throw it away to marry a ne'er-do-well, and a former plumer at that?"

"It wasn't so long ago you had no objections against plumers. All your hats have feathers."

"I've not worn those hats for a long time now."

"Nor has Fin shot a bird." It was quiet a moment before she spoke again. "I know you don't understand," she went on, "so I won't ask your permission. But I will marry Fin, and when I do, I won't be back to Portland for a good long while, so I hope you'll give your blessing."

"You're leaving?" Owen asked.

"Fin's work is in the marshes," Maggie told him. "We'll be heading for Klamath soon." Seeing her father's long face, she added, "I know Fin hasn't always been the pillar we might have wanted, and he's plenty to make up for. But he's worked hard these last few months to right his wrongs, and if I'm willing to stand behind him, you ought to be willing too."

Her parents pursed their lips while they thought. Owen was the first to step forward to offer a hug, while Blythe joined in a few moments later, her back as stiff as a book's spine.

Barely a week passed before Maggie sold Tula the store. She agreed to allow her former partner to make payments, just as she herself had once made them to her father. In those first days after the sale, patrons tolerated rather than embraced the shift in Tula's position, familiar with her previously only as Maggie's dark-skinned baker. Maggie supposed once she'd left town to settle with Fin, some of the customers of the SIMPLY WORTH IT BAKE SHOP would no longer come around. But there would be those who understood and accepted it was Tula's sweet stuff rather than Maggie's that they had always come to purchase.

Though Owen offered to host a reception like no other, neither Maggie nor Fin wished to celebrate their wedding with anyone other than friends and family. Despite Phoebe's urging that Maggie at least consider her father's offer, she declined, telling Phoebe in private it wasn't her style, parading in a flouncy gown with her hair wound tight in ringlets. Nor was a fancy wedding anything Fin wanted, which Phoebe might have guessed.

In 1902, when Fin was twenty-eight and Maggie twenty-three, they married on a fall afternoon in the garden of Owen Elliott. Willa was present, as were her neighbors, Mr. and Mrs. Gary. Fin arranged for Willa's financial support, agreeing once again to send money on a monthly basis, with the promise she'd tote it the bank the same day she received it. Money would be tight for Fin and Maggie, for Fin insisted Maggie stash the money from the sale of her house into the bank, as well as the payments she received from Tula, since she'd earned that money and it was hers alone, and he'd have it no other way. Willa didn't argue, but she had no desire to burden her son and his new wife, and so she made her own plan, which was to bake a cake now and then, sell it to Tula, and purchase the staples she needed. As soon as Fin left for Klamath she would put her plan in motion.

Tula was at the wedding, as were Maggie's parents. Aiden served as best man and Phoebe as matron of honor. Phoebe wore a dress of cream lace, with matching beaded slippers. Her hair, woven loose and lovely, sat atop her head like a smooth gold cap. That she looked prettier than the bride surely crossed the guests' minds, although they would never say so. Rather, in their bedrooms that night, tucked beneath their covers, they'd whisper among themselves that Maggie still held some childlike quality, an aura of innocence, and how it seemed sadly touching somehow.

Aiden secretly worried that Fin might not show up for his nuptials, that at the last minute he'd take off for the Klamath region without so much as a fond farewell. Yet there he was, just as he'd promised, holding Maggie's hand beneath an arch twined with ivy and salmon-colored roses.

Their vows were loving, but simple. Each promised to love one another faithfully and forever, and afterward Fin held Maggie's face in his hands and kissed her full on the mouth. Fin's manner demonstrated a surprising peace, an unusually tranquil calm, while Maggie's demeanor suggested the opposite. Moved almost to tears, she placed her hands on his, her face betraying not only her rapture, but her gratitude as well.

After the ceremony, the wedding guests applauded. Owen kissed his daughter and clapped Fin's shoulder, and Blythe patted Maggie's hand. To Fin she offered her fingertips and genteel congratulations. Phoebe embraced Maggie. Aiden's eyes traveled to his wife, and then darted toward Fin. Even after Fin's apology, Aiden expected a reaction on his old friend's part, some sense he still loved Phoebe. But what Fin felt he kept to himself, and when Phoebe stepped toward Fin to squeeze his hand, Aiden quickly stood between them. He shook Fin's hand and offered congratulations, not caring how it looked. Fin knew as well as Phoebe did that it was best to leave it so; let Aiden make his statement, however awkward it appeared.

It wasn't long before the guests strolled over to the wedding cake. Over a span of forty-eight hours, Tula constructed three tiers of a rum-filled cake filled with nuts and candied cherries, then frosted it with butter cream and arranged baby roses at its bottom. On top, she'd placed a bouquet of violet pansies. Maggie proclaimed it the most beautiful cake she'd ever seen, and the tastiest too. "Oh, Tula," she said when she took a bite, "you've got to put this on your menu."

Tula's eyes danced. "Folks always have need of weddin cakes," she said, envisioning the potential. "Could even name 'em, if I wanted." She looked at her former boss. "This one I'd call *Maggie*." She turned toward Phoebe, saw in her some recipe of gold. "I'd build a yellow cake with lemon custard for you, Miz Elliott, and that one I'd call *Phoebe*."

Not one to be left out, Blythe stepped forward and said, "What would you name after me, Tula?"

This being Maggie's wedding day, Tula couldn't tell her such a beast already existed and they called it Diel's cake; instead, she concocted a kinder story and sprinkled it with sugar. "I'd bake you a chocolate cake with chocolate frosting, and perch a crown on top." Everyone clapped at that, as they were able to picture the cake perfectly; after all, what woman wouldn't want to be thought a queen in the eyes of Portland?

"Come taste, my sweet," Owen extolled, a fork and plate in hand. Blythe glided over, accepting a bite from her husband.

She smiled serenely, conjuring, no doubt, the occasion on which she'd order her own specialty cake, and the tiara she'd select for its top.

# CHAPTER TEN

It was nearly Christmas when Maggie tromped into their house at Klamath, her cheeks flushed with cold. She stamped snow from her shoes, blew on her fingertips, and yanked off her wrap. Fin was sitting in a rocker next to the hearth, where he could jab the fire with a stick when he wanted to, and never get up from his chair. She came up behind him, breathing hard and bending low to brush her cheek against his. He flinched, smiling, saying her nose was cold as a carrot. She rubbed it, sneezed twice, and then once more. Fin recalled the first time the inside of his own nose had crystallized, the little hairs standing stiff with frost. It never got so cold in Portland that a body truly froze, but Klamath was a different story. At four thousand feet, the snow spit as early as October, gathering as high as a man's kneecaps, often by November. Once, Fin recalled, it had snowed on the fourth of July.

Maggie leaned against his shoulders and draped her arms loosely around him. He grasped her hands and kissed them. Ever since they'd arrived in the Klamath country, he often made these gestures, and she loved him dearly for it. But every now and then, when she lay in bed at night and opened her eyes, she sometimes found him staring at the ceiling, lost in some netherworld. Eventually he would look her way, see she was awake and extend a smile, as though surprised somehow to see her. She clung to that small sign of contentment, but when the first year folded into the next and he'd still not said he loved her, she stood in the doorway one morning, hands on her hips, fed up to her core. "What did you marry me for, if you can't bring yourself to love me?"

Blinking, he looked up from his porridge. "What are you talking about?"

"I've waited a whole year now, and you haven't once said you love me."

"Surely I have."

"No," she said, shaking her head. "Believe me, I would have noticed."

Maggie saw the calculations in his head, the visiting and revisiting of all the things he'd told her. He must have realized what she said was true, for in that instant he pushed away from the table, walked over and took her in his arms. "If I haven't said I love you, that's my error, Maggie. Because I do—I love you with all my heart."

She wrapped her arms around him, and laid her head on his shoulder. "And our baby?" she asked, remaining still against him. "Will you love our baby too?"

He leaned back to see her better, wonder in his eyes. Hugging her, he lifted her from her feet and twirled her around, his face buried in her neck. The gesture was so unlike him that she kissed him, and when he set her down, she kissed him again and again.

Once he learned she was expecting, he was sensitive

toward her in a hundred different ways. He put off for days his departure to the marshes, wanting to stay behind and care for her, bringing her tea when she wasn't feeling well, and cake when she was fine. In bed at night, he held her close, his breath warm against her shoulder.

Satisfaction seized her, yet it scared her too, for it was strange and unfamiliar. One evening after supper, she told Fin happiness was fickle and she feared it wouldn't last.

"I ain't leaving, Maggie, if that's what you're afraid of."

"No," she said. "I've taken you at your word, and love you for keeping it." She plucked a plate from the dishwater and laid it on a cloth on the sideboard while she thought on what was bothering her. "I can see your job makes you happy. You come in, beaming, after a week in the marsh, like you haven't a care in the world. What worries me is that man, LeGrande Sharp. What if you come across him again one day, and catch him with his wares?"

"I got to catch him with his wares, Maggie. That's the point of what I do now."

"But who's to say he won't dish out a beating, like the one he gave you last time? Or shoot you, just like he shot your dog?"

Despite his happiness with his new job, LeGrande was never far from Fin's mind. He had every intention of one day arresting the old plumer — if he ever came across him — as well as his shaggy nephew, and Fin often looked for LeGrande's grotesque silhouette and Axel's scrawny frame as he scanned the horizon. He fully expected to come across them one day, but not wanting to worry Maggie, didn't share this with her. He kissed her forehead, smiled, and said, "Audubon Society don't pay me to get dead."

"But there's not much they can do to keep you alive, either."

He couldn't argue with that. Help was what he needed, since covering half of Oregon was too much for one man. His territory was vast and his resources almost nonexistent. Oh, he had a boat, a rifle, and a shotgun, but what he needed was armed bodies willing to fight mosquitoes and sleep in the tules, all for meager wages. And that didn't even take Malheur into account, which Fin hardly ever got to, and which, for the time being stood defenseless against marauders like LeGrande and his companions. Then there were the locals, too, most of whom did not consider bird killing an offense, and who shot birds to put dinner on their tables. Despite his title of game warden, Fin did not fault them and tried to look the other way.

Deep down, he too would always be a hunter.

He supposed he'd never be so reformed that he never thought on hunting again — what it was to scour the woods, a shotgun on his shoulder; it would likely always thrill him. But he was also prepared to acknowledge that he'd done more than his fair share of killing, and that he'd reveled in the tales his mother had told him as a boy. How many times had she recounted her story of growing up in Pennsylvania, when scores of passenger pigeons with rust-colored bellies blackened the daytime sky? Her own mother told of a flock a mile wide and three-hundred long clapping across the country, their wings pealing like sleigh bells.

"It took them hours to pass," Willa had claimed, "if you can begin to imagine."

He *could* imagine, and when he was younger he desperately wished to be part of that killing scene. But growing up had changed him. He'd settled down as most men do, and gained some comprehension of the world. Aiden had offered him a new path, and he now lived and hunted by standards he'd not known before, but which he gratefully accepted.

In summer, he was gone more than he was home, but he happened to be at the house the day in late July, when his son was born. Maggie wanted to name the baby Edward Owen, but Fin said Owen Edward sounded better. Maggie said no, Edward had to be the baby's name, and she would not budge on that. It was a gesture, Fin knew, to bring him closer to his father, to close the wound that after all this time still hadn't completely healed. He gratefully accepted that too.

When little Edward was six months old, Fin bundled him in wraps of wool, sat him on his shoulders, and carted him everywhere. If there was such a thing as a slow month for hunters, it was January, when most of the lakes were frozen and the ducks had flown to California. Fin was home for thirty glorious days then, and during that time he and Maggie regularly donned heavy coats and thick leather boots, and trekked to White Rock ridge. The view was spectacular. Edward enjoyed it too, bouncing on Fin's shoulders — even while Fin stood still — and patting his papa's head. Maggie sometimes packed a lunch of sliced bread, blackberry jam, and a jar of applesauce, which she fed to Edward in a spoon Blythe had sent him. Afterward, they walked home again. Fin collapsed in his wooden rocker, Edward on his lap. Edward's eyes soon grew drowsy, and then Fin's did too, and father and son fell asleep, their cheeks softly blowing.

Maggie could barely contain the gladness in her heart, for it seemed Fin's love overflowed these days. Her only real hardship was letting him go in February, when he resumed his job as a warden. Even after he'd been gone a full month, her eyes welled for days, and she thanked God for sending them Edward, her most delightful diversion. He was growing as quick as a grasshopper, though, and she couldn't cart him on her shoulders the way that Fin could. She constructed a knapsack of sorts, in which she carried him. In summer, she walked to White Rock with him strapped to her belly, released him, then sat on an outcrop and wrote in her journal. There was so much to record — plants, birds, and insects and such — as well as the date, and state of the weather.

Fin had given her the book as a Christmas present, thinking she might want to jot recipes, although she still wasn't much of a cook. She preferred tracking her daily doings in the great outdoors, as well as the elements of nature. She wrote her name inside the book's cover in tidy penmanship, forgetting for a moment she was Maggie McFaddin now, having so few occasions to say or write her name. She accidentally wrote Maggie Elliott, and having no eraser marked out her old name and put in the new. Aiden would have cringed at the scratching she'd made there, but Fin let it go; he thought everything she did of late both bright and marvelous.

And so she sat, sketching bugs and birds and jotting small notes about them while keeping one eye on Edward. He was an early walker, taking his first steps at ten months; now, at the age of one, he was almost masterful. Maggie wasn't worried about him toppling over, and if he did, he was more than adequately bundled: he wore soft leather moccasins, a knitted bonnet with matching sweater, and a dress of lightweight cotton. Every now and then, he curtailed his travels, plucked a pebble from the ground, and popped it into his mouth. Maggie would shoot from her perch, scoop out the rock, and how he would howl in outrage! She'd hand him a cookie and then he was satisfied, waddling over to a bit of dirt and using his biscuit as a shovel.

It was a ritual, and after it passed, Maggie could finally settle in and concentrate on her journal. She longed to write as an author might, telling of her troubles. But she worried Fin might find her book, sit in his rocker next to the hearth, and read her hard-kept secrets. Of the fear she held inside.

She suspected he kept many of his own worries from her, and wished she had someone to talk to about it, Willa perhaps. But lacking a woman's companionship and motherly advice, she looked to heaven now and again, and chatted with God. It was unfamiliar territory and she had no real idea what to tell Him, so she kept it polite and simple. "Keep Fin safe, if You please, Lord, and bring him home to Edward and me." God watched over Fin, just as Maggie asked Him to. LeGrande, though, God frowned on, and his wiry nephew Axel.

Over the years, the lump sprouting from the old man's back had grown ever stouter and had begun to slow his pace. What LeGrande couldn't handle he assigned to Axel, and what Axel couldn't do, the old plumer berated. Still, Axel stood beside him as he'd always done, shooting more birds than LeGrande did now, and skinning the bulk of them. He wasn't tempted to go his own way, for the reasons he'd long ago confided to Fin; he was still leery of his uncle. Axel more or less did what LeGrande told him to, although he had long regretted leaving Fin injured, as LeGrande had insisted. On the other hand, Axel always thought Fin foolish for tussling with his uncle. To make matters worse, Fin had made his way to Malheur, trespassing, more or less, in country LeGrande had long ago claimed for himself. The marsh was big and its borders broad, but the rule was first-come, first-served. If LeGrande saw fit to sneak up on some rookery before Fin found it, so be it; that was the law of the land. But Axel knew, too, this was something he told himself, so he could live with what he and his uncle had done.

Axel supposed Fin had died where they'd left him, that the coyotes had dragged his bones into the sagebrush and had themselves a party. It came as a shock then, when Fin shouted his name, and pointed a gun his way.

"Axel! Put your weapon down! I got a bead on you."

Axel jerked his head up. He had been sitting in a rowboat, holding his shotgun in one hand. A pile of dead birds was stacked two feet high at his feet. LeGrande held a net with a grebe inside it. At the sound of Fin's voice, he startled. The men squinted uncertainly, staring at the apparition bobbing in a boat across the way. Realizing it was Fin, LeGrande spat into the water, but didn't otherwise move a muscle. Axel took his cue from his uncle, and sat perfectly still.

"Took you for a ghost, McFaddin," LeGrande called at last. "I thought you was a goner."

"You left me for one, that's for damn sure." Fin aimed his gun at the men. "But I ain't no ghost, as you can see. I'm a game warden now, and I caught you-all red-handed."

"Game warden?" spouted LeGrande. Fin might as well have claimed he was the King of England.

"That's right—the governor appointed me."

The news was more surprising than learning Fin was still alive. "How can you be a warden," asked Axel, "when you was once a hunter, same as me and LeGrande?"

"I'm hunting plumers now instead of herons, but my aim is just as good." Fin caught LeGrande's gaze drifting toward the bottom of the boat, and guessed the man had stashed a gun there. He tightened the grip on his own shotgun, and hollered, "I'd like nothing more than to take you in, LeGrande, but seeing as I only saw Axel shooting, he's the one I'm fetching."

LeGrande smirked. When he spoke, his voice was calm. "Never thought I'd see the day when a plumer slapped on a badge and called hisself a lawman. Did you, Axel?"

"I never thought on it a'tall," Axel told him.

LeGrande drew his mouth up, and his nostrils flared somewhat. "It was a mistake to leave you layin in that dirt. I ought to have kilt you when I had the chance."

"Well, you didn't, and now you'll get no next-time. I'll watch you like a hawk, arrest you too, first opportunity I get." Fin pointed his shotgun at Axel now, indicating the shore with its barrel. "Put your gun down, like I told you to, and come on in, Axel. Give yourself up now."

Axel hesitated. Fin let only a moment pass before he shot a hole in their boat. The dinghy began to fill with water, and then to rock, the weight of the men leaving it topsy-turvy.

"I can't swim," Axel said, his voice panicky now. LeGrande looked around for an oar, moving as quickly as Fin had ever seen him. When he found one, buried beneath the dead birds, he chucked it toward Axel. Axel grabbed the oar and jabbed it into the water.

"You best row like a son of a gun," Fin instructed. Axel took up the cause.

As soon as they hit the shore, the water in the boat was up to their shins, their guns fully submerged. Fin ordered the men out, instructed them to walk toward a stand of willows. He tossed Axel a length of cord, told him to tie his uncle to one of the bigger trees. "Keep his bonds loose enough that he can eventually work his way out."

Axel picked up the rope and took one step toward LeGrande. The man jerked away, warning Axel with a cruel face not to try it. Axel looked over at Fin as if to say *What do I do now?*

"Do like I told you to."

LeGrande cocked one eyebrow, balled his fist, and raised it at his nephew.

"For God's sake," Fin shouted, disgusted. "Stand over

there, Axel." He indicated a spot about ten feet away. "If you make a move or try to run, I'll fill your back with bullets."

Axel did as he was told, looking over his shoulder as he went. "I ain't one to run," he said, his feelings hurt.

Fin strode over to LeGrande. The marsh dweller barked, "You ain't nothin but a rooster. It's all you ever been."

"Sit down, LeGrande." When the man did not move, Fin hefted his shotgun and pointed it at him.

LeGrande slowly sat. "If you think I'll let you tie me, you got another thing coming."

"I got no plans to tie you," Fin said. "But I will return the favor you once done me, and fall you with my gun here." He knocked LeGrande hard on the head then, and watched the man keel over.

Axel sucked in his breath. "You oughtn't to have done that, Fin."

"Tie him up like I told you to," Fin demanded. Axel did so. When he had finished, Fin tossed him a second rope, told him to strap his own ankles so he couldn't skip off toward the sagebrush.

"Skip off?" Axel cried. "My horse is four miles in the opposite direction—me and LeGrande come by boat." Fin looked vaguely at that far-away place, but never said a word. "How was you aimin to get me to jail?" Axel went on. "Will I be ridin with you?"

"Well, we ain't heading backwards, so I guess you'll be walking," Fin said, motioning again toward Axel's ankles. Axel tied them. Fin set his gun down then, roped the man's wrists, and released Axel's ankles. "It's maybe nine miles to Merrill," Fin told him. "We best get cracking, if we're to make it before dark."

"I can't walk that far," Axel protested. "I'm prone to blisters."

"Then maybe I ought to help you the same as you helped me." Fin was referring to Axel's abandonment those few short years ago. He let the remark sink in. "Oh, that's right," he went on, "you didn't lend no hand at all, you left me there to die." He strode over to the men's boat, snatched up the waterlogged shotguns, and flung them into the marsh. "Get a move on," he told Axel.

"What about my uncle? You gonna leave him here?"

Fin looked over at the marsh dweller, who was splayed like a drunkard on his back. "He ain't hardly bleeding, leastwise not like I was. I guess he'll be all right."

"He'll have hisself a headache whenever he comes to. We ought to leave him some water, at least."

"Leave him your canteen, if you've a mind to. I'll do that man no favors."

The first hour in, Axel was already limping. He looked as forlorn as he had the evening he'd told the story of his sandhill crane. Fin wasn't taken in by Axel's pained expression, or his gyrations. Not that Axel was pretending; Fin knew him to be more or less an honest man, convoluted as that was. But never again would Fin offer so much as a glimmer of encouragement. Axel was an enemy now, and a mortal one at that.

"Them guns you chucked was automatic loaders," Axel complained after a while. "You could have spared us one, at least, without no skin off your teeth."

"Ain't got no skin on my teeth," Fin told him. "Even if I did, I'd not give any to you."

Axel stepped on the wrong side of a pebble. His ankle wobbled and he grimaced, and he began to flap his elbows to help himself along. Fin looked back a few times to make sure the man was keeping up. The day had turned hot, and the sun shone as fiercely as a white-hot poker. He led his horse toward the shade of a stubby juniper and dismounted. Popping the cork from his canteen, he took a long swallow, his eyes fixed keenly on Axel, who was thumping hard toward him. Every now and then Axel glanced Fin's way and licked his lips, dry as they were, and fat too, swollen big as pillows. As quickly as he glanced up, he looked away, and Fin realized Axel wouldn't permit himself to stare; staring announced a body's weakness, and that was something no man wanted another to see.

Axel looked off to the west and his face folded. Fin couldn't know what the plumer was thinking, but he liked to imagine Axel felt sorrow in his soul, that he regretted the being he'd become, just as Fin himself felt remorse for his own misdeeds. The notion that Axel might yet leave LeGrande and start anew made Fin think again that Axel was a man less evil than his uncle.

He called for Axel to come in from under the sun and sit in the shade. Axel clomped over and collapsed against a tree stump, grateful for the rest. He sighed heavily as he leaned forward and pulled off his boots, no easy task with his wrists tied. Wincing with the effort, he peeled off his socks, which were rank with sweat and blood, and propped his heels in the dirt.

"Why don't you get boots that fit you?" Fin asked. "You've had them things as long as I've known you, and they ain't never fit you right."

"Ought to," Axel agreed. "'Cept I hate that trip to town."

Fin could appreciate that. He reached over, untied Axel's knots, then offered him the canteen. Axel took it, permitting himself three long swallows. He wiped his mouth with the back of one hand, then rubbed the sore spots on his wrists.

The two of them sat quietly. After a while, Axel said there

was one thing he couldn't understand. "I don't see how you can be a warden now when you was once a hunter."

"You already said that."

"But I still don't understand."

"I don't know what to call it. Change of heart, I guess."

"Lost the stomach for it?"

Fin stuck the cork back into the canteen, and ground it with his palm. "For a time I did, yes. Turned my stomach when I saw what you and LeGrande had done to those herons back at Malheur." He gazed into the distance, watched a dust devil building on the hillside. "Craving to hunt left me for a while, and I lost my spirit too. Bit by bit, it came back, although it's never been what it once was, which is just as well, I suppose. There ain't that many birds left in this world, and I got a boy to raise. I got a living I can depend on."

"You turned warden so to earn yourself some money?"

"And to live in the marsh again. I like a job that keeps me outdoors."

Axel studied Fin, watched him as he laid his head against the tree trunk, and slowly closed his eyes. Limb by limb Fin seemed to let go, his arms first and then his legs, twitching now and again as he began to relax. Before he drifted off, Axel took advantage. "I wish you'd turn me loose," he said in low tones, as though Fin might open one eye, smile, then bid him a fond farewell.

Fin kept his eyes closed. "Why would I do that?"

"Old times' sake?"

"There ain't enough time in the world to make me do that, Axel."

The marsh dweller was quiet then. He gathered a handful of pebbles and chucked one at the dirt. "Case you're interested, I do wish me and LeGrande hadn't left you to them buzzards.

I always felt bad about that."

Fin sat up and shifted against the tree trunk. "Well, you did, but I guess that's history now." He was quiet again, thinking on the story Axel once told him about how he'd come to live with LeGrande—how his mother had died, and then his pa, how his uncle had adopted him.

"You know," he said, surprising himself that he'd chosen to speak of it, "my pa could be as cruel to me as LeGrande is to you. He had a knack, just like your uncle, for cutting people down. The day he died, we had words, and over the years I've wrestled with that. But I've come to understand that a man can't command respect simply because he's your father, or your uncle, either one. Respect is earned, Axel, and as near as I can tell, LeGrande don't respect you one iota. Yet you treat him like he's God."

"He ain't God, I guess."

"Yet you still refuse to cross him."

"I cross him, he'll cut me loose. Then where will I be?"

Fin scratched his head. "I looked at you back there, struggling in the dirt, and I thought I saw a man who might enjoy a life of his own. A man who, if he wanted to, could find a woman and settle down, wash his hands of his uncle."

Axel snorted. "What woman would have me?"

Fin looked at Axel a long time then. He realized the man would never change, never leave LeGrande, no matter what a body told him. "None I know," he said. He was weary all at once. He closed his eyes again, thinking how badly he missed Maggie and the baby, and his chair beside the hearth.

Axel too was tired. The more he thought about his predicament, the more he worried on it. He'd never been cooped up in jail before, and couldn't imagine what it would be to wake up in the middle of the night and pee into a coffee can. All his life he'd peed in the open, where a man could take some air.

He chucked another pebble. "You sure you won't let me go?"

"I told you, this is my job now."

"Least you can do is let me ride to town on your horse."

"You might escape," Fin told him, "and I'd have to hunt you down and shoot you."

"I don't guess I want to get shot."

"No man does, Axel. You want to live for your sandhill cranes, I want to live for mine."

Fin thought Axel might not understand what he'd meant just then, that he'd take him literally. But a look of clarity crossed the young plumer's face, and he sat quietly from then on.

# CHAPTER ELEVEN

Despite Frank Chapman's never-ending praise and the compliments Phoebe gave him, Aiden managed, with a fair amount of practice, to pocket humility. He'd been working on it since Maggie had accused him of standing too tall. More than anything though, it was his sister's letters that kept him humble, since it was nearly impossible to read her words without contemplating her hardship and feeling sympathy for her.

She was lonely in the desert, and it wrenched his heart to hear it. Twice a month he received her missives, two pages of Xs and Os, descriptions of her life in Klamath and her longing to help Fin.

"He's got his job to tend, I understand that, Aiden — and you know we're grateful for it. If it weren't for you, Fin might be out there hunting *with* plumers instead of striving so to fight them. But he's gone for weeks on end, and each time he ventures out I worry terribly, since he hasn't a sole to help him. It would be an enormous relief if he had a second man, someone to spell him now and again, watch his back when plumers are at their thickest." She asked if he would be willing to approach the Audubon Society and ask if they would consider funding an additional warden to help her husband.

While it was true Aiden had substantial pull and might be able to persuade the society to hire another man, doing so would take time and approval from the board. Until then there was little he could do aside from concentrating on his sister, aiding her as best he could, and offering his support. As children they'd not enjoyed the staunchest relationship, but now that they were adults he was endeavoring to change that.

"Pack our satchels, Phoebe," he hollered up the stairs. "We're off to see my sister."

Phoebe appeared at the top of the landing. "I'll set our suitcases brimming," she shouted in delight. As much as she wished to see Maggie, she yearned to see Edward more, for the years Phoebe dedicated to Aiden's work meant turning from her own. While she'd not regretted a moment of the life she had lived with him, she had recently begun thinking again of how much she would like to teach children. It would be a joy to start with her precious nephew, although he wasn't more than two years old.

Neither Aiden nor Phoebe anticipated that Fin might make an appearance once they got there; their sole purpose in going was to assuage Maggie's loneliness, and keep her occupied while Fin was away at the lakes. He did come home, though, the day after he dropped Axel off in Merrill. A wagon stood in front of his house and two horses in the pasture, telling him instantly Maggie had company. Yet the surprise he received when he walked inside shocked him to his core.

Phoebe stood near his special chair, Edward's blocks in her hands. She quietly gasped at the sight of him, and he stood still as he looked at her. Even after all this time, after all the damage done, his flesh still tingled at the sight of her. Her hair caught the reflection of the afternoon sun, and her face shone earnest and happy. "Hello, Phoebe," he said, surprised that he had stumbled a bit to get the words out.

"Hello, Fin."

"What brings you up to Klamath?"

"We've come to see Maggie, and to meet Edward, of course. He's wonderful, Fin, truly. You're an incredibly lucky man." She smiled, but her voice was sad. She kept her eyes on him.

"I am a lucky man," he said. "Although I don't know that I deserve it."

Hearing Fin's voice, Maggie flew around the corner and into his arms. "You're home! I didn't expect you for another week yet." She kissed his eyes and mouth.

Fin kissed her, too, his hand around her waist. And then the three of them stood, smiling awkwardly, until Aiden walked into the room, little Edward perched on his hip.

Aiden stopped, and then stepped forward to embrace Fin, gently squeezing the baby between them. Edward threw his head back and erupted in throaty giggles.

"The boy's a McFaddin through and through," Aiden said as he handed Edward to Fin. "No sooner do I set him down than he gathers my belongings and drops them in some basket."

Fin held the baby in one arm, kissed his cheek, and then his neck, and tousled his hair. "What's he gathering?" he asked, his eyes wide with pride.

"Anything and everything. He's a collector, like you were, back in the day."

"We had us some fun, didn't we?" Fin asked Aiden,

clapping him on the shoulder. Aiden nodded and smiled, and with the smallest effort, it was like old times again.

The good mood lasted throughout the evening. Fin cooked a snow goose for supper, a lone straggler he'd shot on the way home. As a rule, the bird was held in low esteem when it came to cuisine, and Aiden made a face when he saw it. "We're not eating that, I hope," he said, looking over Fin's shoulder, watching his friend pluck the last of the bird's feathers.

"It beats beans and ham hocks," Fin said, referencing the meal they'd eaten for weeks on end all those years ago. The men were quiet then, each thinking his own thoughts about how far they'd come since Malheur.

Fin sliced the tenderloin next to the breast, dusted the strips in flour, and tossed them into a pan. He browned them in butter and sprinkled them with salt. Maggie whipped up plum syrup from a jar of preserves, which they used as a dipping sauce. Alongside the goose, she served steamed carrots, mashed potatoes with peppered gravy, and rolls she called *Parker House*. She made a lemon pie for dessert, although she scorched the meringue and the crust was soggy. "I never can get this pie just right—sometimes I wonder if Tula left out a crucial ingredient, just to prove her pie was better." She smiled when she said it, however, intending the remark as a joke.

After the meal, they sat back and recounted their favorite stories. Maggie insisted that Aiden tell Phoebe the favorite tale of their childhoods. "The one where you find the robin's eggs." When he balked, she urged, "Go on, Aiden, tell it."

"Fin's heard that story dozens of times," he objected. "He doesn't want to hear it."

"But I do!" Phoebe said, leaning forward.

Aiden looked at Fin, and when Fin smiled and shrugged,

he assumed the role of chief orator and began the story. "When I was twelve, I scaled the branches of an Oregon pine just outside the house. I'd been forbidden to do so, because Father knew a robin had built a nest in the tree and laid a clutch of eggs. As you can imagine, I badly wanted those eggs—"

"—which Father also knew," interrupted Maggie.

"I should say he had warned me plainly that if I took the eggs, he would happily whip me ragged."

Phoebe's eyes grew wide at hearing that, since Owen Elliott had never seemed one to strike a child. Then Aiden explained that robin eggs were considered good omens, and Owen was a superstitious man.

"So," Aiden continued, "I asked Maggie to keep watch at the base of the tree while one by one I gently slipped the eggs into my pocket. As I held the last egg in my hand, I heard the screen door slam. Maggie hissed that Father was coming, and when I looked down, there he was, looking up at me. He ordered me out of the tree. I turned, took a minute to find my footing, and started down. When I reached the bottom, he said, 'Are you hunting eggs, young man?' I said no, I wasn't hunting eggs—because I'd already found them, see? 'Show me your hands,' he said, and so I stuck them out, turned them this way and that. Then: 'Empty your pockets.' So I showed him my pockets, too, which were empty..."

Aiden smiled broadly, and Phoebe smiled back. Blinking, she said, "What happened to them? Did you put them back in the nest?"

"I popped them into my mouth," Aiden said. "Swallowed the entire lot before I jumped from the tree."

"Aiden's first taste of ornithology," Fin said. How they laughed at that.

The room settled and then grew quiet as they thought on

Aiden's tale. Fin was the first to speak. He told them that as much as he had enjoyed their visit and wished he could stay home the whole week and reminisce, he had to return to the field the next morning. "I heard shooting near the border on my way home, but if plumers are hunting in California, I got no jurisdiction." He was speaking of the southern boundaries of Klamath and Tule lakes, both of which spilled into northern California.

"They need wardens there as much as we do here," Maggie said to Aiden. "Until they get some, they'll make no arrests at all. Plumers can continue to kill all the birds they want to."

"Or at least the ones they can find," Fin said, adding, "market hunters too." He wiped his mouth with his napkin. "Hunters like LeGrande Sharp won't never see the light. They'll shoot everything on the planet, and the sun too, if they can get a bullet to go that far."

Maggie sighed. "I wish you didn't have to leave so soon. You haven't been home seven minutes yet, and already you've got to go."

"I put one of LeGrande's men in jail yesterday," Fin told her. "That nephew he calls Axel. He'll be out tomorrow, and as soon as he collects his uncle, they'll start shooting birds again. I'd like to get LeGrande behind bars and keep him there, but I've got to catch him first. My effort so far has been piecemeal, at best."

No one had been paying much attention to Edward, and now he banged his cup with a spoon. It tickled him greatly to see his milk splashing about, and as he laughed in his husky baby voice, his downy blonde curls danced on his forehead.

Maggie reached across the table, replaced his full cup with her empty one. He didn't like that one bit, and began to cry at once. "Edward," she chastised, though it was hard to keep from smiling; he made such a pitiful picture, with his lips so tightly puckered. "I best get him to bed," she said, plucking him from his chair and tucking him into her arms. Phoebe offered to help bathe him. When the women set to fussing over Maggie's golden boy, Aiden and Fin stepped from the table into the parlor, where Aiden lit a cigar.

"I hope you don't mind our coming," he told Fin, blowing smoke into the air. "We thought Maggie could use the company, and you know we've long wished to meet Edward."

"No, no, I don't mind," Fin told him. "It does Maggie good to have you here."

"She's got a case of the lonelies," Aiden went on, "though she works like the dickens to hide it."

"I can't help being gone," Fin said, a little defensive now. "There's too much ground to cover. I either got to spend the entire summer in continuous travel, or pick a section of the country and stick around a while. Either way it ain't enough, for as long as there's a bird with a feather on it, plumers will take their aim. As it is, they've shot out nearly all the herons, and the grebes will soon be gone."

Aiden sucked his cigar. Not so long ago Fin had been there with them, aiming his heavy gun, and now it seemed his old friend was nearly as content hunting plumers now as he'd been hunting birds, and it pleased Aiden to know it. He leaned slightly forward, releasing the smoke from his cigar. "I'm hearing the earliest hint of a rumor," he said, "word that President Roosevelt is talking of setting land aside at Klamath and Malheur, creating reserves just as he did in Florida—that place they call Pelican Island?"

"I've heard of it," Fin told him.

"Audubon Association situated a warden there, a man named Guy Bradley. Ten days ago I received word that plume hunters had killed him." He studied his cigar. "A man named Smith was shooting egrets on Cape Sable, and Bradley went in to arrest him. Smith claims Bradley had his gun drawn—insisted he had to shoot him before Bradley got a shot off first. Claimed it was self-defense." Aiden lowered his voice. "You could find yourself in the same predicament, if you're not careful, Fin. Watch your back every time you turn it, and in the meantime, I'll work as hard as I can to get you the help you need."

"There's only one plumer I worry about," Fin confided, "and you know who that is."

Aiden nodded.

"Thank you for not saying 'I told you so.' That means a lot to me."

"Maybe we ought to pull you in for a while, at least until the sting of arresting Axel lessens."

"It ain't gonna lessen. LeGrande's made it clear he don't want me messing with him, and he broke my nose to prove it. If I run, it'll just send a message that I'm scared."

"Aren't you?"

Fin nodded. " Which means I'll take no chances. I love Edward too much to let him lose his father—I know what it is to face the world without one."

"And Maggie?

"I love her too, Aiden, and it will do your heart good to know I told her so. I wish I'd told her sooner—years ago, in fact."

Aiden sat gazing at his friend, inspecting the lines on his face. Fin was thirty-one now, but looked easily ten years older. Aiden promised himself he'd do all he could to help his friend, for helping Fin was helping Maggie, and little Edward too.

The next morning, before Fin took off for Klamath, Aiden

set up his tripod and camera, insisting on a photograph. He arranged Maggie and Fin on the sofa, with Edward standing between them. Sliding a glass plate into the camera, he ducked under the heavy black drape, focused the lens, and snapped a picture. Edward began to fuss as soon as Aiden had finished, so Maggie got up to fetch him a biscuit. Still standing on the sofa, the toddler leaned into his father, one arm draped around his neck, as he waited for his mother. He laid his head against Fin's shoulder, his cheeks red and rosy, and gazed intently at Phoebe, who sat across the way. The scene so captivated Aiden that he took that picture too.

Phoebe smiled at Edward, trying to solicit a smile in return. But the child stood as stoic as his father once had, so many years ago.

Aiden pulled out the plate, and then placed the negative in its holder. "I'll just get these loaded up," he told Phoebe, "then we'll make our way home—Fin's got work to do." He strode happily from the room, leaving Fin, Edward, and Phoebe to sit quietly without him.

Phoebe got up from her chair, walked over, and sat on the other side of Edward. She caressed the child's arm with one finger, and he tucked his elbow in, like a baby bird might do. She smiled, although the rebuff stung her. Now, she looked at Fin. "When I look at you and Maggie and Edward," she said, "I confess I've mixed emotions. I don't regret the path I've taken, but now that I see what I've missed, I wonder if I might have made some other choices."

There was so much Fin might have said then; he might have begged for a second chance and a brand new life between them. All the nights he'd lain awake, he'd wondered much the same. Had he done right by marrying Maggie, or was he just pretending? Pretending he loved her when it was Phoebe he really wanted? But then Edward's breath warmed his neck, and he couldn't get the words out. Couldn't tell Phoebe he would abandon his son and the woman who loved him and had always stuck beside him.

"There haven't been many times in my life when I've done the right thing, Phoebe, but now I can say I have. You can say it too."

Her eyes welled and she dabbed at her nose. She lifted her chin a bit. "Do you remember that day in the marsh, when you claimed you were a killer?"

He said he did.

"You weren't a killer—not then, not ever, I suppose. Your mind was tangled and your heart was too, but I knew the minute I met you that you were a good person, Fin. And as long as I know you, I'll be proud to call you *friend*." She fixed her mouth to say more, but then Maggie strode in and scooped Edward into her arms, stirring the veil between them. Neither Fin nor Phoebe let on that they'd had a moment, and Phoebe stood and excused herself, saying she needed to help Aiden.

A few hours after seeing the Elliotts off, Fin told Maggie he too had to leave. She deflated at the reminder but stood bravely before him, smiling while he held her face. "I wish I hadn't wasted so much of our lives, wallowing in self-pity. I regret that, Maggie, I do."

She took his hands in hers and kissed his palms. "As long as I live, I'll love you, Fin. I know you'll love me too."

He kissed her hair, her eyes, her forehead, and little Edward's too. A moment later, he disappeared with his gear, and headed for Lower Klamath.

Collecting a boat he'd stashed at the northern shore of the lake, he climbed in and rowed to the mouth of Lost River.

He sat a while, and as soon as the gunshots came, rowed in, angling between the tules and using them as cover. Now and then, he hit a pocket of chilly air and shuddered, feeling almost ghostly. Minding that eerie notion, he hugged the shore, knowing that when he approached open water he'd have to take it easy. A mistake would dearly cost him.

He spotted two men in a boat, knew instantly who they were. Axel stood on the left, near the bow, while LeGrande stood to his right. Axel fired into the air twelve times. LeGrande shot six. Eleven birds fell, and they collected them all with a large steel hook. LeGrande laid his gun at the bottom of the boat and sat on the little seat there.

Axel shot again, fixing his gaze on a bird's downward spiral. As it dropped in front of the boat, Axel caught sight of Fin, sitting in a skiff not forty yards away. Axel stood quietly, the butt of his shotgun still tucked against his shoulder.

Fin sat motionless. There was no breeze at all, nothing to stir the air, and a man's voice could be heard clear to California. Fin pointed his own gun at Axle. "Drop your weapon," he said, just as he had not one week before.

LeGrande jerked up. His mouth went taut when he saw Fin, and he held tight a moment. Subtly, he leaned forward and stretched his fingers, feeling for his gun.

Fin slowly directed the barrel of his weapon toward LeGrande. "Don't be reaching for your gun, old man. I'd truly hate to shoot you."

LeGrande sat up now. "I don't know why—I'd shoot *you* dead, if I had me a second chance."

"Too bad you won't," Fin said, shifting again toward Axel. "I said set your gun down, Axel. Put it on the bow, where I can see it."

Axel stood with locked knees, his finger on the trigger.

"I ain't going to jail," he cried. "I been there once already." His eyes drifted toward his uncle, whose gaze flared cruelly. Some unspoken communication passed between them then, some kindred secret message. LeGrande lifted one eyebrow. The gesture was slight and might have gone unnoticed, but Fin had drifted in and was close enough to catch it. He grasped at once that LeGrande wanted Axel to shoot him.

Almost imperceptibly, Axel raised his gun.

Fin's blood grew cold. He knew in an instant he had misjudged Axel Ambrose, given him credit where none was due. All this time he'd thought it would be LeGrande Sharp who might one day try to kill him, when it now looked to be Axel.

All these years Fin had taken pride in his skill as a hunter, yet now he stood vulnerable, exposed as raptor's prey. The irony did not escape him. When he spoke, his tone exposed his surprise and desperation. "Don't do it, Axel—think on what you'll lose."

"You caught me and my uncle red-handed," Axel said, his face folding in distress. "You'll be trottin us off to jail, like you said you would, but we ain't about to go." Axel didn't want to put a bullet into Fin, but even so, he raised his weapon.

"Shoot him, boy," LeGrande hissed. "Pull the goddamn trigger."

Sweat poured from Fin's armpits and trickled down his sides. His throat went dry. "You shoot me and I shoot you, where will we be then? Think on it, Axel!"

Axel glanced at his uncle. When he looked back at Fin, tears welled in his eyes, and saliva webbed his mouth. "Why couldn't you leave well enough alone?" he cried. "Why couldn't you stay a plumer, like me and my uncle here?"

"Shoot him!" LeGrande spat.

When the old marsh dweller tried to snatch his gun from the bottom of the boat, Fin shot LeGrande. And then Axel shot Fin. The echo of gunfire skidded across the lake, and the air filled with the acrid stench of sulfur. The marsh went quiet and time stood still. Axel stood, his mouth partly open. He snapped from his haze and glanced at his uncle. Fin's bullet had seared the man's cheekbone and peppered his face with shot. He lay unmoving in the boat. Axel looked at Fin. He was seated now, staring at Axel, blood bubbling from his throat. Slowly, he raised one arm and pointed a finger, as if to tell him something. Axel grabbed an oar and rowed furiously toward him. No sooner had he got there than Fin's gaze went glassy and he slumped to one side, saying a quiet word. Axel leaned in, frantic. He grabbed Fin's collar, shook him, and begged him to talk louder. But then Fin's eyes drifted and his breath gave out, and he didn't speak again.

Axel rocked on his haunches, gripped his head, and sobbed. He looked at Fin's shotgun, and without thinking took it up, propped its barrel beneath his chin, and pulled the trigger. Lurching toward one side of the boat, he fell into the water and slipped beneath the surface. All was quiet then.

Two days later, a boy of twelve hiked to the lake from Merrill, hoping to catch some trout. He had poor luck, however, and by noon had caught only a handful of suckers. He switched to gigging frogs, and though his sack wasn't quite full, the wind was blowing and he was tired, and so decided to head home. On the way back, he spotted a rowboat tucked among the cattails. Seeing a dark form lying inside it, he approached cautiously, his heart beating inside his chest, and quietly said, "Hello?"

The next day, two horsemen started out for Maggie's. She was in the yard with Edward, hanging wash on the line. She looked up when she heard them, knew as soon as she saw them what they aimed to tell her. Had they come at a gallop, she would have known there had been trouble—but she would have also known they'd found Fin alive and had only come to tell her. Instead, they rode up slowly, almost at a cantor, their worry wedged between them.

She turned, gathered up Edward, and walked steadily toward the house. Stepping inside, she shut the door and leaned against it. She closed her eyes and kissed her son, her mouth parted at his ear.

"Mama," he said, one hand on her face. Tenderly, she shushed him.

## CHAPTER TWELVE

It was Owen's job to see to the funeral arrangements. He selected the casket, a rosewood box lined in emerald satin. He felt bad to receive Fin as he had, for no man deserved to die so in the marshes. Exposure to the elements had left him bloated and discolored, and there wasn't much Owen could do to set Fin right again. He combed the young man's hair and dabbed on some grease paint, but still wasn't satisfied he'd done Fin justice. He discouraged Maggie and Willa from looking at him, and while Willa acquiesced, wishing to remember her son as the man he was, Maggie insisted on a viewing.

She fixed her gaze on the man she had loved since the day she'd met him. His face carried the sheen of some strange old man, a man she didn't know. The more she looked, the less she knew him, and her heart grew thick and jagged.

She turned to her father. "He looks so tired," she sobbed.

Owen grabbed her arm as her legs went out beneath her. He kneeled on the ground with her, gathering her to him as she cried. Holding her as close, he said, "It's an impossible task, letting a loved one go. As many as I've buried over the years, it never changes much: the dead go where God intends them, while the living pass through Hell." He cupped Maggie's chin and lifted it gently. "Some get stuck and some move on, and I know you're among the latter. You'll find your way like you always have, and make me and your mother proud." He drew her in, kissed her forehead, and then gently let her go.

After they had buried Fin, Tula came up to Maggie and wrapped one arm around her. "Wisht I'd named a cake after him," she said wistfully, "though I never thought to do it."

Maggie's eyes were wet, her face red and swollen. "He would have liked that," she said, trying to roust a smile.

"Might do it still, though he weren't much on sweet cake. Was pie he liked, a juicy peach filling, the crust all crisp and brown." She looked over at Maggie; whatever pluck the girl possessed had clearly left her now. It took some meanness, in Tula's view, to survive a wicked world. Aiden had it, and Fin did too, but Maggie weren't no thistle.

She wondered what the girl would do and where she'd go, now that Fin was gone. She hoped she could maybe help her. "Shop is doin real good these days," she started. "I brung Willa on some time ago, but Morris Kiff has took to courting her, and I reckon they'll marry soon."

"Morris is courting Willa?" Maggie said, her voice craggy, but interested too.

"Likely she would have tole you herself, had Fin not passed away." Tula looped one arm through Maggie's. "I sure could use a helper, with Willa bound to go…seeing as you wipe a table better than anyone other, you want to lend a hand?"

Maggie smiled. "I was good, wasn't I?"

"The best," Tula agreed. She hugged Maggie closer.

Maggie glanced over at Blythe, saw her toting Edward.

All these years the woman had held Maggie at arm's length, never showing so much as a crumb of affection, and now there she stood, planting kisses on her grandson. "I suppose Blythe would happily tend Edward if I were to work at the shop."

"Jes look at her, will you?" Tula said, eyeing the sprightly woman. "Old turkey, coddlin your young'un. Whoever would a thought it?"

Maggie recalled how Fin had kept her at a distance too, all those years ago. But in the end, he'd embraced her, and perhaps Blythe would too. She was thinking on this still, when Aiden and Phoebe approached. She drew a breath, then draped her arms around them. Closing her eyes, she leaned her head back, the sun warm on her face. "No matter what we tell ourselves, it was birds Fin loved, and birds he wanted, and mostly what he lived for." She opened her eyes and looked at these two members of her family, her gaze now strong and clear. "But he loved us too, with all his heart—although it took a while to get there."

"Amen," said Aiden. "Amen."

A heron called, and the three of them looked into the sky. "There it is," Maggie pointed, one finger tracing the horizon.

"And there it goes," Aiden said, as it flew toward the sun.

They all laughed then, for it was easy to imagine Fin chasing after it, his stride so strangely familiar, his smile so bright and new.

# ACKNOWLEDGEMENTS

Writing a novel takes tremendous support. My publishers, Mark Bailey and Kirsten Allen, of Torrey House Press, fueled my determination to work as hard for them as they did for me. My editor, Dawn Marano, provided shape and consistency to the book's early chapters, and offered keen advice on character development. Dave Marshall, Frank Graham, Chuck Henny, Lloyd Kiff, Phil Cuthbert, and Joe Mazzoni shared their knowledge of hunting, oölogy, and bird-skin preservation, and provided philosophical insight concerning men's desire to hunt. Claudia Angle, collections manager at the Smithsonian Institution's National Museum of Natural History, opened the museum's archives to my inspection, and allowed me to study bird skins, and patiently answered my questions. Larry Landis and the staff at Oregon State University archives assisted in my research of William Finley and Herman Bohlman, the men who inspired my story. David Sibley, Bill Thompson III, Tim Gallagher, Fr. Tom Pincelli, and Graham Chisholm offered generous blurbs, and Greg Downing provided the breathtaking cover shot. Joelle Delbourgo believed, and Jennifer Prost helped spread the word. My workshop-mates at Squaw Valley read early on and urged me to write the whole story. But of all my supporters, I owe the biggest debt to Steve Thompson; so many times I went to him with questions about wildlife and habitat, and he answered, or made calls, or introduced me to those in-the-know. He is not only my husband, but my beloved best friend.

# AUTHOR'S NOTE

While researching a contemporary story about water wars in Northern California and Southern Oregon, I came across a historical photograph of William Finley and Herman Bohlman, Oregon naturalists hunkered at their campsite in the marsh of Lower Klamath. I was captivated by the photo, and knew as soon as I saw it I would create a story featuring two similar men. I owe William Kittredge and photographers Tupper Ansel Blake and Madeleine Graham Blake my gratitude for their book, *Balancing Water – Restoring the Klamath Basin*, for it was their work which first inspired my own.

Worth Mathewson's *William L. Finley – Pioneer Wildlife Photographer* provided the background that sparked the creation of Fin McFaddin and Aiden Elliott, as well as the rift between them. Frank M. Chapman's *Autobiography of a Bird Lover* afforded the instruction and conversation for my fictionalized version of the same man. Ted Kerasote's *Bloodties* was instrumental in shaping *Plume's* subtext, which explores the human urge to hunt and kill. Stuart McIver's *Death in the Everglades: The Murder of Guy Bradley* introduced me to the life and death of Guy Bradley, a game warden in Florida who was killed by a plume hunter. Barbara and Richard Mearns' *The Bird Collectors* was invaluable in its historical discussion of the skinning and preservation of dead birds. And T. Gilbert Pearson's experiences as a young hunter and egg collector provided anecdotes and entertainment.

Throughout my novel, I incorporated actual historical figures, but I did so in a fictional manner. In a few instances, I sparingly used the dialogue in Frank M. Chapman's autobiography because I believed it was critical to the understanding of pluming's eventual demise and to the development of my story. Any errors or omissions are entirely my own.

# RENÉE THOMPSON

Renée Thompson writes about wildlife, her love of birds, and the people who inhabit the American West. Her first novel, *The Bridge at Valentine*, received high praise from Pulitzer Prize-winner Larry McMurtry, author of *Lonesome Dove*. Renée lives in Northern California with her husband, Steve, and is at work on a short-story collection.

# PUBLISHER'S MESSAGE

*Wild creatures, like men, must have a place to live. As civilization creates cities, builds highways, and drains marshes, it takes away, little by little, the land that is suitable for wildlife. And as their space for living dwindles, the wildlife populations themselves decline. Refuges resist this trend by saving some areas from encroachment, and by preserving in them, or restoring where necessary, the conditions that wild things need in order to live.*

— Rachel Carson

Until the early 1900s, wildlife protection in the United States was weak or nonexistent. The westward expansion of the nineteenth century assumed abundant resources and seemingly limitless land, and land use policies sought to maximize exploitable yield of unsettled territory. However, by the turn of the twentieth century, America had suffered the near extinction of the bison, increasing devastation of water bird populations by plume hunters, and catastrophic reductions of other once abundant native wildlife species such as the passenger pigeon, which would become extinct by 1914. Sportsmen's groups, including the Boone and Crockett Club which was founded by George Bird Grinnell and Theodore Roosevelt, pressed for protective laws for decades, and Grinnell's writings in *Forest and Stream* proposed the creation of an Audubon Society to protect wild birds and their eggs.

Thanks to efforts by the early Audubon Society, public support increased for more vigorous action to reverse this destructive trend and protect both wildlife and its habitats. In 1900, Congress passed the Lacey Act, the first federal law protecting wildlife by prohibiting interstate trade of poached game and wild birds. In 1901, the American Ornithologists Union and the National Association of Audubon Societies (now the National Audubon Society) persuaded the Florida State Legislature to pass a non-game bird protection law, which effectively established the first bird sanctuaries and provided a policy model that other states adopted. Growing public concern about the decimation of bird populations and the advocacy of Frank Chapman convinced conservation-minded President Theodore Roosevelt to set aside the first federal land for wildlife protection when he created by executive order a Federal Bird Reservation at Pelican Island in 1903. This designation of federal land spawned the beginnings of what would become today's National Wildlife Refuge System.

Though plume and market hunting along with habitat destruction devastated bird populations over one hundred years ago, today the hunters of Ducks Unlimited have helped protect over 12 million acres of waterfowl habitat throughout North America. Founded by Joseph Knapp, E.H. Low, and Robert Winthrop in 1937, Ducks Unlimited arose out of concern for the loss of wetlands and its effects on waterfowl hunting, and habitat loss continues to present the greatest threat to wildlife today. Ducks Unlimited and its 600,000 members protect wetlands and wildlife through education, advocacy, and the direct purchase of conservation easements and wetlands that the organization restores and often donates to the National Wildlife Refuge System for management. Working in partnership, the National Audubon Society, Ducks Unlimited, and the National Wildlife Refuge System offer promise and protection for wild places and wild creatures.

# ABOUT TORREY HOUSE PRESS

*The economy is a wholly owned subsidiary of the environment, not the other way around.*

– Senator Gaylord Nelson, founder of Earth Day

Headquartered in Torrey, Utah, Torrey House Press is an independent book publisher of literary fiction and creative nonfiction about the environment, people, cultures, and resource management issues of the Colorado Plateau and the American West. Our mission is to increase awareness of and appreciation for the transcendent possibilities of Western land, particularly land in its natural state, through the power of pen and story.

*2% for the West* is a trademark of Torrey House Press designating that two percent of Torrey House Press sales is donated to a select group of not-for-profit environmental organizations in the West and used to create a scholarship available to upcoming writers at colleges throughout the West.

Torrey House Press, LLC
http://torreyhouse.com

*Also available from Torrey House Press*

*Crooked Creek* by Maximilian Werner

Sara and Preston, along with Sara's little brother Jasper, must flee Arizona when Sara's family runs afoul of American Indian artifact hunters. Sara, Preston, and Jasper ride into the Heber Valley of Utah seeking shelter and support from Sara's uncle, but they soon learn that life in the valley is not as it appears and that they cannot escape the burden of memory or the crimes of the past. Resonating with the work of such authors as Cormac McCarthy and Wallace Stegner, *Crooked Creek* is a warning to us all that we will live or die by virtue of the stories we tell about ourselves, the Earth, and our true place within the web of life.

---

*The Scholar of Moab* by Steven L. Peck

Through a series of letters, journal entries, and interviews, a mysterious redactor tries to reconstruct events surrounding a curious explosion and disappearance of the town hero Hyrum Thayne and the strange night a baby was born and then vanished in the La Sal Mountains above Moab. A black comedy set in 1970's Moab, Utah, and contemporary Vienna, *The Scholar of Moab* introduces readers to the most comic character since Samuel Clemens gave rise to Mark Twain and uses magical realism to explore the meaning that emerges at the intersection of place, consciousness, and coincidence.